LOST HOURS

ALSO BY PAIGE SHELTON

LOST HOURS

A MYSTERY

PAIGE SHELTON

Minotaur Books

New York

First published in the United States by Minotaur Books,
an imprint of St. Martin's Publishing Group

LOST HOURS. Copyright © 2023 by Penelope Publishing LLC. All rights reserved.
Printed in the United States of America.
For information, address St. Martin's Publishing Group,
120 Broadway, New York, NY 10271.

www.minotaurbooks.com

Library of Congress Cataloging-in-Publication Data

Names: Shelton, Paige, author.
Title: Lost hours : a mystery / Paige Shelton.
Description: First edition. | New York : Minotaur Books, 2023. | Series: Alaska
    Wild ; 5
Identifiers: LCCN 2023023647 | ISBN 9781250846617 (hardcover) | ISBN 9781250846624
    (ebook)
Subjects: LCSH: Alaska—Fiction. | LCGFT: Detective and mystery fiction. | Novels.
Classification: LCC PS3619.H45345 L68 2023 | DDC 813/.6—dc23/eng/20230523
LC record available at https://lccn.loc.gov/2023023647

Our books may be purchased in bulk for promotional, educational, or business use.
Please contact your local bookseller or the Macmillan Corporate and
Premium Sales Department at 1-800-221-7945, extension 5442,
or by email at MacmillanSpecialMarkets@macmillan.com.

First Edition: 2023

10 9 8 7 6 5 4 3 2 1

For the Ernats and Millers of Hamilton.
Sometimes in-laws are Win-laws. Much love to you all.

LOST HOURS

One

lifted my face to the cool wind and breathed in the crisp air. Contentedness washed through me. The calm wasn't completely unfamiliar, but it had been rare over the last year. Something inside me whispered: *This is the life, Beth. Enjoy every second of it.*

I hoped I'd never again take such things for granted.

A year into my escape to Alaska, I was finally on a boat, on my way to see one of the sights that were the reason most people ventured to this part of the world—glaciers.

A year ago, I checked myself out of a hospital in St. Louis and ran away to Benedict, Alaska, gateway and launching point to one of the true wonders of the world. I'd been hesitant to take the tour, having been warned by an acquaintance, Ruke, to stay off the water. Back then, I'd figured that even the big tour boats should be off-limits.

Ruke's intuition had been telling him a different story recently. He'd shared with me that he didn't sense I was in any danger at all, particularly aboard one of the big ships. He did suggest I might not want to kayak in Glacier Bay if I'd never kayaked before, but that was practical advice. I hadn't ever been in a kayak or canoe, and I had no plans to do so any time soon. When it came to boats in the bay, both Ruke and I had concluded that bigger was probably always better.

The mid-July weather was unseasonably warm. While seventy degrees wasn't unheard of, seventy-five was rare. It had hit seventy-six today, though the local temperature was always described using Celsius—*It is almost 24 degrees, can you believe it!* I'd asked why Benedict residents didn't use Fahrenheit like lower forty-eight residents, but no one had known the answer, some folks shrugging and commenting, "It's just the way it is."

Not only was the higher temperature a rare treat, but it was sunny today, too. Benedict and Glacier Bay saw clouds and some sort of rain most days, July included. If it was going to rain today, though, the clouds that would bring the precipitation were still out of sight. The sun's rays were warm and made me smile.

Tex laughed as he stood next to me. "Feels good, huh?"

"It does." I shaded my eyes with my hand and looked up at my tall, broad "man-friend," a title he'd given himself. Most of his self-descriptors were laced with some humor, and it was easy to play along. I continued, "I can't believe you've never done this, either."

"I must admit, this way of seeing the glaciers is much easier than the hikes from the other side, and I've done those a time or two." He looked behind us and into the enclosed area of the ship. "And here there are snacks that I didn't have to pack and carry along. Can I get you a coffee?"

"Yes, please."

"Be right back." Tex turned to make his way to the comfortably stocked snack bar inside the warm and well-protected seating area.

The tour boat was not far behind a cruise ship. I'd seen a few of those ahead of us, and a couple headed back the other direction off our port side. The bay was wide enough, and the ships all moved at a consistent enough pace to not worry about crashes or getting in each other's way. The ingress and egress patterns were obvious. However, there were things other than glaciers to see along the way. Snowcapped mountains filled the distant landscape, but it was the islands in the bay that surprised me the most. Those of us paying attention had been gifted with the sight of a mama grizzly and her two cubs running along the shore of the first one we'd passed by.

Tex had explained that the islands weren't off-limits to anyone. People did take kayaks and canoes to many of them. They hiked the islands and even camped there. I wasn't quite ready to consider a walkabout and campout with the wildlife, but maybe someday.

When I'd first moved to Benedict and asked what sorts of wildlife I might run into, I was simply told *all* of it. I'd had my fair share of run-ins with bears, moose, porcupines, even some fish that were big enough to seem too wild for this giant catfish fisherwoman from Missouri. The big boat's deck was about as close as I needed to get to any of the islands.

With a jolt, as I was surveying an island overflowing with birds, the ship took a sharp, right veer. I gasped and grabbed the railing in reflex. Before I understood what had caused the change in trajectory, the noise of a siren filled the air.

"What in the world?" I looked around but couldn't spot any immediate danger. It didn't appear that we were about to run into anything or be run aground. I had no sense that we could be sinking—I certainly hoped not. I scanned the nearby landmasses, the other visible islands, but didn't immediately spot anything that might be cause for trouble.

"Beth, you okay?" Tex, still empty-handed, came up beside me again, raising his voice above the siren's din. He hadn't made it to the coffee bar yet.

Though the annoying noise continued to wail, the ship regained a smooth course, seeming to head straight for an island that had come into view—not the one with birds nor the one with the frolicking grizzlies but one covered with green trees and what appeared to be forested mounds of earth taking up the southerly half.

"I'm good." I glanced at him. He was fine, too. "What's going on?"

"Not sure."

We both looked toward the island's shore. Mercifully, the siren ceased—just as we, and probably everyone else who'd come out to the deck, saw what must have garnered the captain's attention.

Standing on the shore was a woman. She was distraught, maybe in her thirties, her body language begging for help. She was also covered in blood.

"Damn," I heard Tex utter. "I'm going to see if I can do anything to help. Stay aboard the boat, Beth. You don't know these waters. Just stay here. Don't leave."

I nodded as he hurried away. I wouldn't leave the boat, but I did make my way, again with everyone else who'd come out onto the deck, to the bow. A tinny voice came from a speaker that had been secured onto a pole with a rope.

"This is your captain, Horace Moorehouse, speaking. As you might have noticed, we need to make an assist here. Folks, this happens. It appears that our rescue is standing upright, so we just need to get her aboard and make sure she's taken care of. Please stay out of our way—remain on the main deck as we get to her. As I know you've heard, it's rough country out here. Accidents happen. We'll take care of her. Please, everyone, remain calm, and . . . out of our way."

No one appeared panicked, but concern rumbled through the growing group of onlookers. The blood-covered woman was a terrifying sight to behold, but the captain was correct, she was upright, which was definitely good news.

I squinted toward the shore as we approached, wondering if I knew her or had seen her around, but it was more likely that she was a tourist who'd found herself in some trouble.

She didn't seem to be badly hurt, which was even better news. In fact, despite all the blood, I couldn't spot any injuries.

"Oh no," I said quietly. What if she wasn't the injured one? What if the blood came from someone else? Someone she hurt?

I was sure I wasn't alone in my evaluation. I hoped that anyone who approached her would be careful.

Still, though, my heart rate picked up as other scenarios played through my mind. What if this was a trick? What if she was luring someone to shore to hurt them?

"Oh, for goodness' sake, stop it," I muttered to my catastrophizing thoughts. It was a good thing I was in therapy.

From the bow, it was easy to observe the rescue. Most everyone else was as curious as I was, but some folks cleared off and made their way back to the seating area, where the snacks and coffee could have appealed to them more than what might just be *another day, another bay rescue* to them.

Tex was a local search and rescue expert, so he might have volunteered or been recruited to assist. My thoughts were confirmed as I noticed him with another man and a woman standing on the lower deck, all of them slipping into wet suits and goggles with full backpacks stacked next to them. Their level of preparation eased my worries a little more. As the boat moved closer to the island, full gear probably wasn't necessary, but it was always the right way to conduct any rescue. Even an obviously clear-cut one.

The captain, though not geared up, stood next to them, alternately looking out toward the island and seeming to give the rescue crew instructions, or maybe he was just asking questions. I couldn't hear their words. Nevertheless, thumbs-ups and nods made me think they were all in sync. Tex seemed to be leading the way.

I glanced out again toward the woman, who was now sitting on the ground. When I'd first spotted her, she'd been shaking from

wails or cries for help, but now it appeared that she was just crying, maybe with relief that someone was coming to help.

As I watched, a surprised expression lifted her eyebrows. Suddenly, she was on her feet. She glanced around into the woods and
then back at the ship again, her expression now sheer panic. She
screamed and started running for the water. I squinted at the tree
line that started about thirty feet up the beach. Was someone or
something coming for her?

I couldn't spot anything—not even a suspicious shadow. Nevertheless, it sure seemed like something had frightened her. I gripped
the railing again, hoping she'd make it and wondering what in the
world might be coming after her.

Once she was fully submerged in the water, she swam with a
speed that must have come from fear and adrenaline. She moved
quickly, like a pro.

I hadn't noticed the three rescuers jump into the water, too, but
I saw them now, all headed toward the woman, who would meet
them much closer to the ship than the shore at the rate she was
moving.

I muttered, "Be careful, Tex."

My disaster thinking wasn't triggered again, though. The ship
was close enough to the landmass that the water wasn't deep. It
was almost as if there were too many people in the water, considering the scenario.

I could hear the woman's screams now as two of the rescuers
took hold of her, one on each arm, and made their short way back
to the boat.

Still, nothing came from the trees. I couldn't see as deeply into
them as I would have liked, but whatever she'd seen, it must have
decided to explore a different direction.

I watched as they easily got the woman aboard using a plank
that had been extended from the boat's hull. Tex was the last one
to come out of the water. The captain and the two others guided

the woman inside and out of view, but Tex took a moment to look out toward the island.

He turned and looked up, spotting me quickly. I shrugged; so did he, just before he followed the others out of sight.

The captain and Tex had said to stay put, but no murderous animals or humans had emerged from the woods. The woman was safely aboard, and I still didn't think she'd been mortally wounded.

It wouldn't hurt if I made my way to the lower deck now. Would it?

Since most of the ship's passengers were, indeed, staying in place or lining up at the snack bar again, there wasn't a mad rush of curious onlookers. No one else seemed to wonder about the woman who'd just been rescued. One person wouldn't get in the way.

Without impediment, I took the stairs down to the lower level and paused outside a door to the room I assumed everyone had gone into. I could hear voices on the other side, but I couldn't make out any words. I was pretty sure I'd found the right place. No one gave me a second look as I took the seat nearest the door and hoped to be extended an invitation to go inside the room soon.

Two

I didn't have to wait long. Tex, his hair a little wet though he was already out of the wet suit, came through about fifteen minutes later.

"Hey," he said grimly when his eyes landed on me.

I stood to greet him. "Hey. Are you okay? Is she okay?"

Tex nodded. "I'm fine. I think she is, too, but . . . well, I think . . . This is an unusual situation, but I think we could use your help, Beth."

"Okay."

He looked around and guided us back outside to a spot away from the seating area, near the railing. He looked around again, but no one was close enough to eavesdrop on us.

"What's up?" I asked.

"She was a kidnap victim, Beth. Someone took her from her house in Juneau, brought her out here. She claims that her kidnapper was . . . killed by a bear—and she thought she saw it coming for her as we were conducting the rescue."

"Oh. That's . . . Who took her?" I swallowed hard. "Where is his body?"

"She doesn't know who he was, but she claims his body is probably still there, in the woods. She wasn't aware she was on an island until she ran and came upon the shore."

"Oh," I repeated. I took quick stock of myself, thinking a wave of PTSD might set me off-balance and I would need to set myself straight. But I was okay. Mostly. Anxiety tightened my throat, but it wasn't debilitating. Our stories were similar. I'd been taken by a stranger. I'd gotten away, but unfortunately, I hadn't had a bear nearby to finish off my captor. Travis Walker was in jail, and it wasn't as difficult as it used to be to remember that I was now safe. Completely safe.

"I'm heading back to the island to look for the body," Tex said.

I blinked back into the moment. "By yourself?"

"No, the other two are going with me, but I wondered if you'd talk to the woman. Her name is Sadie . . . That's all we've got. I know enough about these sorts of situations to know that as time passes, facts become murkier. Maybe you could find something out, even help her." He paused but locked his serious eyes on mine. "If it's not something that will upset you."

I nodded. If anyone understood what she was feeling right now, it would be me. The passing of a year hadn't made the memory of that sort of shock murkier. Though I'd worked hard to get past what had happened, that day that Travis Walker took me from my house and the three days he kept me in his van wouldn't be easy for anyone to let go of. I still knew the fear, desperation, and raw rage that came with the aftermath. However, remembering how it all felt didn't mean I would feel it all again anymore.

Even today, though, I thought I could probably kill him given the opportunity. What I would have given for a hungry bear.

"Beth, is this going to be okay?" Tex put his hands on my arms.

"Yes. Absolutely. I wish you weren't going back onto that island, but I can help her. I can try."

"We'll be fine." His eyes held mine for another long beat. It wasn't a romantic gesture. He was wondering if I could handle what he was asking of me.

I nodded. There was a time, not that long ago, that my concern for Tex's, anyone's, safety would take a backseat to my own fear. Not anymore. I was more concerned for him than me. "Okay, let me talk to her."

Tex nodded, too, and then turned to lead us back inside. He hesitated at the door to the room, his hand on the handle, and looked at me. I nodded and he opened the door and went through, shutting it behind us.

The room was simple, with walls made of the same white material—probably Plexiglas—as the floors. As far as I knew, it wasn't a fishing boat, but the room smelled like the ocean, fishy. Light filled the space from a small porthole and overhead fluorescents.

The woman sat on the one chair in the room—more a stool, though. Captain Moorehouse stood next to her. She was wrapped in heavy blankets, and despite the swim through the water, she still had blood on her face and in her hair. Like Tex, the other two rescuers were out of their wet suits. They were standing back, their arms crossed in front of themselves as they both leaned against a wall, appearing to want to be both out of the way and ready to do whatever they were asked.

The captain stepped close to me.

He lowered his voice, but the room wasn't big enough for any conversation to be completely private.

"You've been kidnapped?" he asked with no preamble.

I nodded. "Three days in a van. I got away, too, escaped I mean."

He nodded, his eyebrows coming together. "Okay then. We have her first name. Sadie. She keeps repeating that *he* took her from her house in Juneau a week or so ago; she's not too sure of the time frame. She said that a bear ate him. But that's all we've got.

We could use more. She claims she's not physically injured, but she won't allow any of us to examine her. And I don't know what kind of a mess she's in, psychologically. She could just be in shock, but some real empathy might help. Tex told us a little about what happened to you, said maybe you could help." He shook his head as he looked at me, then continued. "Don't push if you think it's too much. But I'd really like to be able to report a full story here, maybe send some official folks out here to investigate."

"I can try."

"Much appreciated." The captain turned to Tex and the other two. "Okay, the dinghy is ready. I'm not commanding anyone to do this, but the sooner someone looks, the better. Are you sure you want to?"

Tex and the others nodded as they uncrossed their arms and bounced themselves off the wall.

"I know Gril will appreciate your timely investigation, but . . . well, be careful. Err on the side of getting the hell out of there." He looked at his watch. "Check back no later than one hour from now."

An hour felt like an eternity, but I was ready to give the woman my focus as Tex and the other two went about preparations for going ashore, which I noted to myself, did not include wearing wet suits again. They had plenty of gear, including guns, but this trip would be done in a boat not via a swim.

The captain gave his attention to the other three. After they all left the room, I cautiously stepped to a spot in front of Sadie, making sure to keep my distance so as not to threaten her.

She was rocking back and forth, shivering, but she wasn't making any noise. I reached for the cup of coffee that had been set next to her. She didn't seem to notice. She appeared to be checked out.

"I bet you're cold," I said gently. "Here. This could help."

It probably took fifteen seconds of me standing there holding out the coffee for her to finally notice. When her eyes landed on me and focused, they opened wider in surprise, as if she hadn't really seen me before then.

She didn't appear to need any sort of surgery, which messed with my memories, erasing some, delaying others. When I had woken up in a hospital post–brain surgery caused by propelling myself out of Walker's van, I was full of fear and confusion. My mother had been there, in a chair next to the bed, her hand on my hand, her fingers twitching, probably because she'd wanted a cigarette.

"Your hair's all white, dollie," she'd said first. *"But you're here, and you're going to be okay."*

But this moment in time wasn't about me. It was about this woman in front of me, whose eyes had finally locked onto mine. I saw an ever-so-slight wave of calm pass through hers, and I tried to give her a small but reassuring smile. Maybe just having a female for her to talk to was helpful.

"My name is Beth," I said as I moved the coffee closer to her.

She didn't speak, but she did take the cup. She didn't sip from it, though. Only held on to it, let it warm her hands.

"Are you hurt?" I asked. "I mean, should we clean any wounds or anything?"

A long hesitation later, she shook her head. "I don't think I'm hurt. I got away." She sat up a little straighter. "I got away."

"Good," I said. "I'm glad. You're shivering. Is there any chance we could get you out of those clothes and into dry things?"

"No, no. You can't touch me. No one can touch me." She dropped the cup onto the floor, spilling the coffee, steam from the hot liquid rising from the cold Plexiglas floor. She looked at her hands as if she couldn't quite believe what she was seeing. "I'm sorry."

"It's okay. No big deal. I'm sorry."

It was just the woman and me in here, but I still didn't think she'd registered her surroundings.

"You're on a boat. I can get you some dry clothes and you can change on your own. I'd hate for you to catch a chill," I said, sounding just like my grandfather, gone for over a decade now. I suddenly missed him deeply.

He'd know what to do here, how to talk to her. *Okay, Gramps, what should I do?*

I remembered something he'd said. "Want to talk about it?"

I'd heard him ask that simple question often. So many people had been surprised by the power of those words, by how many people really did want to talk about what they'd done or what had happened to them. If given the chance, and someone truly willing to listen, they did want to tell their story in their own words, not by answering a rote set of questions that had somehow been pre-scribed. They wanted to talk.

She shook her head once more. No, she absolutely didn't want to talk about it.

"My name is Beth," I said again. "You're going to be okay now. Everyone will make sure you get home. You are safe."

Those words got her attention. She took a deep breath and seemed to relax even more. She was still wound tight, but the springs were loosening. However, I knew they could tighten back up at any second. A loud sound, something that jolted her back toward those things that she'd gone through, could send her back to that place where she wouldn't want to speak again. PTSD would be her side-car now, forever to some degree, though maybe with therapy she could feel at least somewhat better.

I tried again. "Sure you don't want to talk about it? I'm a friend. I've . . . I've been through the same sort of thing." I understood of course why this was something that might bring us together, but it did feel weird to lean on this commonality.

Her eyes snapped up to mine this time. Suspicious and angry.

"No, really I have. I was taken from my home, held by my cap-tor in his van. I escaped, too."

Her expression transformed, softened, but not by much. "God, I'm sorry."

I laughed once, and then put my hand over my mouth. "That was inappropriate, my laughing I mean. It just came out." I paused as my hand fell to my side. "Look, I don't know what I'm doing here. They just brought me in to talk to you because of our similar horrors. I'm happy to listen, talk, sit next to you silently, or leave if that's what you want. Is there anything I can do?"

She nodded slowly, her eyes meeting mine again. She was fully there now. "My name is Sadie Milbourn." She looked at the ground, the spilled coffee, then back at me. "Well, that's my name now. I used to be someone else, but I've been living in Juneau for six years. I used to live in Connecticut, but I was put into witness protection. I'm not supposed to tell anyone about that, but I don't think the old rules apply any longer. Do you?"

I worked hard to keep my expression normal. I didn't think she was supposed to tell anyone about witness protection, but I wasn't going to admonish her. "I've been suspicious of rules for a long time, Sadie. I think we're all given impossible choices sometimes, and breaking rules is our only option."

"I'll talk to you, Beth. I can tell you're not lying. I'm not going to share my story with a tour boat captain. I might talk to the police, but not the Juneau police. Where are we?"

"In Glacier Bay."

"Near Benedict? Are there police there?"

"Yes, the chief is Gril Samuels. He's great at his job."

"I might talk to him. I'll have to meet him first."

"I hear you." I didn't want to leave her to get another coffee, but I had something in my pocket. I reached in and pulled out a granola bar. "Hungry?"

Her eyes got big. "I'm starving. I didn't even know that until you asked, but yes, I'm famished."

I watched her dig into the bar.

I realized something that she must have picked up on even before it came to me. Why would she tell me she was in witness protection? She and I were suddenly and without any notice at all, connected for life. Even if our acquaintanceship lasted only until this boat re-docked in Benedict, Sadie and I shared something that would keep us from ever being totally separated again, even if we ended up worlds apart.

And I hated it. I hated what Travis Walker had done to me, and I hated what some man had done to Sadie. Neither of us deserved it. No one did.

However, something else buzzed in my intuition. It was something from my grandfather again. He'd been a police chief, too, like Gril, a good one; and though he'd want to help this woman, he knew that it was always important to keep a little doubt in play, if only so some new piece of information didn't blindside those investigating.

"Trust but verify," he might say. If he'd been alive when it happened, he would have kept a pebble of doubt about my story, too, mostly so he would keep his guard up, his alert on high. He'd have probably hunted down and killed Travis Walker, but it was only through deep and thorough questioning that the real answers came to light. He always knew that the answers, the full truth, were the only real way to set any victim free.

There's a whole bunch more to this story, and until you get all the details, don't let Sadie blind you to the full truth. Don't let her get away. Get all the answers.

Okay, Gramps, will do. I waited for her to talk again.

Three

After she finished eating, though, Sadie slid off the stool, sat against the wall, and fell asleep. This was something else I understood—the exhaustion that reared its ugly head during and post trauma. Her body needed the sleep, but so did her mind.

She'd stopped shivering, but the blanket that had been around her shoulders fell to the floor. I grabbed a dry one from a nearby stack and draped it over her—she didn't stir. I used the one she'd dropped to sop up the coffee. Finally, I sat on the floor next to her and waited.

Captain Moorehouse reentered the room a few moments later. His eyebrows rose as he looked at us. "She's conscious?"

I stood. "Yes. She just fell asleep. I gave her a little food, so she does have something in her stomach."

"Good. Did she tell you anything?"

"I got her last name. Sadie Milbourn. But that's it," I lied. "Did they find anyone, anything?" I nodded toward the island.

He patted the oversized walkie-talkie-like radio transmitter attached to his belt. "They just checked in. There's no sign of a body anywhere. No sign of carnage or blood, either. They aren't exploring caves because of the threat of bears, but they haven't found anything suspicious."

"Caves?"

Moorehouse nodded. "Lilybook Island is known for its caves." He sighed. "We lose at least one tourist every couple of years because of curiosity. Bears like caves, too."

"Lilybook? Sounds like a place you'd find a library, not bears."

"No libraries out there."

"Are they on their way back soon?"

"Right now. We need to get Sadie, Ms. Milbourn, to Benedict and have the real investigators take over. I think we've done all we can"—he looked at the woman on the floor again—"and she could use some professional assistance. Dr. Powder will be a good start."

"Gril and Donner will investigate?"

"I don't know, but"—he shook his head and patted the radio again—"we've already got people coming in from Juneau on this one."

I was glad I hadn't mentioned Sadie's witness protection. She had been quick to tell me she wouldn't talk to the Juneau police. Though I wasn't sure if I'd share with Gril everything Sadie had told me, I might figure out a way to let him know that she was concerned about talking to the Juneau folks.

Captain Moorehouse reached for his radio, unsnapping it and holding it to his mouth. He communicated Sadie's last name to a woman who answered as "dispatch."

"Any other identification, Captain?" the woman asked.

He looked at me, his eyebrows raised again. I shook my head.

"Negative," Moorehouse said into the radio.

I would talk to Gril, but maybe I should also have a conversation with my landlord, who was at least unofficially part of Benedict's law enforcement group.

Viola ran the Benedict House, a halfway house for nonviolent female felons. I'd managed to get a room there after a late-night internet search I'd conducted when sneaking into a doctor's office in the St. Louis hospital I'd been taken to after escaping the van. During my hurried hunt, I'd missed the fact it was a halfway house. I enjoyed living there. I loved my room, having only that small space as mine. Even though my captor was now behind bars, I wasn't in any hurry to return to St. Louis, with Viola and the Benedict House among the biggest reasons.

As he peered out the porthole, Captain Moorehouse communicated to dispatch that the rescuers were returning from their look around the island. He asked for clearance to turn the boat around and "bring it home." Dispatch told him she would seek approval and get back with him quickly. He reclipped the radio to his belt and then gave his attention to some instruments attached to another wall.

I walked over to the porthole. The rescuers were riding in the dinghy, almost to the still-extended plank. I was relieved. No one appeared hurt, but the expression on Tex's face told me he wasn't happy.

They were aboard quickly, and the room felt too small again when we were all in there, though Sadie remained fast asleep, her chin to her chest.

Tex and I told the captain we'd be in one of the seating areas if he needed either of us; getting out of the way seemed like the right thing to do. We took seats near the same one I'd waited in earlier just as the captain's voice came over the speakers again.

"Folks," he said. "Apologies, but we're going to have to turn around and head back to Benedict. You'll all be refunded for the ride, and we hope you'll be around long enough to try again tomorrow."

It wasn't good news, but if anyone hadn't seen the bloody woman firsthand, they'd heard about her by now. Complaining, no matter how much someone might want to, wouldn't be appropriate.

Tex and I were at the end of an aisle, away from most everyone else. If they'd paid attention to who'd been involved with the search and rescue, no one seemed curious enough to ask Tex what he'd found. Except me, of course.

"Tell me," I said.

Tex looked around again. He was good at checking for unwanted listeners. "We didn't see anything suspicious. It's a small island and we didn't venture inside the caves—though we did inspect the openings. There was no sign of any problems. We couldn't even find a trail of blood left by the woman. It was . . . unexpected."

"Sadie Milbourn," I said. "That's her name."

"Sadie Milbourn. Good job, Beth."

"She offered it up pretty easily." I paused. "It's strange you didn't see anything, though. No blood at all?"

"No. If what she said happened, there should have been . . . something."

"Could the body have gone into the ocean?"

"Yes, but I do think there would still be something somewhere, and if a body did go into the water, dragged or another way, currents might bring it ashore again."

I thought a minute. From all I'd seen, everything in Alaska was extra-dynamic, in constant motion, changing all the time with the assistance of a big breeze or a rainstorm or a mudslide. The rivers could rise quickly, the sky could cloud over before you noticed the blue had disappeared.

"Something could have washed it all away," I said, though it didn't make much sense.

"I don't know. We haven't seen any rain today." Tex paused. "Did Sadie say how long she'd been on the shore?"

"I didn't get the chance to ask, but it seemed like she hadn't been there long."

"Knowing that time frame might help answer some questions. I'll come back out if Gril or the Juneau people want me to. We didn't have tranqs, and that would be the preferable way to come upon bears—not just spray or lethal force."

"I know you'll be careful."

Tex nodded in passing. This was a new thing for both of us—checking in with someone, letting someone we cared about in on our plans in case they had some issue with those plans. Telling each other to be careful. We'd both been single for so long that coupledom was still sometimes awkwardly executed, though we were both trying. I also knew I could trust Tex without reservation.

With that in mind, I made a quick decision, lowering my voice. "Want to hear more about Sadie?"

"Absolutely."

I told him about Sadie's witness protection admission.

"That's news," he said after I whispered the surprise twist.

"I didn't want the captain to know. Sadie doesn't want to talk to the Juneau police, so I don't know how that will all go. She shouldn't have told me. I shouldn't have told you, but . . ." I thought about her comment about rules not applying. "The circumstances seem extenuating and with no body, unresolved. I'd hate not to have shared something if it would help Sadie's situation in any way."

"Right. I wonder if the reason she was put into WITSEC will tie in with what happened to her out here," Tex said, using the abbreviation for witness protection.

"Same. In fact, I wondered if she suspects that she might be in further danger. She didn't say that aloud, though."

Tex's eyebrows came together as he looked around again. There were no obvious threats anywhere. "We need to get her back to Benedict."

"Agreed. We aren't a bad team, you and me," I said.

Tex smiled under all his facial hair. I could see it in his eyes.

My mother and I had been a team for years but far from an equal one. When my father had disappeared when I was seven, I'd gone with her to search for him throughout Missouri. Come to find out all these years later, we'd wasted a lot of time and gasoline. He'd been in Mexico the whole time.

Now, however, he was in Benedict, having come to see me, attempting to make a relationship with the daughter he'd abandoned. It had been an unwelcome addition to my Alaskan adventure but hadn't been as contemptuous as I might have predicted. Dad—Eddy—was good at reading my mood and stepping back if he thought I didn't want to talk. He hadn't pressured me at all.

Currently, it was my mother who was off the radar. I was worried about her, but even Eddy had said a few times, *"Mill can take care of herself. She always has."*

Until Tex, I'd never felt a part of a cohesive and equal team. It was proving to be my favorite part of the relationship—the sense that someone, even if they didn't agree with me, was willing to listen to my side, and always had my back. You and your teammate against the world, whatever form that took.

"All right, folks, we've got the all clear. We're on our way back to port. It shouldn't be too rough, but hang on and we'll be docked in about half an hour," the captain's voice came over the loudspeaker again.

Tex and I climbed the stairs to the upper deck, and he made another attempt at getting coffees, but by then they were all out. We'd grab something back in Benedict before he traveled back to Brayn that afternoon.

Tex had stayed with me in the Benedict House some, and I'd spent a couple nights in Brayn, but that was trickier. Tex had two daughters, and we didn't want to confuse them or cause them any concern or discomfort. His mother loved watching them, so that worked out every now and then.

Though we cared for each other, neither of us was ready to

call what we had permanent, or even semipermanent, by living together. We knew we got along well, but the list of unknowns was long. A kidnapper, a trial, my missing mother, my now overly present father . . . and those were just some of *my* things. Tex had things, too.

"So no glaciers today," I said, wondering if I should take this as another hint from the universe that I should, in fact, stay out of and off the water.

"Apparently not." Tex smiled again.

Just as we settled into some chairs again and after the ship had made a full turnaround, noises came from the starboard side. Once again, Tex and I stood and hurried to the railing to see what was going on now.

"Hey!" a man in a small fishing boat called to the captain, who was now leaning over the bow railing. "You're about hit us!"

"Sir, did dispatch not tell you we were turning around? We were given the all clear."

"I don't care what you were given. I'm right here. I have three people aboard. You could have killed us all."

It wasn't that the man in the fishing boat didn't have a point, though I didn't understand why someone hadn't warned him we were coming his way or if he'd ignored the communication. What I did know—or I should say *who* I knew—was the man. He was my father, Eddy Rivers, fishing guide. Based on experience and the fact that he hadn't had much time in his new career, I would bet he'd been the one to make the wrong choices.

"Beth, is that . . ?" Tex asked.

"Yep," I said. "My father."

"We have a medical emergency aboard," the captain called to Eddy. "We need to get moving, but you and I can discuss this after we dock. Come find me later."

"Oh, I will!" Eddy said.

A tiny thread of concern wavered through me. The boats *were* too close for comfort, though I didn't understand the regulations or rules for how far apart they should be.

I was relieved when Eddy steered the smaller boat around the bigger boat's stern and out of the way. But then something else got my attention.

"Tex, isn't Eddy going the wrong way? Isn't all the traffic in this lane going the other direction?"

"It is." Tex turned from the railing and walked toward the other side to see what Eddy did next.

I followed his quick steps.

"There, he straightened it out." Tex pointed.

Eddy had come around the ship the wrong way as if he was going to go against the flow the whole way, but he expertly managed to move over into the other "lane," the one that took people out toward the glaciers instead of into the dock.

"I guess that worked out okay," I said as Eddy's small boat moved through the water.

"Uh-huh," Tex said, "but what was he doing in the inbound route in the first place?" He shook his head. "I guess we don't know the particulars. All's well that ends well, right?"

"Something like that."

The rest of the short trip back to the dock was, mercifully, uneventful. Once there, though, it seemed that Sadie's circumstances and presence in Benedict had garnered lots of quick attention. There were several official personnel there to meet us. I wondered at the layers—what specifically was going to be investigated? The Juneau folks had gotten there quickly, or I assumed that's who I was seeing in the police uniforms. How would Sadie handle their presence? I was glad I'd told her about Gril. Maybe she would seek him out.

As we disembarked, my eyes caught the police chief's. He frowned and nodded. Of course, he probably didn't know I'd talked to Sadie. He appeared surprised to see me there but otherwise busy with too many other folks to take the time to ask me about my journey out to see the glaciers for the first time.

I nodded, too, hoping he could see my curiosity and might be able to appease some of it later. I had wanted to tell him about Sadie's reluctance regarding the Juneau authorities, but the timing didn't feel right for that, either.

I'd seek him out when the time was right. He'd know I wouldn't be able to resist.

Four

Tex and I managed to grab coffees, along with lunch, at the one downtown Benedict restaurant, conveniently named CAFÉ.

As we ate and the restaurant filled, we heard people talking about what we'd witnessed firsthand. It was a perfect lesson in not trusting rumors. We heard everything from "a woman killed a bear" to "a bear killed everyone aboard a small fishing boat." No one seemed to have the correct story, and we didn't offer it up. Shoot, we didn't even think we had the full story, and we'd been there.

I whispered to Tex, "At least no one is mentioning witness protection."

"You probably weren't supposed to pass that along to me," Tex said just as quietly as he reached for a french fry from the shared basket in between the two of us. "I won't tell."

"I know. It will be our secret. For now. I'll probably tell Gril."

"Makes sense." He put the fry back into the basket and gave me a long look.

"What?" I asked.

"Maybe for now it should be our secret, so much so that we don't ever bring it up again, even to each other."

"I hear you." I leaned toward him and lowered my voice even more. "What secret?"

"Exactly." Tex retrieved the fry.

I'd brought it up a few times now, but I asked again, "You didn't find anything suspicious on the island?"

"Not one thing, Beth. It's not unusual to find blood in the wild, remnants of an animal kill, but we didn't even spot any of that. I'd like to be called to search again. I don't think we rushed, but it was unusually void of wildlife."

"Have you ever explored the caves?"

"Sure, many times."

"Come upon bears?"

"Not every time, but absolutely."

"That has to be terrifying."

"It was an adventure when I was a stupid kid, but yes, scary now. I don't go in unprepared, though. We should check the Lily-book caves. I assume someone will, even if it isn't me."

I didn't say aloud that it would be okay for someone else to do it, but I did think it.

We finished the meal, and he took off for Brayn, with a few planned stops along the way. He hadn't received a message from Gril or anyone that he was needed further, but because communication was so spotty, he decided to drive by the cabin that housed the police station and then back to the dock to see if any of the officials could use an extra search and rescue person. We made a date to talk at nine P.M. that night, me on the Benedict House landline, him on his landline at his house. It was an often-used way to say good night and one we both looked forward to, though we were flexible enough to know that other things could get in the way of the calls.

I waved as his truck turned onto one of the main roads through town and then disappeared out of sight. Clouds had filled the sky and I missed the sunshine but only a little bit.

As had been happening lately, a wave of something that felt similar to homesickness wavered through me. But it wasn't me missing Missouri; it was melancholy at the thought, or maybe just the idea, of someday leaving this place.

I had a home—a house—in St. Louis. It was a very nice place, something I'd purchased when my books first started taking off. I'd run away so I couldn't be found, but my captor's capture had been big enough news that, for a short time, my location in Benedict had been part of the stories. My secret identity in Benedict wasn't really a secret anymore. One photographer had snapped a picture of me walking into the *Petition* shed. My short, white and somewhat unruly hair had made quite the picture. I was freaked out at first. I'd become used to the cover I'd created. The exposure had felt violating, but Travis Walker was locked away now, so I wasn't frightened for my safety. I'd hoped the story would, like most news, pass quickly.

My looks had been fodder for social media commentary. "Her hair!" "God, was it that bad?! She looks so different!" But kinder voices had spoken up, too. "Elizabeth Fairchild is a survivor." "That hairstyle and color will be a trend now!" That didn't happen, but I hadn't commented and had just continued with my Benedict life.

I remember thinking that if my mother saw the picture, it might trigger her to reach out and admonish me to get that cut she'd requested right before she disappeared. It hadn't, and the media had become bored with my story rather quickly.

It was no longer a secret in Benedict that I was also thriller writer Elizabeth Fairchild. And, frankly, no one cared. I was known here as Beth Rivers, which was my real name, so that's what everyone continued to call me.

I'd been hiding so well that I'd become a different person, or was it the person I was meant to be all along? It was a strange twist, but I fit in my skin better here.

Was I going to turn my back on this new me, this contentment just because I had a house in St. Louis?

"Beth!" a voice called from the Benedict House. Viola was leaning out the front door.

"Hey!" I pulled myself out of my reverie and jogged over to her.

"I need your help," she said quietly when I reached the threshold.

"New client?" I went inside.

"Not exactly." She shut the door behind us and did the strangest thing. She locked it. She took off down the hall. "To my office."

I followed behind. She surprised me by shutting her office door once we were inside, too.

She always locked the front door at night, but since the Benedict House was an old inn, each of the rooms had its own locks. She kept the front door unlocked during the daytime. Something was up.

"What's going on?" I asked as she sat in her chair, signaling to the one opposite of her for me.

I did as she instructed and waited as she put her hand on a closed file on her desk.

"We will have someone staying with us, but this time it won't be a client. A woman was found hurt out in the bay today—"

"Viola, I was there. Sadie?"

She squinted. "You were in the bay?"

I hadn't told her my plans for the day. "I was. I . . . well, I talked to Sadie for a few minutes." I outlined for her the sequence of events, though I didn't tell her about Sadie's involvement with WITSEC. "Gril didn't tell me you were there," she said.

"I saw him at the dock, but it didn't seem like I should interrupt him and tell him I'd talked to Sadie. I was going to later."

"I see. Well, okay then, I'll tell you what he said I could share."

I nodded.

"Sadie Milbourn will be staying with us. She was found out on Lilybook Island out in the bay. She isn't hurt but she claims that a man was with her and that a bear hurt the man, killed him, probably ate him. That jibes with your story so far?"

"Mostly, but—"

She continued, "Good—"

"Wait, Viola, You locked the front door. You shut your office door, and you're being very precise with your words."

She held up her hand. "I am, Beth. There are things about Ms. Milbourn that aren't for public consumption, and I just want to be careful." She cleared her throat. "Ms. Milbourn might be in danger"—Viola looked at me—"or maybe she's the danger."

"I see. Gril is suspicious." These were the same thoughts I'd had.

"No, Beth, everyone is suspicious. Not just Gril. It's all suspicious."

"Okay. Why?"

"Can't tell you those details. She's not going back to Juneau yet, so she's staying here, and when I say 'here' I mean here at the Benedict House."

"I guess that kind of makes sense."

Viola shrugged. "It's at least reasonable."

"Right."

"Anyway, Gril would like for you to leave."

I sat up straight. "What?"

"Yes, just for now. He'd like for you to stay someplace else. He's rounded up a few options for you. He can set you up at the *Petition* shed, or maybe you could go to Tex's. Orin says you can stay at his house, too. If none of those work, we can figure out something else."

Orin was a friend and the local librarian, who also sometimes worked for the government helping with covert operations. I'd set up a cot where I worked at the *Petition*, but it wasn't the most comfortable.

"So the help you need from me is for me to leave?"

Before she could answer, a scratch sounded from the door. I looked at Viola for permission to open it. She nodded.

As the door swung open, Gus, the purebred husky who had become my and Viola's dog, trotted in, the look on his face a mix of question and concern. It was rare that either Viola or I came into the house and didn't greet Gus first thing, and I had been gone all morning.

"I'm fine," I said as I rubbed his neck and allowed him to kiss my cheek. "Viola's fine. Come sit with us."

I closed the door again. Even Gus wondered what in the heck *that* was all about. Viola didn't even close the door most of the times she had meetings with her clients.

I turned to her and asked again, "You want me to leave?"

"No, Gril wants you to leave. Just temporarily."

"Is it an order?"

Viola hesitated but then said, "Yes. An order from Gril."

"What do *you* want me to do?" I asked.

"I'd like for you to be safe. But this is your home, Beth. I would never kick you out of it unless I was one hundred percent convinced you were in danger." She glanced at the door. "It's just you and me in here. I didn't want to be overheard, particularly if I'm not . . . enforcing Gril's orders."

"I see. And you're not convinced that it's not safe?"

"I think there's some risk. I can't tell you everything about Sadie, but I do think there's some risk with having her around, though I really don't think it's a big risk, considering . . . time and location, I guess." She frowned at her own cryptic words. "Gril is always extra cautious."

Viola and I got along so well partially because we lived our own lives, did our own things, cleaned up after ourselves or each other without mentioning it. As good as she'd been for me, as wonderful as her company was, she'd told me I'd been good for her, too. I'd been happy to hear that and didn't want to do anything to be a less desirable housemate.

I'd enjoyed the clients I'd come to meet at the Benedict House as well. They'd been a mix of messed up, manipulative, and over the top, but they'd been interesting people.

"I think I can help with Sadie," I said. "Gril might not know yet, but the captain asked me to talk to her because she was taken from her house." I paused to gauge if Viola wanted me to go on or if I should stop talking. I continued, "The man she was with, I know he *took* her, Viola. I know much more than Gril thinks I do. I've been through some of what Sadie went through."

Understanding and relief relaxed her expression. "Okay, no, I don't think he knows, but . . . well, yes, you and she have lived through some similar things." She paused and gave me a level look. "Maybe you can also suss out if her story is or isn't true. I'm not saying I feel one way or another, but we all need to proceed cautiously as well and keep her protected."

"I agree. I got no strong indication she was lying, but we didn't talk long. Having more time around her would certainly help."

Viola nodded. "I'm telling Gril you'd like to stay."

"How about telling him I'm insisting upon it? Too much?"

"I'll see what mood he's in, and I'll let him know the two of you already spoke. For now, our guest is currently with Dr. Powder, but she'll probably be here within the hour. I've got her room ready, the one next to mine. I'm going to run out to do some grocery shopping.

Now, while you don't have to move out, would you mind heading into work for a few hours so I can have Sadie to myself for a bit?"

"That I can do." I put my hand on the dog's neck. "I'll take Gus with me."

"He'd like that."

Gus and I were packed up and on our way only a few minutes later. I gathered my laptop and the last burner phone I'd brought with me a year earlier. I still hadn't gotten rid of it. I barely used the burner, but it was the number my mother had to contact me, and I didn't want to miss her.

In fact, I thought of Mill almost every time I picked up the phone these days. I glanced at the screen before I put it in the backpack. "Do you think she'll ever call?" I asked Gus.

Of course, if she came back to Benedict, the man I assumed she left with, someone known as Elijah, might come back, too. He might want his dogs back, and I couldn't imagine Gus not in my life. "Over my dead body," I said as the random thought popped into my head.

Gus whined agreeably. I plunked the phone into the pack and then put my laptop inside.

"Shed?" I said.

Gus's tail wagged double time.

An old hunting shed with a tin roof, it was where my original cover job had taken place—editor for the local weekly paper, the *Petition*. The paper was more a listing of local events than anything else. Gus and I spent a lot of time inside it because I also wrote my books there. While it was near the library where Orin worked, it was otherwise surrounded by woods that Gus had come to love exploring while I used the library's internet as well as its sometimes-reliable cell coverage.

Gus had also come to enjoy the library and his visits with Orin. It had happened organically one day. Gus and I had been outside as Orin had walked out the library doors. All it took was one friendly wave for Gus to see it as an invitation to take off down the connecting dirt road, greet Orin, and receive love in return.

Now at around three o'clock every afternoon, we'd all go outside, and Gus would run to visit Orin. Sometimes he'd stay at the library for a couple of hours, hanging with anyone else who might be there.

Of course, Orin wasn't always at the library, so there were days when three o'clock rolled around and Gus and I would step outside, but Orin wouldn't. Unfortunately, the nature of Orin's secretive retirement career meant he didn't always get to give me a heads-up when he was leaving, though we all knew that the disappointment Gus felt when Orin wasn't there would break the librarian's not-so-hard heart if he could see it.

Gus looked toward the library as we got out of the truck.

"It's only two," I said to him and headed toward the shed door.

Resigned to hanging with only me for now, he followed me inside.

I got to work on my real job, the novel that was due in two weeks. I was on track, on the third draft. It had been smooth sailing until a week ago when I'd found a huge plot hole. I'd been working for a week to fill the hole, and I thought I was almost there. If nothing else got in my way, two weeks would be just fine.

From the depths of my backpack, the burner phone rang. I'd set the ringer to sound like a bird whistle, but it rang so infrequently, it always surprised me.

I wrangled out the phone, glanced at the ID, and answered, "Detective Majors?"

"Hi, Beth."

She'd worked my case from the beginning, been there the whole way. She'd been the one to drive me to the airport when I'd escaped St. Louis. She'd known where I was going and told only Gril, just so he would have a heads-up. It was largely because of her efforts that Travis Walker had been caught, tackled in a gas station in my hometown by the current police chief, Stellan Gray-stone.

"I hear something in your voice. What's up?"

"Everything is okay. I just wanted to give you a quick update on a couple of things."

"I'm listening."

"First of all, Travis Walker has acquired an attorney. Have you ever heard of Clara Lytle?"

I laughed once. "The defense attorney who represented the Hollywood movie star who admitted to killing his wife, but she was able to defend so successfully that he wasn't convicted and has gone on to have a whole other career? Yeah, sure, I think I've heard of her. Why in the world would she want to represent Travis Walker? Surely, he doesn't have enough money to pay her retainer."

"Well, I don't know about the money, but she has, in fact, taken him on as a client."

"Goodness, that's . . . disappointing."

"He's guilty and everyone knows it. Maybe that's why Clara took him on—maybe she loves the idea of a challenge. I don't know. But he's guilty. Even she can't help him get away from this."

"If anyone can, it's Clara Lytle."

"The district attorney feels like it's an airtight case."

"Yeah, the Hollywood DA probably thought the same thing."

"Hollyweird is a different world."

"Right." I sighed. "Has a trial date been set?"

"Ms. Lytle has gone in front of the judge, stressing the 'speedy trial' part of the defendant's rights, asking for a fast track. It appears the trial is set for October."

"*This* October?"

"Yes, three months from now."

"Good grief."

"Yeah. Something like that."

"I'll be there, of course. The DA already told me I'll be testifying. I wouldn't even try to get out of it."

"Right. I wanted to make sure you heard from me that it's right around the corner. The DA's not my favorite, either. Though, of course I want him to win more than he does."

"I appreciate that. I'm confident Travis will be convicted." I was slightly less confident than I'd been before the call, but still, how could he not be?

"There's more."

"Oh boy. I'm ready."

"Clara is asking for a change of venue, wants to move the trial to another county."

"That doesn't bother me too much."

"No, me neither, but she's got something up her sleeve. I heard it through the grapevine that she's going before the judge tomorrow. I'll keep you up to date."

"I appreciate that." I paused. "Okay, is there more?"

"A little bit."

I braced myself. "I'm still listening."

"I think your mother has been spotted."

"Where is she?"

"She's in Missouri."

Detective Majors didn't need to say another word about her thoughts regarding the reasons my mother might be in Missouri. It took me only a few moments to conclude the same thing. Millicent Rivers was in Missouri to make sure that Travis Walker paid for his evil, paid for his crime, probably paid with his life— because if there was any chance at all that he wouldn't pay, she was going to nip that in the bud.

"You should find her, maybe bring her in," I said. It went

against everything I'd wanted—I'd been protecting her. But this news changed things. I was relieved that there was a real chance she was alive. But I couldn't imagine her making her way back to Missouri with anything other than destruction on her mind. No one would benefit from that.

"For what?"

She'd shot Travis Walker in the leg, but he had said he didn't know who'd done it. There had been no other witnesses.

"We broke into houses when I was a kid."

"I'm sure the statute of limitations has run out on all that, Beth. Not only that, just because she's been spotted doesn't mean it really was her or that we'll be able to catch her. I just wanted you to know."

Of course I was relieved, glad to know it was likely that my mother was still alive. I was also terrified. There was no doubt in my—in anyone's—mind that she would try to kill Travis Walker.

"Shit," I said.

"Yeah, that sums up my feelings pretty well, too." She paused. "We're looking for her. I've spread the word, though an APB is out of the question. As far as we know, she's done nothing wrong. But we'll figure something out if we find her."

"Have her call me, Detective. Let me talk to her if you can somehow do that. . . ."

"I hear you."

We were both silent for half a minute or so.

"You okay, Beth?"

"I'm good. I . . . I appreciate the update."

"I wish I'd called with all good news."

I laughed. "This isn't the worst news."

"All right. I need to get back to it. Have a good afternoon, Beth, and I'll be in touch."

"Talk to you soon, Detective Majors."

We ended the call, and I texted my mom, at least on the number I had for her.

Come see me. Don't do anything stupid. I'm so good. Don't mess it up.

"Do you think she'll listen to me?" I asked Gus.
I was pretty sure he rolled his eyes.

Five

It was after seven by the time I pulled into my parking space next to the Benedict House. It was still bright out: the sun rose between four and five throughout July and set around ten.

Almost every window had blackout curtains, the window in my room included. It was easy for me to close the curtains and sleep when I needed to, but tonight I felt a sense of anxious confusion creeping in—that wired-tired that came with the light not aligning with the time I expected it to be.

My anxiety had ramped up even more today as I noticed a couple things out of the ordinary in the small, downtown area. A Juneau police car was parked at the end of the other line of downtown shops for one. It must have come over on the ferry, which seemed odd. Why wouldn't they fly and just use a van left at the airport or ride around with Gril? Two uniformed Juneau officers were walking along the boardwalk. Donner, the park ranger who assisted Gril, was sitting in a chair outside the bar, wearing clothes that weren't the green and brown of his normal ranger's attire. In fact, I didn't remember ever before seeing Donner in jeans.

I could tell he was also trying to look casual, but he and the uniformed officers were alert to everything.

"Goodness," I said to Gus. "Things are serious around here."

We hopped out of the truck and walked directly to Donner. At least his expression wasn't one of complete irritation.

"Hey," I said.

"Beth, how are you today?"

"I'm great. You?"

"I'm good." He chewed the inside of his cheek a moment. "I'm kind of working."

"I figured." I stepped to the side in case I was somehow blocking his view, but Gus didn't care and walked right to Donner for some attention. Donner behaved appropriately.

"Can I get you anything?" I asked him.

"No, thank you."

"I've never seen you in civilian clothes."

"Most of the time I'm not a civilian." He sent me a wry grin. He had as much facial hair as Tex, so like with Tex, I had to read Donner's eyes.

"How did the car get here?" I nodded in that direction.

"On the ferry."

"A Juneau cop car, uniformed officers? They don't appear to want to be subtle."

"No, I don't think that's their goal."

"How worried are you about all this?"

"Me? I just do my job. I don't worry. Gril is concerned, so I'm going to be as available to him as I can be. This shouldn't be for more than a day or two."

"Did they find the man's body? The one allegedly attacked by the bear?"

"Not as far as I know." He lifted an eyebrow. "In case you hadn't heard, Tex is out on the island, searching."

I nodded. I hadn't heard, but of course, had known that might be a possibility. "I hope they find something helpful. I'll ask him about it later."

"Be alert, Beth. Viola told me you won't move out of the Benedict House."

"I'm okay."

Donner looked around as if assessing the situation. "I think all will be well, but be careful."

I sensed he was torn. He thought a lot of ado was being made of something that didn't require it, but he was also a cautious man. And fiercely loyal to Gril.

"I will. Is Sadie over there now?" I nodded toward the Benedict House.

"She is."

"Okay then. Let me know if you need anything."

"Thank you."

Gus and I made our way back to the Benedict House. Normally, downtown was quaint, calm, and comfortable, and I didn't like the tense air tonight.

Even Gus was a little out of sorts. He picked up on the changes, the seriousness, and he didn't like it, either. His trot was a little too enthusiastic, his ears a little too perked.

"It's okay, boy," I said as I opened the front door. "No one messes with our place, at least for long."

Gus took off to find Viola, so I followed behind. She was in the dining room, along with Sadie, another officer from Juneau, and Gril. The officer was standing at the doorway. He took a step toward the entrance as I approached and as Gus made his way around the man's leg.

"Hey, Gus," Gril said as the dog went to him and sat close to his leg. He always did that with Gril. "That's Beth," Gril told the officer. "She lives here. She'll probably be leaving for a few days, though."

I shared a look with Viola, but I didn't argue with Gril. I looked at the officer. "Pardon me for interrupting."

"Beth, hello," Sadie said. "Oh, it's good to see you again. Every-one here is making such a fuss over me. I want to go home. Can you explain to them how much I want to go home?"

I'd wondered if she remembered talking to me. In fact, I'd al-ready told myself she probably wouldn't. Clearly, I'd been wrong. I nodded. "I can try."

"Thank you."

"Sadie mentioned that you and she spoke on the boat," Gril interjected before I could attempt to make a case for Sadie's return to her home.

"We did," I said.

Gril rubbed his chin. "Have a seat, Beth. We just got here our-selves. We want to figure out what happened, and there is a chance you could help."

"I'm not going to talk with him in here." Sadie crossed her arms in front of herself as she sent a fleeting glance toward the officer. "I already talked to them when I got off the boat."

Not only did it appear she was going to stick by her guns re-garding the Juneau police, but she also wasn't going to hide her disdain for them.

"Okay," Gril said a long beat later. He looked at the officer who, to his credit, didn't appear bothered about Sadie's remark. "Officer Natno, you mind stepping out for a bit?"

"I don't think I should." He looked at Sadie. "You didn't give us much."

Sadie didn't budge.

Gril took a deep breath. "Please. Just give us a few minutes."

Officer Natno wasn't a kid. He was probably in his fifties, and he gave the impression he'd been around the block a time or two and might be concerned about Gril's small-town policing abilities. I didn't feel it was my place to speak up and defend the police chief, but I wanted to. Instead, we all just waited until the offi-cer came to the reasonable conclusion of doing what Gril asked, because it was probably the best way to get anything helpful from Sadie.

Once he was gone and we heard the front door shut, Sadie turned to Gril. "I don't trust them, the Juneau police. I just don't trust them."

"I got that. Why?" Gril asked.

Sadie shook her head and pursed her lips tight. She crossed her arms even more tightly.

"Sadie," Viola said. "It's okay. Take your time answering any of these questions. I know you just met all of us, but we *can* be trusted."

"That's the first thing people who shouldn't be trusted say."

"Well, there is something to that." Viola looked at me and then back at Sadie. "We're friends, the three of us. We need answers. We are on your side."

Viola was rough and tumble, a gun in a holster around her waist, literally. But when she wanted to, she could bring sympathy and empathy in ways most people couldn't—genuinely. Sadie's hackles had risen, but they lowered a little now.

Viola and Gril shared a look. He nodded and then looked at Sadie.

"Sadie, would you prefer for me to leave, too?" he asked.

She looked up at him like she was surprised by the offer. "I'm . . . I've been scared for so long. The police haven't been . . . fair." She said the last word as if she wasn't quite sure that was the one she was looking for, but she didn't retract it. "I trust Beth. If she says you're okay, I'll trust you, too."

"They're okay," I said quickly. "They're the best, in fact."

"Gril is always fair," Viola added. "You can trust all of us in this room. You don't have to talk about why you don't trust the Juneau police right now. Let's talk about the man who was on the island with you."

Sadie bit her bottom lip and looked at us, one at a time. Finally, her expression and her crossed arms relaxed a little more.

"Okay. I don't know his name, the one who took me. He never told me something to call him, even a lie. I don't know who he is. Was? I don't . . ."

"Did you see the bear attack him?" Viola asked.

"I saw the bear slash at him, then I . . . froze maybe. What I remember is that I turned away and crouched, covered my eyes with my hands." Tears filled her eyes now. "The man's screams were awful, I'll never forget them." She paused as the tears rolled down her cheeks. "I was happy he was being killed. I felt relief, but it was still awful."

"That makes sense, Sadie," I said. "He hurt you."

She nodded, sniffed, and wiped her cheeks with her hands. "And then everything got so quiet. I don't know how long I crouched there, but I suddenly realized there were no more noises. Not even birds. It was so, so quiet. I stood up and turned around, and there was no sign of either the bear or the man."

"How did you get so covered in blood?" I asked.

"I have no idea," she said, shaking her head.

I'd experienced my own trauma-induced amnesia and had remembered most things from those three days with Travis Walker only over the last couple of months. It was easy to see that this sort of forgetfulness was a way to protect the psyche. But Sadie had remembered me, which didn't mean she should remember anything else. It was just something I noted to myself.

She'd been cleaned up. I hoped someone had flown some blood samples to a Juneau lab for testing. There were so many possible ways to ping DNA these days that it was amazing that anyone got away with anything. But they did.

"Sadie, do you remember when the man took you from your house? Do you remember the details?" I asked.

"I do." She nodded and put her arms on the table, folding her hands together in a composed fashion. "I was working in my front yard, in my flower garden. I'm pretty sure it was a week ago?" She looked at Gril.

He nodded. "The best we can pinpoint is that you disappeared six days ago, so last Tuesday. That's when a neighbor found a gardening bucket overturned in your yard."

"Okay, that probably makes sense. Anyway, the man drove up in a small blue van-like car. You know, something like a delivery vehicle."

"I heard about the van from one of the officers you spoke with briefly. I have some pictures." Gril opened the file in front of him, retrieved pictures of different sorts of vans, and slid them in her direction.

Sadie studied the pictures and pointed at a small, white, boxy van-like vehicle. "Yes, I think that's about right. A dark blue, though."

Gril nodded and took the pictures back. "Okay. Go on."

"He got out of the car and just walked right to me. He didn't carry anything. I thought he was going to give me a message or a package or something." She closed her eyes tightly now, but the tears had stopped. "He just grabbed me. Picked me up and put me in the back of that van. I screamed and yelled. No one helped."

Gril had mentioned neighbors. My house in St. Louis was tucked in the middle of lots of trees. It was feasible that no one had heard or seen what had happened to me, but that didn't seem right for Sadie.

"Do you have nearby neighbors?" I asked.

She opened her eyes and looked at me. "Yes, I live on a street in Juneau. In fact, the houses are crowded together." She sounded angry that no one had helped her.

She wasn't necessarily wrong to be angry. There was a chance someone had witnessed what had happened but just didn't want to get involved. I hoped that hadn't been true, though.

"Maybe your neighbors were all at work?" I offered.

"Yes, of course, but still, someone's always around. I'm around a lot, too. Why didn't someone help me?"

"Sometimes people are just able to do things unnoticed," Viola said. "Some of us can't get away with anything; some of us can. I'm afraid it's just the way it is. You're here now, though."

Sadie nodded as she looked at Viola and then fell back into her story.

"He threw me into that van and then drove away. There were no windows in the back, and he'd put up a sheet of Plexiglas between the back and the front—"

"Same thing happened to me," I couldn't stop myself from adding.

Sadie looked at me. "It was so frustrating. I could see the man who did this to me, but I couldn't get at him."

I remembered. "Exactly."

I could see resolve wash over her, her chin lift a little, her shoulders come up from a slump. "Okay. Okay. He drove out of there and took me to some . . . warehouse or garage or storage place or something."

"Hang on," Gril said. "Tell me more about that. Do you know how long you traveled before you got there?"

"I was panicked the whole way, so it wasn't enough time for me to come down from that fear. I've been trying to understand how long it might have been, but though it felt like hours, it couldn't have been. I mean, we never boarded a ferry. We stayed on land, so it couldn't have been too far."

"Tell me about the warehouse. Colors, how big, whatever you can."

"Drab colors, tans maybe. It seemed like the place he drove us into was about four times the size of a single-car garage. I could only see out the front window of the van, and I'm pretty sure I saw other similar buildings as we made our way. I didn't see any other people."

"Maybe like a barracks or a small airport?" I asked. "We have an airport here. There is only one of those types of warehouses, but that's what first came to my mind."

"Maybe. I didn't see any planes. No, wait! I saw weeds . . . coming up from cracks in the pavement. You know, an old, small airport *could* have been where he took me." She closed her eyes again. "I don't know, maybe I'm just hoping . . . It was abandoned, I'm sure of that. Not in use. The building he drove us into could have been an old hangar, though I didn't see a plane or plane parts . . ."

Viola and Gril shared a look, as if they both had the same idea. I was curious, but I didn't ask about it right then.

"What did he look like?" I asked Sadie.

"I've already told the police." Her tone was clipped, as if she didn't want to talk about his looks ever again.

She would be asked the same question at least a few more times, and even through her irritation, she knew it was important.

"Sorry, but would you mind repeating?" I said.

She sighed. "He was probably in his forties or fifties. He had salt-and-pepper hair, but his face wasn't wrinkled except for laugh lines around his eyes. He had brown eyes. He was . . . a nice-looking man." She swallowed hard. "I hate even saying that I noticed that, but I did."

"We'd like you to talk to a sketch artist," Gril said. "We're trying to set up a call with one in Juneau. It's not the most ideal, but everyone thinks you should stay here a day or so more, until the Juneau folks get some answers there."

She glared at Gril. "They'll never do it right. I want to go home, but not until all of this is resolved, Chief. Please don't make me work with them."

"Why?" Gril asked.

"I can't . . ."

Gril nodded. "Are you okay talking to a sketch artist?"

"I suppose I am."

"What happened after you got to the warehouse?" I asked.

"You want to know what he did to me?" she asked.

"I . . . I guess the police would like to know *all* the details. I'd also like to know what he said to you. Did he tell you why he took you?" I said.

"At first, when we were in the warehouse and I wouldn't stop yelling, he kept telling me to shut up. He told me that no one would hear me, that he was tired of all my noise. After that, he didn't talk to me. He tied my wrists and ankles, put a gag in my mouth, and then took a call on his cell phone, though he asked whoever was on the other end to hang on a second. I couldn't see him leave, but I heard a door open and then shut, and it was quiet again."

"Cell phone?" I looked at Viola and Gril. "If you two have a place in mind, would a cell phone have coverage there?"

"I think so," Viola said.

"It's out from Juneau a bit, but I think it would," Gril added. "I'll have them check the nearby towers, see if that offers any clues." He looked at Sadie. "This was all the first day?" She nodded and he continued, "Okay, what else happened that day?"

"Well, I'm not sure I can separate the days. From there on, it was him just watching me. He gave me food. At first, I yelled and screamed when he took off the gag, but then I stopped even trying. He gave me a bucket for a toilet . . . that was awful, but at least he gave me something to use. I slept at night, sort of. The light wasn't diffused, and I couldn't keep track of much of anything. It seemed like the days went on and on. I don't know when he slept because every time I woke up, he was there watching me. I couldn't get away, no matter how hard I tried." She lifted the sleeves of the jacket someone had given her, displaying abrasions where ropes had rubbed her raw. "I have the same things on my ankles."

I hadn't noticed those injuries before. "Did he otherwise hurt you?"

"No. He didn't rape me, didn't even try. He didn't hit me. He wouldn't talk to me, other than telling me to shut up. I would recognize his voice if I heard it again because of the times he talked on the phone."

"Did you get anything from those calls?" Gril asked.

"Not a thing. He was careful enough to leave before really talking, but he answered in front of me."

"That's good." Gril's tone prompted her to go on.

"I tried to keep track of time, but kept getting myself confused, so I don't know how many days we were there. Then one day, he gave me breakfast and something to drink, and I passed out. When I woke up, we were on that island, though I didn't know it was an island. At first, I just thought we were outside, around a bunch of trees. I was groggy for a while. He untied me, and I remember thinking I was going to run the first chance I got, but then the bear showed up."

Sadie fell into thought. We were quiet as we waited. She looked up at Viola a long moment later. "I didn't even realize I was covered in blood. I have no idea how that happened."

"Okay," Viola said.

"And then I ran. It didn't take long for me to come to the ocean. I saw a bunch of ships, so I just started waving. And then they came and got me." She turned her gaze to Gril now. "I know I'm missing some moments, but I swear, that's all I remember."

"You've done great, Sadie," Gril said. "Really great."

The front door of the Benedict House opened. Gus stood and we all turned toward the dining room entryway to see who was coming inside. Officer Natno stopped there and looked directly at Gril.

"We've got a body."

As Gril stood to join the officer, the only other noise came from Sadie. She made a sort of squeak or squeal as more tears ran down her cheeks. Viola put her hand over Sadie's and let her cry.

Six

"You found the body?" I asked Tex when he, surprisingly, answered his phone.

"Yes, ma'am. It was me." Tex sighed through the phone line, giving the noise some extra static.

"Oh, Tex, that had to be awful."

"I've come upon worse."

"I'm so sorry."

"Mother Nature can be brutal, even given only a few hours to do her work."

"An officer from Juneau, Officer Natno, came in and told us a body had been found, then two other officers came in and got Sadie, Gril, and Viola. I think she's supposed to stay here at the Benedict House, but I haven't seen her come back. She wasn't happy to go with them, but it appeared she had no choice, and Gril and Viola went with her, too. They also seemed genuinely concerned about her safety. Donner told me you'd gone back out to Lilybook. I'm glad you're home now." I was trying to get all the words out.

"Yeah, the other two rescuers who were with us earlier went

as well. Their names are Jenny and Ted and they're from Juneau. Nice enough. Thorough, I think. We didn't talk much, but they were looking forward to getting home.

"Can you tell me any details?" I leaned back in Viola's office chair. The door was closed, though most of the time I left it open when I was talking to Tex. I thought tonight's conversation probably shouldn't be overheard.

"Once on the island, we split up, though that wasn't my decision. I would have recommended a full team of four, splitting into two teams of two. Doesn't matter. We had who we had. I'm familiar enough with the island to know where the caves are located—they aren't hard to find, so I told Jenny and Ted, who said that today was their first time on the island, to be careful around them. They weren't bothered and we had weapons, both lethal and tranquilizer guns. I took the east shore. There are a couple rocky outcroppings over there; I thought either of those inlets would be a great spot for a body to get caught in. Turns out I was right. I'm assuming the tide took it over there at some point, though I'm not good enough to guess where the body went in the water. There he was—it wasn't pretty. I'd glanced in that direction earlier but hadn't noticed the body, so I'm assuming it wasn't there the whole time."

"Oh. That had to be awful," I said again.

"He was already unrecognizable. We did search for a wallet, but no luck."

"Were you supposed to do that?"

"I made the decision. You don't want to miss a chance to identify a body and you don't want to mess with evidence, but I erred on the side of getting this guy's name as soon as possible if we could. Whatever evidence might have been on the body was probably washed away anyway. You don't want to risk a wallet being lost in transit."

"That makes sense. Was it . . . slashed up?" I wrote some of the most graphic and terrifying thrillers in the genre, but when it came to real life, the vivid pictures didn't want to find a place in my mind's eye.

"No, it wasn't. In fact . . ."

"What?"

"There were holes, like stab wounds, but no slashes anywhere."

"Stab wounds? Really?" I paused. "A bear wouldn't have done that. You think Sadie actually killed him?"

"I don't think anything except I know there were no claw marks on that body."

"Interesting. Baffling."

"I agree. I told Gril, but the other two with me seemed not to want to say much."

"I wonder why?"

"Don't know. I'm glad we found the body, though—glad it wasn't found by some hikers or campers."

The memory of my father and the fishing boat popped into my mind, as they seemed to be heading in that direction even though I hadn't witnessed them stopping anywhere. What if he, along with his paying customers or a group like them, had found the body? "That *would* have been worse. Did you see any bears?"

"Not one. And the other two didn't make it to the caves by the time I found the body and radioed them over. There might be something in the caves that would help, but, Beth, this man wasn't killed by a bear. That much I know for sure. I've seen that enough times to know."

Noises as if people were coming through the Benedict House's front door reached me.

"Shoot. People are here. Can we talk later or tomorrow?"

"Tomorrow. I'm beat."

"Thanks, Tex. Get some rest."

"You too."

We disconnected the call, and I went to see what was going on.

Though it sounded like a big group, it was only Viola and Sadie returning. Gus, who'd been resting in Viola's office with me, hurried to greet them. Sadie lit up when she saw the dog this time. She seemed less . . . haggard.

"Hi," I said.

"Beth." Viola nodded at me.

"Did you hear if it's been confirmed?" Sadie looked up from petting Gus. "He's dead. They found him. He's dead."

"I did hear."

Relief bordering on a little forced glee lined her voice, and as much as I wanted to pump my fist in solidarity, that didn't feel quite right. I did have something to say, though. "You'll sleep well tonight."

"I will! That is true."

I spotted a wave of somber roll over her. She wasn't done dealing with everything yet, and though her captor was dead, the horror didn't immediately disappear.

"I'm going to get Sadie all tucked in," Viola said. She turned to me. "We still need to discuss chores for tomorrow."

That was most certainly code for "I need to talk to you." Viola and I had never once discussed chores—today's, tomorrow's, or any other day's.

"Sounds good," I said. "I'll be in my room."

Gus and I stepped outside so he could attend to his necessaries before bedtime. Donner was no longer sitting near the bar, but the chair was still there. The Juneau police car was still parked at the end of the building, but I didn't spot the uniforms walking around.

I suddenly thought about Orin. He would probably have access to all the details of Sadie's insertion into WITSEC, if that was a true story. It wasn't that I didn't believe Sadie, but I wasn't sure what exactly to make of anything at the moment. There were unknowns that made me doubtful about everything. Orin hadn't met

Gus and me today, but I made a mental note to call him first thing the next morning.

Just as Gus finished up, I noticed someone step out of the restaurant. He held three Styrofoam containers of food. If I hadn't been watching him, he might not have sensed eyes on him. But he did.

"Beth!" Eddy called.

I hadn't noticed his car—an old sedan that Gril had rounded up for him—but there it was, parked in front of the restaurant. I quickly calculated how long it would take Gus and me to escape into the Benedict House and if we could lock the door before Eddy reached us. It would have been a rude gesture, and one I wouldn't act on, but I couldn't stop the thought of it.

"Hey," I said as he approached. I'd try to be friendly. You would think I would want to get to know this man, but the resentment I felt at his abandonment kept showing up. I nodded at the containers. "Dinner?"

"Yes, I'm running them over to my clients at the inn." He paused. "You know, I'm actually making enough money to pay Gril some rent. If this keeps up, I might be able to get my own place in a month or so."

My heart squeezed just a little at that. He was trying to impress me, tell me he was serious about life, work, paying bills, sticking around. I couldn't fault him for trying. I wanted him to leave, though. And I wanted him to stay. I wanted him to leave me alone. I wanted us to go get coffee, until I didn't. I wished I could sort it all out better, but it wasn't easy.

He seemed to understand my chaotic emotions, though, and remained patient.

"That's good," I said.

"Right. I'm taking them out fishing again tomorrow and the next day. We don't have a full boat, so you are welcome to join."

"Oh. Uh. No. Thanks, though."

"Okay." Eddy looked well, healthy. The young guy who had left when I was seven was fading from my memory as this older man started to look more familiar. "Next time."

"Sure. Next time. Better get the dinners over there."

"Okay." I nodded and forced a small smile.

As Eddy made his way to the car, Gus and I went inside and to my room. I left the door open, hoping Viola would be there soon.

I sat on my bed and didn't think about Eddy. He did take up too much headspace sometimes, but now there were more important things to consider—Tex discovering a body that had been stabbed, the inconsistencies in Sadie's story. I hoped Viola had more . . .

"Beth?" Viola said from the door.

I looked up. "Hey."

"Can I come in?"

"Of course."

She closed the door behind her as I scooted over to give her room on the bed.

"So we're going to talk about chores?" I lifted my eyebrows.

She snorted. "I wonder if I was subtle."

"I doubt Sadie was paying a bit of attention."

"Yeah, she's been through the wringer."

"You don't sound completely convinced."

"Oh, Beth, you know me, I'm suspicious of everyone. Turns out, though, this time my suspicions might be warranted."

I sensed I knew what she was going to say, but I didn't know if Tex was supposed to have filled me in. "What's up?"

"A bear didn't kill that man. He was stabbed, most likely with a stick, a strong one, but something natural."

"Sadie could have done that?"

"I think anyone can pull something like that off if they're motivated enough, running on enough fear or adrenaline."

"But wouldn't it be justified? I mean, if she killed the man who kidnapped her?"

"Yes, of course. If that's really what happened."

"Obviously, there's some doubt."

Viola sighed. "The good news is that we've got the body. We can go from there, but Gril doesn't think we've been given the whole story."

Again, I wasn't sure how much I was supposed to know or if Viola knew about Sadie's alleged WITSEC. I suddenly decided that maybe I shouldn't interject unless I had something verified. First, I'd talk to Orin tomorrow.

"The Juneau police will be staying the night?" I asked.

"Yes, in Benedict, but not here with us. What Sadie said about the police—that they haven't helped her, that she seems adamant about not wanting to work with them—bothered Gril. He's told the police they are not allowed to stay inside the Benedict House, but they are welcome to watch the place all they want."

I nodded and lifted a sarcastic eyebrow. "That's pretty thoughtful of him."

"He's always on the side of law enforcement, but the way Sadie was earlier, it sat funny with him. He wants her to be able to relax and recuperate."

I nodded.

Viola looked at me with an even more scrutinous gaze. "Beth, there's more going on here than meets the eye. Of course, I'm going to defend this place"—she patted the gun—"with everything I've got, but I don't know . . . Consider staying somewhere else for a few days?"

I shook my head. "No, I'm not going anywhere. I'm fine. None of this has been too triggering, and I do think I can help Sadie, if it turns out she needs that sort of help."

Viola frowned at me.

"Also," I continued. "Those chores."

She laughed, though it faded quickly. She was tired and worried. "All right." She stood. "Lock your door."

Viola petted Gus. "Watch over Beth."

Gus nodded that he had it covered.

Viola left my room, her mind so otherwise occupied, she didn't even say goodbye. What I didn't tell her, what I wasn't even sure I had a right to feel, was that I was going to stay in the Benedict House for her, too. Sure, she had the gun, but I would be worried about her if I left now.

She'd laugh at me if I told her that much. It seemed a bit over the top even to me, but my decision was made.

Nope, I wasn't going anywhere.

Seven

couldn't sleep. I sat up in bed and looked at the digital clock on the nightstand. It was after three, but not close enough to four for me to get excited about the idea of getting ready for the day. I wasn't in the mood to read or work or watch anything. I was antsy.

Maybe I was just hungry.

Gus was passed out, snoring hard in his bed on the floor next to me. I even asked him if he wanted to join me in the kitchen, but he answered with only another snore.

I left the door open a crack so he could find me if he woke up and wondered where I'd gone.

Dim, red night-lights glowed in the hallway, giving it a creepy ambience. I'd mentioned to Viola that a different color might be more soothing, but she'd only shrugged and said she'd bought what she could find at Toshco, our local Costco-like store. I imagined that many houses throughout Benedict had become home to nightly red corridors. We were all at the mercy of the available inventory.

I padded to the kitchen, giving a cursory glance to the end of the other hallway but not noticing any room lights on before I headed into the kitchen.

I didn't think I really was hungry, but maybe a snack would help me feel tired enough to sleep for a couple hours. I opened the refrigerator and freezer doors and looked around. Both sides were well stocked, but nothing looked particularly appealing. I finally settled on a package of string cheese, which was one of Viola's favorites.

Just as I closed the fridge door, I heard the front door open. My first reaction was to call out for Viola or just announce that I was in the dining room. Instead, something inside me thought better of it, so I remained silent in the dark kitchen behind the dark dining room, holding the cheese in one hand as I waited for whoever had come in to walk by.

Sadie hurried past the entryway, not giving the kitchen a second glance. Remaining silent, I listened as it seemed she made her way into Viola's office. I could hear the chair squeak, just like it had earlier when I'd been talking to Tex.

Extra curious now, cheese still in my hand, I walked lightly out to the hallway and then down it, stopping outside Viola's office door, just as the keys on her keyboard started to clack.

"Shit," Sadie said another moment later. "No internet?"

I'd flattened myself up against the wall. No, Sadie, there was no internet connection. Sometimes Viola used her landline to dial up a connection, but the turtle-speed of that sort of internet only made her want to shoot her computer, so she didn't resort to that very often.

I was lucky, though, in that it appeared that Sadie liked to talk to herself. I did, too. Though I mostly rationalized that I was speaking to Gus, even when he wasn't with me.

"Damn," she said. "Come on. Goose Creek. Goose Creek. I just need Goose Creek." She paused. "There is literally no internet here," she said, astonished.

She'd get used to it if she stuck around long enough.

Why was she looking for something called Goose Creek? And why did that sound familiar, even though I knew there was nothing nearby with that name? Tex had educated me on the local geography, thinking it important for me to know names of places and when the best times were to walk through or visit them—and when to stay away from them.

But there was no Goose Creek in Benedict. Again, though, it sounded so familiar.

"Shit," Sadie said again, as it sounded like she lifted the keyboard and dropped it, though not with a force hard enough to break it, hopefully.

I could have tried to hurry back to the dining room or even to the other hallway toward my bedroom, but instead I stayed where I was. If she saw me, we could talk. If she didn't, I could talk to Viola tomorrow and then she, and maybe I, too, could have a conversation with Sadie.

The chair complained again as she stood and then made her way out of the office. I remained where I was, my back still to the wall, under the red glow as Sadie went directly to her room and then inside it. She didn't even look in my direction.

I hurried back to the front door, unlocked it again, and went outside. At almost three-thirty now, there were hints of the early sunrise and I felt momentarily discombobulated. I hadn't slept much, and still might get some sleep if I tried, but the sun was about to get the day started. I shook off the feeling and looked around.

No one was in sight. Sometimes I could see a light on in the bar in the middle of the night and I knew Benny was working, cleaning, or just "puttering around" as she called it. But the bar's window was dark. So were all the others.

The chair Donner had sat in was still there, but Donner wasn't. I couldn't immediately see the police car, but as I took a step out toward the town square, light from somewhere gleamed off a bumper; the car was parked farther back.

I hadn't put on any shoes, but I marched in that direction, through the dewy grass that made up the center of the square. My feet got wet and cold, but it wasn't terrible. They'd been colder and sometimes wetter inside winter boots.

I approached the passenger side of the police car slowly. I couldn't immediately see inside, but startling someone with a gun was never a good idea.

As I came around, I could see Officer Natno. He was awake, his eyebrows lifting and his eyes growing wide before he hurried out of the vehicle.

"What's wrong?" he asked.

"Nothing," I said. "I just couldn't sleep."

I'd explored to see if I could understand what Sadie had been up to. The urge to look inside the police car had just come upon me. I'd heard and seen enough from Sadie that I didn't want the Juneau police to think she might be up to something, even if she was.

"Okay," the officer said. "Beth, right?"

"Yes."

"Can I help you with anything?"

I shook my head. "No, I . . . well, I guess I just wanted to see who was still out here." I held out the cheese. "Need a snack?"

"No, thanks." His eyes went to my feet. "Bare feet around here aren't a good idea."

I laughed at his weak but sincere mansplaining. "You are right."

"Okay then."

I couldn't help but ask him. "Why didn't Sadie want to talk with you around?"

"Oh. Well, you should probably ask her, but yes, there is a history between Sadie Milbourn and the Juneau police. It's nothing you need to concern yourself about."

"It isn't? I mean, you don't think it has anything to do with everything she's been through?"

Officer Natno was about to lose patience with me. I knew the look. Instead, though, he seemed to choose some careful words. "No matter what the history is, the police are here to protect her, even if she doesn't believe that."

I nodded. I wished he'd give me more, but he wasn't going to. "Did you see anything suspicious tonight?"

"No, I didn't. Do you have something you would like to share with me?"

The car had been parked enough to the side of the building that Sadie could have easily come outside and moved around on the boardwalk without being noticed by Natno. I couldn't figure out why she'd do such a thing, but I was pretty sure he hadn't seen her. He would have escorted her back inside, wouldn't he? I still wasn't quite sure who to trust.

"Not a thing," I said, surprising myself by how truthful the lie sounded.

He nodded. "You should get back inside. Get something on your feet."

"Yes. I will. Have a good . . . morning." I turned and made my way back to the Benedict House, the red glow still lighting the way in the hallways.

No one was out of their rooms, including Gus, who was still fast asleep on his bed. I dried off my feet and climbed back into my own bed, grateful for the blackout curtains and hopeful for at least a couple hours rest. I ate the cheese and then tried to sleep.

If I could just turn off my mind.

Eight

I woke up at seven, having gotten a few hours of rest. Gus was awake too, sniffing the cheese wrapper I'd left on the nightstand.

I laughed. "You snooze, you lose. All right, we're going to make this a great day."

Once I was cleaned up, I ran Gus outside—still no Donner. No police car, either. Gus and I searched for Viola and Sadie but found neither. I wondered if they'd run over to the café for breakfast. I didn't want to leave Gus alone in the house today—though he'd done fine alone many times, I just felt like I wanted him to be around one of his people.

However, as welcome as dogs were around Benedict businesses, taking them into the restaurant was frowned upon. I spotted the open light on at the bar, so I decided I'd see if Benny wanted some Gus company for a little bit. I knew she would.

Benny, Viola's sister, was just as integral to the town, though she didn't carry a gun.

"Hey!" she said when Gus and I came through the front

door. Her smile widened when she spotted him. "Come here and see me."

Gus trotted to her. She'd started keeping a canister of dog treats under the bar. Gus knew where it was, and he knew she was always happy to give him one.

"You'll spoil him," I said.

"I certainly hope so."

Benny loved dogs. Dogs loved Benny. She'd been listed as a possible owner for one of Elijah's crew, but she'd disappointedly declined. I'd overseen the rehoming of the dogs, and she'd told me she was afraid she couldn't give a dog enough attention. The bar needed her too much, and she didn't want to force a dog to spend most of its life inside a bar. However, she had taken to watching Gus every now and then, and Gus hadn't minded his days hanging with Benny and her customers.

Once they were done greeting each other, she stood up straight and looked at me. "What can I get for you?"

"I'm going to run over to the restaurant, see if Viola and our guest are there."

"Sadie something-or-other?"

I cocked my head at her tone. "Yeah, Sadie Milbourn. Know anything about her?"

"That she's not who she says she is, but that's all I can tell you."

I felt a sense of being left out, even though I was hiding information, too. Sadie had told me about WITSEC, but I was pretending I didn't know. Benny wasn't working too hard to hide what might be the same story. I took a chance.

"Do you mean the witness protection?" I said quietly, though there was no one in the place but us.

She raised her eyebrows at me. "You know?"

"I do, though Viola and Gril don't know I know."

Benny crossed her heart. "Won't tell."

"How do you know? Does everybody know but are pretending like they don't?"

"Oh no. I overheard the cops talking about it in here last night." She rolled her eyes at me. "No one thinks the bartender is paying attention, but everyone wants us to solve their problems. It's a thing."

I sidled up to a stool. "Ooh, I'd love to know what else you overheard." I reached in my bag for my wallet. "I'll have a tomato juice, no bloody to it."

Though Benny made the best Bloody Marys I'd ever tasted, it was too early for me.

She set a glass of tomato juice in front of me. "Not much more than that really, except that they kept calling her Sadie with a tone that made me think that wasn't her name. That's what got my attention first—their tone."

"Any chance they mentioned her other birth name, I guess?"

"No, I hoped they would, but they didn't."

"Connecticut? That's where she said she was from."

"No."

"Huh."

Benny put her hands on her side of the bar and leaned. "Sounds like this girl has some things going on."

"It does."

"All the attention they're giving her." Benny paused. "But Connecticut? I mean, it's not a hotbed of crime syndicates, is it?"

I shrugged. "Summer home for a mafioso?"

"Maybe. I'd sure like to know what went down."

"Me too."

"I'm not just saying that, Beth. I wonder if Orin could help us figure it out."

"I had the same thought. I was going to try to talk to him this morning. I wonder if he also knows Benedict's worst-kept secret."

"Probably. It's hard to keep a secret around here. Let me know what he says, 'kay?"

"Sure, but why so curious?"

"Just naturally curious, I suppose, but she is staying at the Benedict House. Viola's great with nonviolent stuff, and of course she's prepared for something worse, but I'd like for us all to be aware of what she has on her hands. Mostly, though, I'm nosey."

"That makes sense. I'll let you know what Orin says."

"Thanks. Also, the two guys last night clearly don't like Sadie, and that bothered me. They're supposed to protect and serve, right?"

"Of course." I thought about my conversation with Officer Natno. It seemed sincere enough, but Benny's words made me second-guess my assessment.

"They were clearly doing their jobs with a chip on their shoulders."

"And you couldn't figure out why?" I took a swig of the cold juice.

"Not really. The only thing they said that might have something to do with it was that she'd 'screwed them before' and they 'weren't going to let her do it again.'"

"I wonder what she did to them? Maybe she filed some sort of complaint against an officer or something."

"That crossed my mind, too, but they didn't share any more."

"Want me to try to get Orin to work on that, too?"

"Sure." Benny paused again. "I think we count on Orin to share too much sometimes."

"I thought it was just me."

Benny shook her head. "No, we're all curious, and Orin has such good intel."

I nodded and then finished off the juice. "He does. Hey, mind Gus hanging out for a few minutes?"

"Why don't you leave him here all day? You might be busy, talking to Orin and all."

I turned and looked at Gus, who was sitting behind me but peering up at Benny. I laughed. "I think he'd like that."

"See you later, Beth. I'm looking forward to any answers you want to share."

I saluted her as I left and set out on the short journey past the mercantile and into the café.

Viola and Sadie were there, sitting at the back corner table, which had become Viola's favorite spot to bring all her clients. It was private enough.

As I wove my way toward them, I had the distinct impression that maybe they wouldn't welcome a visitor. But I'd come that far, and it would be weird if I turned around now. The restaurant wasn't big enough to miss my entrance.

Donner wasn't there and I didn't spot any police officers. I wanted to talk to Viola about Goose Creek before I brought it up with Sadie, but I'd see if a good moment presented itself anyway.

Viola sent me a quick nod of hello, but Sadie's eyes brightened as I approached the table. "Beth, hello!"

"Good morning."

"Where's Gus?" Viola asked.

"He's with Benny."

"Good." She looked at Sadie and then back up at me. "Okay, Beth. No more options. You need to move out of your room for a few days."

"Wait. Why? What happened?"

Viola looked back at Sadie, who nodded.

"Have a seat, Beth." Viola scooted her chair closer to the wall so I could move easily into the one next to her. She looked around the restaurant. There was no one suspicious inside. I recognized everyone there, in fact. By now, I knew most of them by name even if we hadn't had a conversation.

"What's up?" I asked in a hushed tone.

"I'm not . . . I told Gril and Viola that I let you know I'm in witness protection," Sadie said. "I was giving Viola more of the details after she spoke with your police chief this morning."

"Coffee, Beth? Anything to eat?" Donna stood next to the table, a mug and a full carafe in her hands.

"Coffee's great. Thanks, Donna," I said.

She set the mug down and poured the coffee. She must have sensed the heavy air around us.

"All righty then. Tell you what, I'll leave you three be, but just let me know if you need anything. I'm a holler away."

"Thanks, Donna." Viola would leave a good tip.

Once Donna had moved on to the next table, Viola, Sadie, and I hunkered even closer together.

"The police don't think the man who took me had anything to do with my past," Sadie said.

"In Connecticut?" I asked.

"Right. And they think I killed him."

"Did you?" I asked. I didn't even need to add that it would have been her right to do such a thing. It would have been in my book, and if things had gone down the way she said, there wasn't a person in Benedict who wouldn't support and defend her. I still didn't understand what the problem was with the Juneau police, but if they somehow held her feet to the fire, Gril would make sure she wouldn't have to pay for saving her own life.

"I don't think so." Sadie shook her head. "I don't remember doing so, but I really don't think I could." She held out her hands, palms up. "Look."

Her hands were mostly injury-free. There was one small abrasion on the inside of her thumb, but it wasn't bad.

She pulled her hands back and looked at them herself. "If I had stabbed him with . . . anything, wouldn't my hands be more messed up? It's the first thing I thought of, my hands. They aren't even sore." She flexed her fingers.

"Did you point that out to the police?" I asked.

"I did, but they didn't have any comment."

"So why wouldn't they err on the side of caution and just get you out of here, move you somewhere? Isn't that what happens in witness protection?"

Sadie nodded enthusiastically. "Yes, but they . . ." She looked at Viola.

"Gril has suggested they get Sadie out of here just in case, but the police aren't the people who control her status as a protected witness. They want to make sure Sadie didn't just randomly kill a man. The US Marshals are in charge of WITSEC, and, well, the police . . ."

"They don't trust me. They don't like me," Sadie said.

"Why? What happened? And you killing the man who took you seems justified."

Viola frowned. "That's what I was talking to Sadie about. The police have questioned her neighbors. Two of them claim to have seen Sadie get into the van with the man willingly."

I looked at Sadie.

"That's not the way it happened. It's not." Her voice was firm, her gaze into my eyes steady.

"Okay," I said. I thought a moment. "Is that why they don't trust you, though? I was under the impression that it was because of something before . . . all of this."

Sadie frowned. "There was an incident in Juneau a while ago. I was present when a murder took place. The police think I let the killer get away."

"Okay," Viola said. "Details?"

Sadie shook her head. "Really, it doesn't matter."

Viola frowned. She was used to being the one to determine what did and didn't matter.

"Why were you put into witness protection?" I asked.

Sadie sighed. "That's why you need to go someplace else, Beth. I shouldn't have told anyone about my witness status. My handler is on his way here and he's angry. I can't share more." She looked at Viola. "Even with Viola or Chief Gril. I'm sorry." She paused. "Look, if it were up to me, I would just leave, go back to Juneau, pack my bags and go someplace else. It's a big world. I would find a place. But I don't have that sort of freedom. One, because I'm being protected by the government. Two, because of the reasons why."

I didn't want to leave the Benedict House, but realized that Sadie had somehow convinced Viola that the danger was more real than any credence I'd given it.

I looked back and forth at them. "Okay, what about the van? It might hold evidence to show the truth."

Viola bit her lip and nodded slowly as if she'd thought of this a long time ago. "Right. They haven't been able to find it."

"And I don't know where it is," Sadie exclaimed, and then lowered her voice again. "From all indications, he drugged me, and I woke up out in the middle of nowhere, where there was a bear, for god's sake. I don't know where he parked that stupid van."

Tears filled Sadie's eyes, but I watched her blink them back. She didn't want to waste time crying right now. I knew that feeling, too.

I turned to Viola. "Where could it be? No, more importantly, how could he have gotten Sadie to the island? We can backtrack from there."

She lifted one eyebrow. "Exactly."

"Oh. That's what you two were doing."

Viola nodded.

"Okay, so what did you come up with?"

"Planes and boats, that's it. A seaplane, maybe a smaller, rented boat."

"From Juneau?" I asked.

Sadie jumped in. "Or very close to it. Had to be. I was drugged in the warehouse, I'm sure. He couldn't have boarded the ferry from Juneau with an unconscious woman hoisted over his shoulder. He might have put me on a plane but those logistics and me waking up on that island don't add up. How did I get off a plane and onto the island? There was no landing strip. I doubt I would have fit inside a suitcase. So somehow, he got me on a boat, probably by himself. But if so, where was it first docked, and then where did it go? I don't remember a minute of it."

"Because the Juneau police are being so obstinate," Viola said, "Gril is going to jump on a plane and head over to an old airfield outside Juneau. Maybe that's where Sadie was kept. It's the most logical option, at least with the information we have."

"When?" I asked.

"Soon, I guess. He was headed over to the airport half an hour ago."

I had so many more questions for the two of them. I wanted to talk to Orin. I did not want to move out of my room at the Benedict House. And Goose Creek—what in the world was Goose Creek?

I also wanted to look at the old airfield.

"Think I could go with Gril?" I asked Viola.

She laughed once. "No, Beth, I don't."

"I'm going to see," I said as I stood from the chair. I grabbed a ten from my wallet and left it on the table. "I'm going to see if he'll let me come along."

"Beth . . ." Viola began.

I couldn't stop myself. "I'll be back if he says no."

"Beth!" Viola said, firmly enough to get my full attention.

I looked at her. "I'm sorry, Viola. I need to try. I'm curious."

"I know," she said. "And, honestly, I don't think it's a bad idea, but Gril will."

"Oh. Okay."

Viola held up a hand. "I think that whatever danger might have at one time been there, it's not anymore, so I'm not worried for your safety. Just tell him you'd like to take the plane over for research for your books. And, well, tell him I wanted to get you out of my hair, so I sent you to ask him." Viola smiled, though it wasn't a happy expression. "I bet that will do the trick."

I returned the frown. "Thanks, Viola. Be careful. You too, Sadie."

Viola patted her gun. "Always."

My smile faded as I realized that she was probably just trying to get me out of there. She might sense there was actual danger nearby. I wanted more answers from Sadie, but I also wanted to go with Gril. And now, Viola wanted me to go with Gril, too.

I sent Viola one more nod, and then I turned and headed out of the restaurant, only to have my journey inconveniently thwarted right outside the door.

Eddy was walking with three people toward the restaurant. They were already in front of the mercantile, so there was no way for me to get away from them.

"Beth, hello!" Eddy said as I looked longingly toward the parking lot with my truck.

"Good morning," I said as politely as I could.

"Meet my clients," he said cheerfully.

My mother might have been one of the most direct and rudest people I'd ever known, but with the intervening influence of my grandfather, it was difficult for me to bring myself to be that way. I relaxed into a friendly greeting.

"Hello," I said to a man, a woman, and their teenage daughter.

They were friendly as they all nodded hello.

"This is my daughter, Beth Rivers," Eddy said, way too proudly.

"What a pleasure. We're the Duponts, not those Duponts." The woman laughed. "I'm Betty. My husband is Greg, and this is our one and only, our daughter, Gracie. Say hello, Gracie." Betty winked at me. "Get it?"

I didn't immediately get it, but once I did, I smiled at her reference just as Gracie let loose the biggest eye roll I'd ever seen. An old comedian, George Burns, used to end his shows with, "Say good night, Gracie." Gracie Burns would then proceed to say, "Good night, Gracie." It was a very cute routine, if I remembered correctly.

"The Duponts are from Des Moines, Iowa," Eddy said.

"Yes, we are," Betty said exuberantly. She was lovely, in that middle-aged way when one no longer seems to care about her hair or makeup but somehow was all the better for it.

Greg wore a look that told me he was tired of practicing patience. Or he'd just zoned out. His big black-framed glasses were in vogue again, though something told me he'd had them through the non-vogue years. An "Alaska Fishing" cap covered his hair, but brown tufts stuck out around it.

"Ms. Rivers, a pleasure," he said.

As he and I shook hands, I realized that Gracie had started looking at me intently. She'd even taken a step closer to me. "Wait a minute . . ."

"Gracie, please be polite," Betty said.

"You're Elizabeth Fairchild, that author who ran away after that man took her. That's you, isn't it? When I heard we were coming to Alaska, I actually thought about trying to track you down, but here you are. I wanted to come here because of you! Gosh, it really is nice to meet you."

"Thank you," I said, finding the fact that I was going to become recognizable here in this desolate place particularly bothersome.

Gracie might have been sixteen. My books were written to thrill and terrify, and though I was a big believer in not censoring anyone from reading anything, I wondered how someone so young had even discovered them.

"Mom, this is that writer I like so much. She writes the best books!"

Betty blinked at her daughter. "The scary ones?"

"Yes!" Gracie laughed.

Betty looked at me. "Well, I tried to read one, but I have to tell you, there is no way I'm ever opening one of them again. You scared the bejesus out of me."

I smiled at her. "Well, thank you for giving them a try."

"Oh, I'll read every one of them," Gracie said. "Keep writing. Please."

"I'll do my best." I looked over them all; Eddy, too. "I'm sorry. I don't mean to be rude, but I have an appointment. I hope you all have a great day. Nice to meet you."

"Yes, so nice to meet you!" Gracie said, drowning out the others' friendly words.

I waved and then turned to head toward my truck. I hoped I hadn't missed Gril. My eyes automatically went up to the partly cloudy sky, but I didn't see a plane anywhere.

"I'll be around town tonight if you want to meet for dinner or something," Gracie called.

"Gracie!" Greg said.

"What?" Gracie said.

"I'm sure I'll see you around," I called over my shoulder and then, hopefully without looking like I was running away, hurried to my truck.

By the time I pulled out of the parking lot and had put talking to Orin in the back of my mind, Eddy and the Duponts (a good band name if I ever heard one) had gone into the restaurant.

It didn't take long to get to the airport, where I found a full parking lot and a small plane sitting on the runway. I didn't recognize the plane as one I'd seen in Benedict.

When I found a parking spot, I turned off the truck and looked toward the plane for a moment. I was in a hurry to see if I could find Gril but suddenly remembered when I'd first come to Benedict on one of the Harvingtons' planes. It had been a terrifying flight, something that had felt like a free fall into another world— and come to find out that's exactly what it had been.

Other than my trips to Brayn, I hadn't left Benedict. Until the day before, I hadn't even ventured out on a tour boat. I hadn't taken the ferry back to Juneau once.

As I looked at that plane and so very much wanted to board it with Gril and go see the place he and Viola had remembered, I wondered if I had it in me to yank those roots up and give the rest of the world a try again.

Well, there was only one way to find out, and everything always started with a first step.

I hurried to find Gril.

Nine

eth, what are you doing here?" Gril asked as I made my way
out to the runway, where he and Fred Harvington were standing, near enough to the building that I hadn't spotted them immediately.

I'd simply passed through an open gate. There was no security
here, no one guarding anything. If someone stepped outside and
if a plane was taking off or landing right in their path, it was their
fault. The Harvington brothers did try to remain alert and stop
the wayward person or occasional moose.

"Viola said I should go with you," I began, figuring I should
start with the strongest argument and hope for the best.

"Why?"

I shrugged. "To get me out of here, I think."

"No."

"Is there room on the plane?" I nodded toward it. I'd come to
Benedict on a two-seater; this one seemed slightly larger.

"Four passenger seats," Fred Harvington said to Gril.

"Donner's coming with me," Gril said.

"Still four seats," Fred said, sending me a furtive wink.

Fred was on my side here. I didn't know why, but I appreciated it.

"I could use it as research for a book." I paused. "I haven't left Benedict, Gril. I've been here for a year. Sure, I've driven to Brayn, but I'm not sure what's going to happen when I leave. I'd like to find out. I won't get in the way. If it seems dangerous, I'll keep back. And if that's where Sadie and her captor were, the danger is probably long gone now."

Gril sighed. "Leaving Benedict is as easy as coming here to the airport, Beth—one step at a time. You could pick any other day to hop on a plane or the ferry."

"I promise I won't get in the way. For some reason, Viola thinks it would be safer for me to get out of here." I worked hard to keep my expression normal, but I was pushing it, I knew.

"Shit. Okay. But *do not* get in our way."

"Thank you!"

Fred winked at me again. "Climb aboard. Gril and I just need to go over a few more things before we take off. Donner's already on the bird."

"Thank you," I said to them both.

And then I hurried onto the plane before either one could change their mind.

"Beth," Donner said as I stepped inside. "What are you . . . ? Ah, I see you worked some more magic out there."

There was a smile to his voice, which surprised me.

"I'm thrilled I get to come along," I said.

Donner laughed. "I bet. No complaining, though."

"Why would I complain?"

"Have you ever been in one of these planes?"

"I rode the two-seater into Benedict." I didn't add that it was a horrifying journey.

"Got it. Just remember, though. No complaining."

"Cross my heart."

There were, indeed, four seats. Donner and I sat in the back two while Gril had the front row to himself. Fred Harvington flew the plane, no copilot in the remaining empty seat next to him. To my knowledge, the Harvingtons had never been involved in any crashes, but there was always a first time.

I told myself to stop disaster thinking.

The ride was rough, but I didn't complain once, as I held my hands in tight fists on my lap, where Donner couldn't see. I only looked over at him one time during the entire thirty-five minute flight: when the plane took what I thought would be its biggest dip. As it turned out, it wasn't, but I kept my eyes forward after that.

The views were spectacular. Mostly we flew over the ocean, which, when the turbulence kicks in big, looks like the open maw of a giant creature that wants to swallow you right up.

Not far past Juneau and cut into the land covered with trees, a bald acreage came into view. As I looked closer, I spotted what must have been an airfield, the two landing strips intersecting at their middles, though even from up here, the whole place appeared to be in rough shape. With two large hangars and five other smaller buildings that might have also served as hangars for smaller planes, it looked almost haunted. There were no planes in sight.

I leaned forward so Gril would hear me. "This the airport?"

He nodded but didn't try to raise his voice above the loud roar of the engine.

"Hold on," Fred announced.

I knew he wasn't kidding. I made sure my seatbelt was secure and gripped the armrests.

We headed downward—almost straight, but not quite. Fred leveled out and managed to land on the cracked and weedy runway. We, shockingly, remained secure on the landing gear's wheels.

"You nailed it, Fred," Gril called.

"I always do."

May his successful streak continue. I swallowed hard, hoping I wasn't green at the gills but knowing I'd recover quickly if I was.

"You okay, Beth?" Donner asked, sounding genuinely concerned.

I nodded and gave him a thumbs-up as I swallowed again. I was going to be fine. In a few minutes.

We disembarked. I planted my feet on the ground and took a couple of deep breaths. No one was paying me any attention. Fred was walking around the plane, and Gril and Donner were discussing the best way to investigate the large area and all the buildings.

It was unclear how long the airfield had been abandoned, but the buildings didn't appear to be about to fall down any time soon. Though the landing and takeoff strips weren't in pristine condition, I inspected them again from this vantage point. Fred might just have to veer around a couple of small potholes on takeoff, but the one we'd landed on would get us out just fine.

There was no one around. You could feel the emptiness, that sense of time being left behind. The cloudy weather that we'd taken off in when we left Benedict had followed us here. It was probably only about sixty degrees Fahrenheit, and the wind was mild. If it didn't rain, our explorations might not be disturbed by weather.

And there was a lot to explore. Even if it was a small airfield, it was hundreds of yards across and up and down, if you measured the intersecting lanes.

"I'm heading to the big buildings," Gril said to me. "You come with me. Donner will take the smaller ones. Fred, you want to go with Donner?"

"Sure. Do I get to carry a weapon?"

"No."

"Shoot. I was hoping."

"Donner will keep you safe."

"Good deal."

"Come on, Fred," Donner said.

Police work in Benedict was often improvised. Gril and Donner had done a great job from all I'd seen, but I knew that Fred and my joining them on this search wasn't exactly authorized. We'd both stay out of the way.

I stood next to Gril as he watched Donner and Fred head toward the smaller buildings. He turned to me.

"Do I need to remind you to follow my orders?"

"No, sir."

A smile quirked at the corner of his mouth. "Beth, you've never called me sir. Don't start now."

"Got it. I'll do as you say, Gril."

"Good. Okay, stay behind me as we approach the buildings. I really don't think there's anybody here, but let's be cautious."

"Of course."

The larger hangars were both domed brown steel structures. The first one we walked toward had a sign above the door that said HANGAR 12.

"How long has this place been abandoned?" I asked.

"Twenty years, as far as I know. This field was originally used for smaller planes—seaplanes—but as Juneau grew, controlling the air traffic became a concern, so this one was shut down or maybe just moved farther south. There is one down there, but I don't know if the same people who ran this one run that one. Fred wasn't sure, either. Sometimes it's not easy to get answers."

"The Juneau police didn't want to come out here?"

"I didn't tell them I was coming, Beth. I don't think they believe all Sadie is saying."

"But you do?"

"It's my job to investigate to see who is telling the truth."

"Isn't that all the Juneau police's responsibility, too?"

"I thought so."

A metallic clang came from Hangar 12. Gril put his arm out in front of me as we both stopped.

He reached for his weapon. "Stay behind me."

"Of course."

With his gun drawn, Gril approached the hangar with me behind him. No other sounds came from it. No one came through its front door.

Gril motioned me to the side of the door before he opened it.

"Benedict police. Show yourself!" he exclaimed.

No one appeared. Gril stepped inside. I heard him move around, but he didn't yell or cry out with any distress.

He peeked his head out, the gun aimed downward. "Come on in. I don't see anyone. Maybe the building settled or maybe it was an animal, but it would be hard to hide in here."

I joined him inside. He was right; it would have been very hard to hide in here. It was just a big, mostly empty, building, about the size of half a football field. Though we'd gone through a regular door, all the hangars also had one big sliding door that must have been used frequently back in the day. Since there were no working light fixtures and we weren't going to pull up the sliding door, the far corners were shadowed until Gril aimed his flashlight toward them. The shadows gave way to stark nothingness.

It wasn't a *completely* empty building, though. A dust-covered table sat against one wall, two pieces of filthy canvas littered the floor and were under one lone, forgotten propeller arm.

"No other rooms?" I asked. "A bathroom, break room?"

Gril took his time moving the light along the walls. There were no windows on the building at all. The sudden flap of wings got our attention. A hawk's nest had been constructed at the pinnacle of the rafters, where it appeared there was also a hole in the roof.

I couldn't see how the bird that was now flying above us could have made the noise we heard, but maybe it had.

"I think we've trespassed where we aren't welcome," Gril said, his light now trailing the impressive raptor.

"Do you suppose the noise came from the other hangar?" I asked.

"I don't know." Gril steadied his light over the walls again, taking slow sweeps up and down.

"Ah, I think I see it."

Gril took off toward the far wall. I followed behind him. What he'd begun as a walk turned into a quick jog.

"Come on, Beth, we're missing them."

I had no idea who *them* were, but I hurried. Once at the back of the building, he handed me the flashlight and told me where to aim it. I did as he instructed as he reached to the bottom of the wall. With his fingertips, he was able to easily peel a whole panel away from the footing—it hadn't been attached.

The noise it made as he maneuvered it sounded like what we'd heard.

"Someone left out this way," he said. "Can you hold this for me so I can get through there?"

"Sure, but can't we just go out and run around?" I grabbed the panel and pulled it open wider.

"We're behind as it is. That's it. All right." Gril squeezed himself through.

After he was on the other side, I angled myself through the opening, glad I didn't crush either Gril or myself, and stepped next to him.

We were peering into the forest. It was dark, thick with spruce, and unwelcoming.

"Hey, we just want to talk to you," Gril called out to the woods, the sound somehow echoing back slightly.

"Should we chase them?" I asked.

Gril shook his head. "No, I don't know this forest, and it's just us out here. It's likely the person was just someone using this place for shelter anyway. They might be able to tell us something, but there are too many unknowns."

I suspected Gril would go if I weren't there, and for a moment, I felt bad about that. But I decided to focus on the fact that maybe he was safer not going into those woods, so me being there was a good thing.

"Gril!" Donner called from the other side of the building. "Gril!"

"We're in the back. We're coming around."

Instead of trying to work our way through the loose panel again, we trudged through weeds and around to the front of the building.

"I think I found something," Donner said from outside a small hangar.

We hurried over to join him. These were made of the same material but unpainted.

Donner led us inside HANGAR AB, according to the sign above its door.

He held out his arm and stopped us right inside. Fred was next to the door, seemingly sticking close to the wall. "There. You can see tire tracks. I took pictures. We'll have to see if they could belong to the sort of van Sadie mentioned. There's a chair over there and a table. I explored the perimeter, and you can't see from here, but there's rope on that table, also a food wrapper. A commercial cupcake. I don't know if Sadie said what she was fed, but maybe."

"Let's take pictures, bag up what we can, and take it all with us," Gril said.

"Will do."

"Good job." Gril shone his light throughout the building.

This one had a window on each sidewall, though they were both grimy and cracked. The dust at the bottom of this hangar's sliding door had been disturbed and wasn't as thick as what I'd seen in the other one. It seemed obvious that someone had been in here recently. Maybe it had been Sadie and her captor; maybe not.

"Fred and Beth, step outside. Be alert and stick close by. Donner and I need to process this scene."

Fred and I did as Gril instructed. Once outside, we talked about exploring on our own but thought better of it.

"Thanks for helping encourage Gril to bring me along," I said.

"You're welcome. I thought you could use an adventure; maybe make up for your first flight in. Two-seaters can be pretty rough.

"I appreciate it." I didn't tell him the recent ride hadn't seemed much smoother. I appreciated his efforts.

It wasn't long before I spotted a movement at the side of the building Gril and I had been in. I did a double take, thinking I was seeing a person. They pulled back from peeking around the corner. Now I was sure I'd spotted someone.

"Fred, get Gril. I'm going to head over there and see if I can talk to the person watching us."

"What? No, you're not."

"Get Gril." I turned and ran across the cracked and weedy runway.

I had to know who it was.

Ten

decided quickly that the person was male, and it took only a second longer to realize he was running along tire tracks, a worn path. Gril and I hadn't spent enough time looking into the woods or we would have surely noticed the forged area. It wasn't too difficult to keep my footing.

"Beth!" Gril yelled from somewhere behind me.

"Follow the tire tracks," I called back.

I kept my eyes on the man ahead of me. He ran fast, but no one could outrun Alaska's nature.

Including me. But I hadn't given chase so I could capture or even talk to him. I'd only wanted to keep my eyes on him because I knew Gril or Donner would be right behind.

It was Gril, who was much older than me, who caught up to and then passed me quickly. I stuck close. It wasn't the first time I'd been surprised and impressed by his speed and agility.

"Stop. Benedict police. I will shoot!" Gril's voice bellowed through the woods.

The man hesitated as he doubtlessly considered Gril's order, but then he took off again.

Gril had his gun out of the holster and aimed toward the man even as we all continued moving. Until Gril pulled the trigger.

The shot popped and boomed through the trees, bark and needles splintering from a spruce that took the bullet. I involuntarily screamed, hunched over, and covered my head.

"Stop! I mean it," Gril yelled. "Next time I won't miss."

Finally, the man slowed and then came to a stop, resignedly raising his hands into the air.

"Keep your hands up and turn around slowly," Gril ordered.

Once again, I was amazed by his stamina as I noticed my own somewhat labored breathing.

The man turned. I hadn't seen him before, but he had the look of many of my fellow Alaskans—scruffy, slightly unkempt, and dressed in layers. His brown hair needed a cut and his beard showed early signs of the gray that would take over soon enough. I thought he might be about forty. If the dead man found on the island wasn't the one who'd abducted Sadie, this man could almost match the description she'd given.

"I didn't do nothing," he said, his voice deep.

"I just want to talk to you," Gril said.

I wanted to ask the man why he'd run if he hadn't done anything, but I didn't think Gril would appreciate my intervention; he was probably going to lecture me about my bold move to give chase. I'd worry about that later.

"Why? I didn't do nothing," he repeated.

Gril holstered the gun. "I hear you, but there was some trouble out here recently, and I'm hoping someone can help me with answers to some questions."

"Trouble? What kind?"

"Come talk to me, and I'll give you the details. All I want to know is if you saw anything that might help us."

The man's face fell before he looked back in the direction he'd been going. Gril moved his hand back to his gun, but he didn't draw it. He didn't have to. The man finally turned again and started to make his way back toward us.

"Thank you," Gril said as the man stopped and looked at Gril and me. "I'm Gril Samuels, Benedict police chief. This is Beth."

"Benedict? What are you doing here?"

"What's your name?"

"Buster Carmony." He shook his head. "I don't bother no one, Chief. I promise."

Buster was scared, but there was something about him, more than his obvious fear, that told me he was exactly who he said he was and not a danger to either Gril or me.

My grandfather wouldn't be pleased by my quick rush to judgment, but he'd be as kind as Gril was being. They were both patient, intelligent, and kind men. Those traits went a long way, even when trying to find bad guys. Maybe especially so.

Both Gril's and my grandfather's kindness would only go so far, though. If Buster ran again, impatience and insistence would take over.

We trudged our way back to the airfield, Fred greeting us at the edge of the woods with a nod that I thought was a mix of anxiety and relief.

"Donner said you told him to stay behind?" Fred asked Gril.

"I did. I didn't want someone to remove some possible evidence from the hangar while we were distracted. Donner did right to keep working. Are you okay?"

Fred nodded. "I heard the gunshot and couldn't see you, though."

"We're fine," Gril said to Fred, putting his hand on Fred's shoulder. Fred seemed to be better because of it. Gril returned his full attention to Buster. "Do you live here?"

A long moment later, Buster nodded. "Yeah."

"I'm not here to kick you out. Just show me."

Buster directed us to the other big hangar. Fred left us to rejoin Donner, who was probably anxious to hear what was going on.

"I'm not hurting anyone here," Buster said.

"I'm not going to arrest you for squatting. You have my word," Gril said.

Buster faced Gril. Tears filled his eyes and he sniffed. "I guess I'll have to take you at your word. You're the one with the gun."

My heart melted a little. Either this man was a great actor or circumstances had put him here, living in an old, abandoned hangar, where the wilds were taking over what once had been a pocket of civilization.

However, if the man touched on Gril's sympathies at all, Gril kept it hidden. "Let's go inside, Buster."

Buster nodded and pushed on the door, opening it wide. Though Buster's living space only took up a small part of the hangar's expanse, it was immediately recognizable as someone's home.

A mattress was stuck against one wall. A stack of rusty, old folding chairs had been placed behind the mattress. Buster had acquired a few high-quality sleeping bags which I knew were necessary if you were going to try to sleep in the outdoors in this state.

However, there was something amid the setup that would probably cause Gril to have to go back on the promise he'd just made. He might not arrest him or kick Buster out, but something would have to be done. He had created an indoor firepit out of old bricks. Wood was stacked against the wall, ready to burn. Ashes filled the pit and the whole place smelled strongly of woodsmoke.

Once he finished surveying the space, Gril's eyes went up to the ceiling, as did mine. Just like in the other building and at the peak, an opening had somehow been created. I suspected this one had been cut out, though I couldn't imagine the tools needed and how anyone could get to the top of the building with anything but a fire truck ladder.

"Yeah," Buster said. "Ventilation."

The floor was concrete, but the mattress and sleeping bags were highly flammable. And no matter what, an indoor fire was never a good plan.

I didn't know this man or how he came to be living here like this, but my soul emptied a little as I pondered what must have been his happiness at finding a place to land, if only temporarily, and in an airfield hangar.

"I see that," Gril said. "Okay, can we grab some chairs?"

"Sure."

In an odd sort of line, we each grabbed a chair from the stack and then unfolded them. I hoped none of us got cut on any of them, or tetanus shots would be in order.

"Want me to start the fire?" Buster said.

"No, we're okay." Gril sat back in his chair. "Buster, we are trying to understand what might have happened to a young woman from Juneau. We think maybe she was brought out here."

"I never touched no woman." Buster tensed.

"I don't think you did," Gril said, though he kept his demeanor calm. "We think someone else brought her out here last week or so, a man maybe your age, with gray hair at his temples. He brought her out here in a blue van. We just wonder if you happened to see them."

Buster pursed his lips and looked at the ground as he shook his head. "People are always trouble, you know."

"Yes, Buster, I do know. Did you see them?"

"I didn't see no girl, but I saw a man and . . . a van. Well, the van when he was leaving. But just the man before that."

"That's wonderful. Thank you. Now give me all the details you can: days, times, circumstances. Okay?"

Buster nodded and then closed his eyes tight. He tapped on the fingers of one hand using his index finger from the other hand, counting off something as his lips moved silently.

Gril and I waited.

Buster opened his eyes. "It was five days ago, I'm pretty sure. I'd been gone for a few days, so I can't be sure exactly when he arrived, but he was here when I got back from some exploring." Buster pointed toward the building that Donner was currently processing. "He was in there, walked outside at the same time I came out of my place. We froze, just looked at each other a long time. He spoke first, said he was just parked in that building for a few days and was it okay? I told him I lived here, and I didn't much care what went on in the other buildings if he just left me alone. He liked my proposal." Buster looked pointedly at Gril. "Mr. Police Chief, I don't care who goes into the other buildings. As long as I'm left alone, why would I care?"

"I get it," Gril said. "So did you see him more than that first time?"

"I did, but we didn't say nothing to each other. I just went about my business, and he talked on his phone, pacing back and forth in front of that other building."

"Did you hear anything from inside?"

Buster shook his head quickly. "No, sir. If I'd heard something, like a girl or something, I would have gotten the police. I mean, I'm all about minding my own business, but if I'd heard someone being hurt, I'd've run back to town, gotten help."

He seemed sincere, but it was impossible to know. Buster was in such dire straits that I could see how maybe he'd be persuaded to look the other way, even for a small amount of money. But that didn't ring immediately true.

"Did you overhear any of his phone conversations?" Gril asked.

"No, sir," he said too quickly.

Gril took a deep breath and let it out. "Buster, the man you saw, we're pretty sure he was killed yesterday. Okay?"

"Oh. Okay. I didn't kill nobody. Never."

"I know. But he's gone. And more importantly, he kidnapped a woman, tried to hurt her. We think she was here the whole time. I need to know everything you witnessed when it comes to him. What else can you tell me?"

Buster slumped in his chair. "Right. Okay. Yeah, maybe I heard some of what he was saying on the phone. Mostly, things like, 'everything is under control,' and 'don't need to worry about anything.' But then two days ago I think, the day I saw the van leave, he was freaking out, wondering where the 'goddamn plane' was and why it was late."

"Okay. Good. A plane?"

Buster nodded again. "Yeah, but no plane ever came that I saw. Not until that one out there that brought you all."

"And you saw the van leave?"

"Yes, sir. I was just glad he was gone. I don't want to know nobody's secrets. I don't want to know nothing." He bit his bottom lip and his eyes unfocused as if he might be remembering something.

"What, Buster?" Gril pushed, his tone a smidge more demanding than it had been.

Buster sighed heavily and made a wet noise with his tongue. "Every time something starts to go okay for me, something spoils it."

"What do you mean?" Gril asked.

"Every time I find a place, something happens, and I get in trouble."

"You're not in trouble." Gril looked at the firepit and then back at Buster. "Well, we do need to talk about the fire in here, but you're not in trouble."

"Well, I might be now." Buster stood. "Come on. Might as well get it over with."

Buster led us out of his building and into the woods again, along the path we'd chased him down before. I'd seen the geography from the plane. The airfield wasn't far from a main road that snaked close to the ocean. I suspected we were headed directly toward the water.

I guessed we traveled about a half a mile. We could hear the ocean before we saw it, and when we finally spotted the never-ending sparkling dark water, a van was parked right next to it.

"There it is." Buster pointed, though Gril and I had already seen it.

The van matched its description: small, not very old, and a bright, metallic blue.

"You're gonna take it from me, aren't you?"

Gril nodded. "Yes, Buster, I'm afraid we are."

"Damn. Like I said, just when something good happens."

Gril extended his hand to Buster, palm up. "Keys?"

"They're in it. Half a tank of gas, too. Damn."

Gril looked at me. "I'm sure that any sort of evidence has been completely compromised, but I need to take a look for myself. I'll drive it back to the airfield, but you all will have to walk back. I'm not sure it matters, but let's keep it as clean as we can."

"Must have caught a boat from here," I said to Gril.

"I didn't see no boat," Buster said.

"Too bad," Gril said with a sigh. "All right. See you back there."

The van started right up when Gril turned the key. Buster and I gave him a wide berth as he steered it back onto the old road and headed toward the airfield.

"Any chance I'll get it back?" Buster asked me.

"I don't think so," I said.

"That's what I thought," Buster said. "Easy come, easy go, I suppose."

I knew what was truly coming. Gril couldn't keep the police out of here now. Buster was about to be found out, no matter what Gril had promised him. I just hoped they'd help him.

I'd seen my grandfather in similar situations and how he sometimes got around the rules. Gril would do the same, but I doubted that Juneau officials would.

"I'm sorry, Buster."

He shrugged. "I wish I'd seen more now. I wish I'd seen the girl. I would've helped, I would have."

"I know." I glanced over my shoulder at the ocean as Buster and I walked together in that companionable silence that can be immediate for some people. It was for us.

But I couldn't help but wonder—where was the boat?

Eleven

Gril made a couple phone calls, requesting more assistance from Juneau officials. He let Fred and me look in the windows of the van, but we couldn't touch anything. He and Donner spoke to each other, away from the rest of us, as Fred and I investigated.

I saw the Plexiglas between the front and cargo areas—I noticed it was much cleaner than the grimy piece Travis had used to separate himself from me.

A mattress had been placed in the back of this one, as well as blankets and pillows. These were also cleaner than any sort of bedding I'd had and would probably prove to hold the lion's share of evidence. I didn't see the bucket Sadie had mentioned nor did I see food wrappers, though other things might be hidden by the bedding.

When we'd had our fill and while Gril was talking to Buster in the same hushed tones he'd used with Donner, Fred said, "Come on" and led me inside Buster's hangar.

Earlier, I'd only taken in the big picture, just the first layer—the bedding, the chairs, the firepit, the hole in the ceiling. But there was something about the way Fred looked at things that made me focus harder.

Everything was dirty—Buster's things, the floors, the walls. Fred crouched and concentrated on the bedding. I crouched next to him.

"What are you looking for?"

"I'm not exactly sure, but I'll know it when I see it."

"Were you in law enforcement at one time?"

"Not officially."

"What does that mean?"

Fred shrugged. "Before Donner started working with Gril, I made myself available to him."

"You did? Tell me more."

"When Gril came to town, we were close to a free-for-all, a little bit of the Wild West. I mean, I've got plenty of my own guns, but some folks were starting to think it was okay to draw them and threaten people in public."

"That's not good."

"No, it wasn't. Gril needed help. He deputized me for a while."

"That sounds official."

Fred smirked. "I don't think there was anything official about it. One day he just said, 'Okay, Fred, you're a deputy now.' I didn't even get a badge."

"I see." I looked at the sleeping bags and didn't spot anything suspicious.

Fred lifted one, disrupting them more than I would have. A business card fluttered across the dirty floor.

"Oh." I grabbed it and read aloud. "Robin's Nest Cleaning." I looked at Fred. "A place in Juneau. I can't imagine Buster needed a cleaning service."

"No, a leftover from another time, I bet."

The blue card with yellow writing was worn, the corners curled and separating. "Yeah, probably." I pocketed the card. "Do you see anything else, Fred?"

"I see the life of a man down on his luck and doing his best." He frowned. "I thought maybe I'd spot something to tell us Buster was lying. Gril usually likes to rule things out, and I thought we could help him that way."

"Makes sense. Gril didn't search through things earlier. How deep do we dig?"

"Just lift the bags again, look around."

As we did that, it was impossible not to come to the conclusion that Buster was a man of very few possessions: the sleeping bags, some extra socks and underwear, and some granola bars.

"How does he do it? Live like this?" I asked.

"One day at a time. I don't see anything suspicious here at all, Beth. No tokens from kidnapping a woman, nothing that might have been in the van. Buster appears to be who he says he is."

"You really thought he might not be?"

"I know how Sadie described her kidnapper. I know a body was found, but Buster resembles the description she gave."

"I thought the same thing."

"If it was him, he's done a good job of hiding all the clues. I really don't think it was, which I'm sure Gril has already figured out or he would have taken Buster in."

"Gril's good, but I think Sadie confirmed that the body was the man who took her."

"Yeah." He lifted an eyebrow.

"You don't trust her?"

"I don't trust anyone until I do, so not yet."

"Right. I hope the Juneau folks leave Buster alone."

"Me too." Fred looked at the firepit and then up and the small ventilation opening in the ceiling. "Even if it might not be the safest."

"Fire would be bad for the woods."

"Bad for everything, but . . . well, we'll see." Fred shook his head slowly. "Life sure kicks some people in the ass, doesn't it?"

"I'm afraid so."

We heard the arrival of other vehicles, so we made our way back outside.

Two Juneau police cars with two officers each and a crime scene van with one more officially dressed investigator had arrived. They all converged on Gril and Donner. Buster was no longer in sight. Fred and I shared raised eyebrows, but we wouldn't wonder aloud where he'd gone.

We observed as Gril and Donner were questioned. They kept their cool, but there were plenty of confusing moments with Juneau officials who didn't think Gril should have headed up any of this. Gril remained patient and told them he was investigating something that happened in his jurisdiction, and he couldn't find any interest from any Juneau officers to do this for him. If he wanted answers, he was left with no choice but to find them on his own. That seemed to stall further discourtesy on the part of the Juneau people.

Mostly, Fred and I were ignored. Calmly, Gril told them why we'd come over from Benedict—Fred was the pilot, and I was Gril's assistant. I did feel one tiny twinge of regret that I'd put him in a position to lie, but he'd used the same line at least once before.

Once everyone understood what was going on and the potential ties it might all have to a dead body found on an island in the bay, we were excused, told to head back home, and informed the Juneau people had it from there and that they'd get back with Gril with anything they found.

After we boarded the plane and Fred steered it toward the part of the runway with the least amount of cracks and weeds, I asked, "Where's Buster?"

"I told him to take a literal hike," Gril said. "I let him know that these new officials might force him to move on, particularly if he was there as they investigated. They'll find his fire setup and be none too happy. They'll wait for him for a few hours but probably not into the night. I suggested he come back tomorrow if he could swing it. I also told him I could help get him into a better situation, a shelter, but he declined."

"Yeah, I'm worried about the fire or him somehow asphyxiating himself," Fred said. "But I've seen more precarious setups. You do what you gotta do."

"I'm worried about the whole thing, but I don't have a better answer for any of it at the moment. Fred, you and Beth looked around his stuff, didn't you?"

"Yes."

"Find anything?"

"Nothing suspicious."

"Didn't think so, but thanks for checking." He looked at Donner.

They shared a knowing nod and Donner patted his backpack. Of course, I was dying to know exactly what he'd gathered from the scene, but I didn't waste my breath asking. They wouldn't tell me, at least not now. Maybe later.

I peered out the window. It was the first time I'd been out of Benedict in a year, and though we'd crossed over ocean to get to the airfield, we hadn't gone far. The people below, the land, the trees, they soon gave way to the water again and I sensed home, Benedict, getting comfortably closer.

I still didn't like the ride, but I trusted Fred. If there was any way at all to keep us from crashing into the ground or the sea, Fred would do all he could.

That's not saying I wasn't glad to land.

"Thanks for letting me tag along," I said to Gril after we disembarked and were walking to our trucks. "I'm sorry if I put you in an uncomfortable position."

"It was no problem. I hope you can use it for research." Gril smirked but then bit his bottom lip and looked off in the direction of the now distant airfield.

"What's on your mind?" I asked.

Gril turned his attention to me again. "I'm going to be overly honest here, Beth. I don't know who to trust—I mean when it comes to anyone outside of Benedict. I need to understand what happened to Sadie and why she was put in WITSEC and why she doesn't trust the Juneau police. I've called a friend in the US Marshals but haven't heard back from her. Sadie's handler is supposed to be here, but I don't think he is yet."

"Could Orin help?" I said.

Gril nodded. "I hope so. I talked to him this morning. We'll see. What I'm saying, though, is that I trust you, and I was glad to have you along. I don't want to put you in danger ever, but I like your style. I'm sure your grandfather felt the same way."

I thought about adding a self-deprecating comment but instead I said, "I think he did."

"Not surprised." Gril sighed. "Be careful around Sadie. I don't trust her yet, either. The body we found wasn't killed by a bear."

"Her hands weren't cut up," I said, remembering her words from that morning.

Gril nodded again. "Well, maybe ask Tex about that. Just be careful, Beth. Okay?"

I couldn't wait to ask Tex, but something else occurred to me. "Gril, you don't suppose Sadie made it, or part of it all, up because of me, because people now know my story and know that I live here? Someone just recognized me this morning."

"I can't imagine why she would do that."

I shrugged. "To get someone on her side. I mean, I know it's paranoid to think that way, but . . ."

"No, I really don't think it's that. I think that once we find out what happened to her in Connecticut, we'll know more about what's true and what's not. I doubt your story has played a part in any of this."

I'd had plenty of moments of paranoia over the last year, but his words eased my concern. Mostly. I thought back to my short time on the boat with Sadie and how forthcoming she'd been with me. Was that strange or something that could be expected with trauma? I had no idea.

I wanted to believe her completely—I never wanted to doubt a victim—and Gril probably did, too. Still, the unknowns were there.

"I hope the marshal clears it up."

"Me too."

I nodded. "I think I'll run by the library."

"Have Orin call me if he's got anything."

"Will do."

Gril took fast steps to his truck. Donner had left quickly without saying anything to anyone, though he and Gril had communicated silently with a shared glance. Fred and his brother, Frank, were attending to the plane.

I'd seen Gril stressed before. I'd watched him spend many sleepless nights in a row making sure his community was getting the attention it deserved, even though he was only one man, two when Donner helped.

A chill ran up my spine as I heard the shrill scream of a hawk. I spotted it flying above the trees on the other side of the airport. The sound had the same sort of semi-echo I'd heard as Gril had yelled into the woods earlier. Here or there, near or far, some things were the same everywhere. I shouldn't have had to leave Benedict to know that, but the short trip realigned my perspective a little.

I hopped in my truck and made my way directly to the library.

Twelve

didn't realize how wound up I was until I felt the relief of spotting Orin's truck in its spot at the library.

A few months earlier, I'd finally seen the inside of his house—a technological dream, as well as a place where he liked to tinker. It had been Gril who'd given me the tour when Orin had been out of contact for a secret mission he'd been called to do. Since then, I'd visited the house only a few times. Orin was more at home in the library than he seemed to be anywhere else. It was either that or maybe he just liked to be alone at home and having people there made him uncomfortable. Though he was gracious and kind, he'd never been married, never in a long-term relationship. He seemed content with the solitary lifestyle.

I made my way inside and wove around the crowded tables. Like at the airport, lots of people visited the library simply for the internet access, and today it was almost overflowing.

I knocked on Orin's office door.

"Come on in."

I opened it wide. "I'm probably going to be a bother. That okay?"

"Always." He looked around the laptop he'd been working on. "Come in, Beth, and tell me what you know about our new visitor—Sadie."

Decorated with all different sorts of peace signs, mostly in print or picture form, Orin's office always smelled like weed—his drug of choice for helping with his back injury. He must have been having a mild pain day; I could take a deep breath and probably not experience a contact high. Strong or weak scent in the air, though, his mind was always sharp as a tack.

Orin watched as I shut the door and waited for me to sit before he said, "I know everything, by the way. Witness protection, man not killed by a bear, et cetera. Gril has me working."

I nodded. I was glad we didn't have to go over those secrets first. "Good. Orin, I think she's afraid of the Juneau police or at least what they might or might not do to help her. She's the one who was so forthcoming about her WITSEC status, and she offered it up pretty quickly to me. Do you know why she doesn't trust the Juneau authorities?"

"Right. Most people are more scared of it being figured out who they really are because of the situation that put them there than what will happen with their local authorities. Gril said she hasn't told anyone why she was put in protection in the first place. Witness protection records are one of the things that I don't have immediate and easy access to, but I'm trying to get some help. I decided to start my research with Juneau and any possible criminal record."

"She said she witnessed a murder—"

Orin nodded. "I didn't find any sort of criminal record for her, but I think I found what you're talking about."

"You dug deeper?"

"I didn't have to dig all that deep. First of all, I couldn't even find a traffic ticket for her. However, since I have access, I managed to search for her name in a different database, one that lists witnesses to other crimes. And I found her." Orin slid a piece of paper around for me to read. "Right here. Sadie did witness a murder."

"In Juneau?"

"In Juneau, as Sadie. I understand what you're thinking, though, that witnessing a murder just might be the reason she was put into WITSEC."

"And who witnesses two murders in their life?"

"Very few people, I would think, but I don't have the statistics."

"So if something like that happened in Connecticut, and the Juneau authorities knew about her status, they might have been suspicious."

Orin shrugged. "Maybe, but we're speculating. Still, though, it's a weird set of circumstances."

"I don't disagree." I reached for the paper and pulled it close and read silently to myself.

One year ago, a young man stabbed a woman at a shoe store in Juneau. Sadie had been among the three customers in the store, and she'd been asked to write down her account of the events she'd witnessed. I hadn't seen her handwriting yet, so I couldn't confirm without a doubt that she'd actually been the one to compose the accounts, but the blocky letters were easy to read.

I was shopping down aisle 3, trying on shoes, when I heard a woman scream. I froze for a second, but I don't know why. When I realized someone was truly in trouble, I ran toward the front of the store and then found the victim on the floor on the other side of a stack of shoeboxes. At first, I didn't even notice the man with the bloody knife standing at the door. Two other customers joined me as we knelt by the victim. I think she was already dead. None of us could get a response from her, but one of the other customers put a scarf over the wound in her side and applied pressure.

The other customer (not the one with the scarf), stood up and yelled at the man at the door to just get out of there before they hurt him. I was confused and worried about the victim, but I guess the customer told the guy to leave to keep us all safe. I don't know.

I didn't get a great look at the man with the knife, but I think he was probably in his twenties. Skinny. Dark brown, short and straight hair. Pointy chin. Dark eyes. Nothing else stood out.

Though her name, address, and phone number were listed at the top, she wrote them in at the bottom again.

I looked up at Orin. "Did they catch the killer?"

"They did. The killer turned out to be the victim's son."

"Oh dear."

"Here are some of those details." Orin turned his laptop so I could read an article from the Juneau newspaper, dated two days after Sadie's witness account. "Read closely. I think you'll find a twist in there."

"Okay."

The headline read: *Local Woman Stabbed by Biological Son*

"Even the headline is intriguing," I said.

"Keep reading."

Long-time Juneau resident Margaret (Maggie) Somersby was stabbed to death in a downtown shoe store two days ago. Fifty-three-year-old Somersby moved to Juneau in 2001 and worked a number of retail jobs over the years but wasn't employed at the time of her murder.

The alleged killer, Albert Jackson, was apprehended at Somersby's residence on Konda Way. Jackson claimed to the authorities that he was her biological son and had come to find her only two weeks earlier. He had been given up for adoption as a newborn 23 years ago. He claims that he wasn't the one to stab his mother and had only been shopping with her when the murder occurred.

According to an unnamed source, when Jackson was asked by the authorities why he had the knife in his hand as he ran away from the scene, he claims that the killer told him that he too would be killed if he didn't run. He claims he didn't have the knife; it hasn't been found by the police. He was the one to call the police from Somersby's residence to report the incident as well as his whereabouts. As of this reporting, Jackson has still not given a description of the killer he claims to have seen. In fact, he's said he can't remember the details.

Below the article were two pictures, one of Maggie Somersby and one of Albert Jackson. Jackson's mug shot was surprisingly blurry.

"I don't think I'm getting what you wanted me to see," I said to Orin.

"Look under the pictures."

My eyes went to the very small font that was used to identify each picture. One said: Margaret Somersby, Juneau resident. The other one said: Albert Jackson, Westport, Connecticut.

"Connecticut? Where Sadie said she came from originally?" I asked.

"Yep, which could mean something or nothing at all, but it sure has my attention."

"This is from two years ago." I pointed at the laptop screen. "What happened to Albert?"

Orin signaled for me to turn the laptop back in his direction, which I did. A few clicks later, he aimed it back in my direction. "This happened."

I read the headline from five days ago of an article I should have read, would have read if I hadn't been working on a book deadline: *Escaped Prisoner!*

"Uh-oh," I said.

"I agree. He escaped from the Goose Creek Correctional Center in Wasilla. He hasn't even had his trial yet. It was scheduled for next month."

"Goose Creek!" I exclaimed. "Orin, I overheard something that might be pertinent."

I told him what I'd overheard the night before as I stood outside of Viola's office.

"She actually said the words *Goose Creek* aloud?" he asked.

"Yes. I wondered where I'd heard it before. I'm sure it's come up in conversation with Viola. She talks to wardens all over the state."

"Interesting." Orin tapped his finger on his lips as he fell into thought. "I guess for now, the connections are Connecticut as well as Sadie and Jackson were both at a murder scene and she spoke the words *Goose Creek*." Orin shrugged. "Maybe that traumatic moment pushed them to form some sort of friendship. All circumstantial, though bothersome."

"Weird."

"Agreed. Read the article. Let me know if anything stands out to you that I might have missed."

It didn't say much more than Orin had just shared with me, though the writer also pointed out the strangeness of the fact that Jackson had traveled far, from Connecticut to Alaska, just to allegedly kill the woman who gave birth to him.

"I don't see anything else that stands out," I said.

"Well, your addition of overhearing Sadie might be the most important surprise, but there is one more juicy bit that I think you will like. I know I do, and I'm sure Gril will love it when he gets the message."

"What's that?" I prompted.

Sometimes Orin liked the slow dissemination of information. He wasn't one to drop everything at once. He also liked prompts, just so he knew his audience was truly listening.

"Mr. Jackson's attorney has a cabin in Benedict. She loves to fish out here."

"Oh, that is interesting. Mind telling me the attorney's name and where she lives?"

"In fact, I do not. Her name is Gina Rocco. She lives out in the west coordinate, just off County Road 4. You will find it easily, though, Beth, I do have to recommend not bothering the woman. However, again, news about Sadie is spreading like wildfire. If Gina is in town, she's sure to hear that a witness to her client's crime is nearby. I think there's a potential for everything to get very messy, even messier if the witness protection element comes into play." Orin frowned. "May I recommend that you stay out of her way, at least for now? I'll share with Gril what you heard."

I nodded. "Sure, I won't knock on Ms. Rocco's door, but I might ask around about her, ask Viola, give her a heads-up. What more do you know about her?"

Orin shrugged again. "She's exactly like you might expect a criminal defense attorney to be."

"Which is?" I thought about the news I'd received about Travis Walker's attorney.

"Confident. Cocky. No-nonsense. She's also one of the best around, or so I've heard. You want her on your side if you're fighting that sort of battle."

Well. Crap. Maybe I would meet her, get a head start on how to deal with Walker's. I sat back in the chair. "I can't even begin to understand all the possible conflicts of interest that might sprout up around this."

"Well, like I said, it could get messy, or Gril will just put everybody back on a plane to Juneau. Might not be a bad idea."

"I would agree, but he's genuinely worried about Sadie's not trusting the Juneau police. It's bothersome, though I admit that what you've uncovered might help push him in the direction of washing his hands of all of it. I think if he wasn't worried, he'd be done with them all by now, but until he understands what's what, he's going to keep investigating."

"I'm glad I found what I did then. If I can get the WITSEC information, or if Sadie tells him the details, he can make a completely informed decision."

"Well, her marshal is supposed to be here soon. We might all learn more than we even want to know."

"Oh, I can never know enough. The more the better."

"You've found some great stuff."

"Thank you, and, Beth . . . we all should probably be on the lookout. I'm not talking about what happened to the man on Lilybook if Sadie wasn't the person to kill him; I'm talking about Albert Jackson. There's something weird going on. Maybe Gril will get something from Sadie regarding Jackson, but still . . ."

I heard his concern. Orin wasn't a worrier, but something about what he'd found had given him pause.

"I could put out a special edition of the *Petition*, telling everyone as much. I wouldn't have to give it any context," I suggested.

Orin frowned. "You know, I like that idea, but let me double check with Gril. I don't know how much he wants to release and how much he doesn't. I'll let you know as soon as I do. I'll get ahold of him as quickly as I can."

"That works." I sensed I'd taken up enough of his time, so I stood. "Thanks for sharing."

"My pleasure," he said, but he was distracted, probably already composing an email to Gril.

I made my way out of the library with the goal of heading to the *Petition* shed, where I could get ready to publish a "be on the lookout" edition if Gril approved. Also, maybe I could get some work done. That deadline was still there, waiting for me to give it my full attention.

As I stepped outside, I spotted another vehicle now parked next to the shed.

Eddy was there. I hesitated. Should I just stay at the library until he left, or should I be rude and tell him to go away? There was no way out of the library parking lot other than the one road.

"Beth!" Eddy called from the back of the building.

He'd seen me before I could hide. I waved back and then sent him a signal, telling him I'd be there in a second. I sighed and loaded myself into my truck to make my way over.

Thirteen

t's weird to love and be so angry at someone that you might mistake it for real hatred sometimes. The pendulum did swing some. Some days I would spot my father—on the boat, in town, eating lunch—and my heart would swell a little, that organ remembering how much the little girl me had loved her daddy. He'd been a great father. Until he wasn't, of course.

So while my heart was doing its thing, my head might do a fast process of the strangeness of the whole situation. Him disappearing, my mother dragging me all over Missouri to search for him, and now his being in Alaska, where I was, where I'd run away to. I hadn't yet been able to talk to him about his time in Mexico, where he was before, and where I imagined he'd lived a pretty good life, filled with sunshine, fruity drinks, and delicious food. Yeah, I wasn't ready to have those conversations yet.

How in the world did things like this happen? How is life so darn messy sometimes? I didn't know, but I knew there were only two things to do: One, work to accept the reality of it if you are able. Two, see what happens. Everything else is out of our control anyway.

Tex had asked me how I'd feel if Eddy left. I'd felt my answer in my gut before I could give it words. I would be sad. I would feel like I'd missed the chance to get to the other side of my anger so I could get to know him again. Still, I couldn't rush myself.

If my mother had known that Eddy was in Mexico all those years, my childhood would have been different. Maybe. Mill Rivers was a piece of work. If she hadn't had my father's whereabouts to obsess over, she might have found something else, some other wild goose chase to drag her young daughter on.

As my father made himself comfortable in the chair I'd come to call my "guest chair" inside the shed, I wondered at his boldness. Yes, he'd apologized over and over again. I'd heard his words and sensed his genuine desire for me to forgive him.

Sometimes, though, he behaved normally, as if we didn't have a history that should get in our way. Today, he'd stopped by as if it was just another day to drop in on his daughter and say hello.

"I'm waiting on a call from Orin," I said as he stretched his legs out in front of him and tucked his thumbs into his jeans' waistband.

"Oh? What about?"

I raised my eyebrows at him.

He shook his head. "Oh, sure, not my business. Sorry about that."

A beat later, I shook my head and said, "It's okay."

"Let me rephrase. Are you and Orin working on a project together, maybe something for the *Petition* or one of your books? Does he help you with research?" The corner of his mouth quirked as if he wasn't sure if he should smile or not.

My heart softened again, the heat of anger mellowing more.

Of course, I'd talked to my therapist about all of this. Leia was good at guiding, even better at not telling what I should and shouldn't feel. With her help, I'd decided that I could be angry as long as I wanted to be, but also, I could work to forgive. Maybe something good could come out of this.

I took a deep breath and tried to find my friendly.

"Have you heard about the woman in town?" I asked.

Eddy's expression relaxed some. He probably saw I didn't need to fight today. He nodded. "I have. The one brought in from the island. She was the victim of a bear attack. She was why a big boat got in my way out there."

I knew how rumors spread and transformed, but I was in on this one, so I felt confident in giving him a straighter story, and since I was working on letting it go and all . . .

"She wasn't part of a bear attack. In fact, she wasn't physically hurt. Allegedly the blood was from a man, whose body was later found on the other side of the island."

Eddy frowned. "What? Was he killed by a bear? How did a bear get in this story?"

"I don't think the cause of death has been determined yet, but the woman, her name is Sadie, says that a bear killed the man."

"Holy moly. Only in Alaska, I guess." Eddy shrugged.

"Well, there are bears lots of places, but I suppose the whole set of circumstances is very Alaska-like." I paused. "I saw you on your boat yesterday. I was on the tour boat."

"You were?"

"I was. My first time giving it a try, but I still didn't make it out to the glaciers."

"That's too bad. Hey, I can take you." He sat up.

"Thank you. I might take you up on that someday." I doubted I would, though.

He nodded and relaxed back again. "That captain thought I was going the wrong way. I wasn't."

I remembered wondering what Eddy was doing and that he

LOST HOURS · 113

was, indeed, traveling outside the appropriate path. I also remembered how he seemed to straighten out his course. I just nodded.

He continued, "We talked later. It's all good. He actually said I didn't mess up. I'm glad."

"You like the boat?"

"I love it. I always wanted one down in . . . well, Mexico, but it didn't happen even though I rode on quite a few. I enjoy everything about them. I'm not looking forward to the winter, when I won't be able to go out—at least as much."

"Will you stick around here?"

"I think so." He paused. "You were right in the thick of it, then? With that woman?"

"I was."

"Wow. What else do you know?"

I shook my head. "I truly don't know much more, but Sadie is staying at the Benedict House, too. I'll probably spend a little time with her." I remembered Viola's order for me to leave. I really hoped she would change her mind by the time I made it back there today.

"Who was the guy who was killed?"

"Not sure yet. Nothing's been confirmed."

"That's crazy."

"I know."

Eddy nodded and studied me.

"What's up, Eddy? Something else on your mind?"

He nodded. "Beth, darlin', I have a big favor to ask."

I remembered our happenstance meeting outside the restaurant. "Oh. You'd like me to have dinner with you and your customers?"

Eddy cringed. "It's bigger than that even."

"Okay? What?"

"Is there any chance you would come out with us tomorrow morning?"

"On your boat? Fishing?"

"Yes, please. Gracie, the teenager, thinks you're the bee's knees. She has been begging me for some time with you."

"I'm not comfortable going out on the bay in a small boat."

"Why?"

I didn't want to take the time to explain Ruke's early-on admonishment and his current redirection to my father.

"Well," I began. "I grew up in Missouri, didn't even see the ocean until I moved here, and I'm somewhat intimidated by it."

"Okay, I get that."

"However, I really wouldn't mind dinner," I said, though I knew I would probably regret the offer. It simply seemed like the lesser of the evils.

I loved my readers, but having dinner with a real fan while my father was there wouldn't give me the ego boost that one might think it would. I would probably just feel uncomfortable, but still, I was trying to forgive, let go.

Eddy nodded. "That would be great, Beth. Thanks. I'll tell them."

"You're welcome."

"Well . . . but, hear me out, okay?"

I laughed. "Okay."

"We won't go out past the first part of the bay. I'll tell you what: we won't go any farther than that island where everything happened yesterday. It's called Lilybook, right? Plenty of good fishing right there."

"Wouldn't that put your boat in the way of the traffic patterns?"

"No, no, it's a wide swath, and I know where we can go and where we can't. In fact, lots of people explore that island."

"I heard. Even with the bears?"

"Sure, though I've yet to see a bear there."

I perked up. The idea hadn't even occurred to me—to go to that island and look around. I would be surprised if it was allowed. Wasn't it a crime scene? Maybe not by now. Here was an unexpected opportunity that I suddenly felt like I shouldn't pass up.

"Could we go on Lilybook and look around a little?"

"Sure, sure." Eddy laughed. "In fact, Gracie's been talking about visiting the islands. I think she'd be thrilled. Sound good?"

"Just half a day? Would we be back by noon?"

"I could get you back by then. I think Gracie would love a morning with you. Yes?"

I thought for another long moment. "Yeah. Sure."

"Thank you."

I got it then. This was not about Gracie Dupont. This was about Eddy looking for a way to spend some extra time with me. I felt both duped and impressed at the same time. And also, admittedly, thrilled to explore the island.

And, darn it, my heart softened a little more. "How early should I be at the dock tomorrow?"

"Five A.M.?"

I laughed. "I should have asked that before I agreed."

"I'll have coffee and donuts."

"Okay, Eddy. I'll be there."

"Thanks again." He looked at me for a long moment and then realized he should probably go—because we'd talked enough or he was afraid I'd change my mind, I couldn't be sure. He stood. "Thanks, again, again."

"You're welcome."

We didn't hug. We weren't there quite yet. He nodded and smiled quickly as he made his way out the door.

Once he was gone, I sighed. I wished Gus had been with me so my next muttering wouldn't be to only myself.

"This crazy life," I said quietly.

A knock sounded on the door. I thought Eddy might have more for me, but I wasn't one to just say, *Come in.*

I stood and made my way to the door, opening it as carefully as I always did. Orin was on the other side.

"Your dad's a great guy, Beth. I really think he is." Orin looked toward Eddy's retreating vehicle.

I opened the door wide and signaled for him to come in. "I hope so, but the jury is still out."

"Understood." Orin joined me inside. "I got the approval from Gril. He *is* worried about Albert Jackson maybe being out here somewhere. He'd like for you to write up a BOLO edition of the *Petition*."

"Really? Well, let's get to it."

Most editions were simply calendars of local events, classes offered at the community center, maybe a special food the café would be offering because of some good deal they got or because something had been brought over from Juneau.

Most people read their copy on paper. Distribution consisted of me dropping off copies at the mercantile, the library, and the community center. However, I'd also created a website, even though most people, even though they ventured to the library or the airport for their internet, preferred a hard copy. The views were ticking higher, but I didn't see a time when I could do virtual only.

Using a stencil I'd created for all of the editions since I'd been put in charge, Orin and I quickly put together the BOLO edition as we discussed his conversation with Gril. Orin had told Gril what I'd overheard, and that had been the real impetus in Gril wanting to get the word out. He was trying to protect as many people as he could.

"It looks great, Beth," Orin said as he peered at my computer screen.

"It looks a little terrifying," I said. "I've never seen such a blurry mug shot. Usually they're pretty clear."

"True. Well, it will get attention, and that's what we want."

Albert's booking photo took up most of the page. He looked

angry enough that you really wouldn't want to approach him if you did happen to come across him.

Because of the spotty communication in the area, Gril had asked to put his phone number and the station's landline phone number on the bottom and then to also add the Benedict House's and the library's landline numbers as well.

Orin and I decided on brief and simple copy.

Be on the lookout for this man, known as Albert Jackson. He escaped from Goose Creek Correctional Center in Wasilla. We have reason to believe he might be in the area. Do not approach. Call one of the numbers below or notify Police Chief Samuels in-person to report his whereabouts. Be cautious.

"Albert has menacing eyes," I said.

"Or our imagination has made them menacing."

"Either way, I hope he's not around, and if he is, I hope someone finds him before he hurts anyone," I said.

"Same."

We printed out a few hundred copies, then packed up and made our way into town.

Fourteen

Each of us armed with a stack of *Petitions*, I took the downtown distribution points, and Orin headed out to the community center, deciding to also drop some off at Toshco.

I stopped at the small post office, the restaurant, and the mercantile before making my last stop at the bar, where I could gather Gus and spend some time with Benny.

Considering when I woke up that morning, it was late, almost eight, so even with plenty of light still left, I was weary. I probably wouldn't even need the curtains to sleep tonight.

Gus was happy to see me, even if I could tell he'd had a fabulous day with his favorite bartender.

"Fully loaded Bloody Mary?" Benny asked as I sidled up and onto a stool and gave Gus's ears some scratch attention.

"No, thanks. I'll have a diet soda, though."

"With a cherry?"

"Of course. Two if you can spare it."

Benny smiled.

There were only two other people in the bar, a young couple

who'd moved to Benedict a month or so earlier. The Oosterhouses. I'd been near the ferry when they were first unloading, so I'd offered to help. They'd been surprised by the number of people who'd joined in. A group of us had gotten their things to their cabin quickly.

They'd purchased a place near the airport, though not in view of it. I'd looked at the cabin myself, considered buying it. It was small, with one loft bedroom and the rest of the living space on the main level. I'd loved everything about it.

But even though I kept coming up with arguments against it, my thought process had always been that Benedict was a temporary place to hide. My captor was behind bars, and I would have to attend and testify at his trial. I still hadn't convinced myself that that was anything but a one-way trip.

The biggest reason I hadn't purchased anything, though, was that I loved living with Viola in the Benedict House more than I could picture loving anything else.

I waved at the couple. They waved back. They looked good, happy, though they hadn't gone through a winter yet. Time would tell if they were made for this world.

"My goodness. I've never seen so much activity in our little old downtown. What in the world is going on? Did you learn more?" Benny asked as I handed her a stack of *Petition*s. She glanced at the top one and then looked back at me. "Now we have a fugitive on the loose?"

"Well, we don't know, but there is a chance, and Gril wants people to be on the lookout. I think he's going with better safe than sorry."

Benny looked at me again and then put the stack of papers on the end of the bar. "I've never seen anything like this in Benedict." She lowered her voice. "Do we know more about Sadie? Orin have new intel?"

I nodded and then told her what Orin had found and

what had led to the special edition. She listened with rapt attention.

When I finished, Benny shook her head slowly and then reached for a third cherry, plopping it into my drink. "Crazy."

"What's been going on down here?"

"The Juneau police have been walking around, going into places, looking around, and then leaving again. They've been in here three times in the last couple hours."

"Just looking?"

"As far as I can tell."

"Maybe they're searching for Albert, too. The ferry manifests—wouldn't Gril know if Albert was here? He's keeping track of people coming over."

But I caught the chink in my logic right away. Of course, there were other ways to get to Benedict via boat. I didn't completely understand all the potential pathways, but I now knew there were more than I'd realized.

Benny frowned at me. "Well, we know that's not perfect."

"Right," I said.

The door swung open, and we all looked in that direction. The man who came in wasn't familiar, though he could have been a resident based on his clothes: jeans, a flannel shirt, and work boots. I glanced at Benny, who shrugged.

"Help you?" Benny asked him.

He looked toward the bar, his stern expression not wavering, at least for a few beats. His eyes scanned the small space again, then he said, "Mind if I open that door over there?"

It was the door to Benny's back room, which was, for all intents and purposes, a small bedroom where she could stay when she didn't want to make the trek back to her own place deep in the woods. It was also the room Dr. Powder used to examine patients when he was downtown.

"Um." Benny paused, though she was probably coming to the same conclusion I was. This was another law enforcement officer. "Okay. Sure. Make yourself at home."

Benny, the Oosterhouses, Gus, and I watched the officer make his way to the door. His legs were so long that he covered the space quickly. Carefully and with one hand where a holster might be if he wore one, he opened the door, peered in, and then went inside.

"This is the third time someone's done that," Benny spoke quietly to me over the bar. "The other times were uniformed officers."

I nodded as he exited the room, shut the door, and turned to face the rest of us.

"All clear," he said. "I'm looking for Sadie Milbourn."

I sat up straighter in my seat, and Gus whined a little. I put my hand on his head to reassure him that everything was okay.

"She was over at the Benedict House last I saw." I turned on the stool. "I can take you over there."

"I just came from there. No one's home."

"I'm sure they'll be back soon." I hoped everything was okay.

The man, with much less serious footfalls, made his way to the bar, sat on a stool, and looked at Benny. "I would love a glass of water."

"Of course. Welcome to Benedict." Benny reached for a glass and filled it, placing it in front of him quickly.

"Thank you."

I suddenly thought I knew who he might be or at least who he worked for. I kept my voice low again. "Are you a US marshal?"

He sent me a distinctly sour impression. "Your dog friendly?"

"Very."

"I have one just like him. Mind if I pet him?"

I relaxed. "Sure. His name is Gus."

"Hey, Gus." He reached toward the dog.

Not discriminating at all, Gus would take ear scratches from just about anyone, strangers included.

The man spent a few moments giving perfect dog attention. Then he turned on his stool and took a sip of water. "So what if I am?" he asked a long moment later. "A marshal."

"Sadie hasn't been as secretive as you probably want her to be regarding her status," I said, not really meaning to throw her under the bus, even though that's exactly how it sounded. I cleared my throat. "I met her when she was brought onto the boat." I paused. "I was kidnapped, too. I'm Beth."

"You're Beth?" he said, his eyebrows raised.

"I am." I nodded across the bar. "This is Benny."

He nodded at both of us. "Sadie told me that she talked to you, Beth. She didn't mention Benny."

"I haven't told a soul," Benny said.

I sighed. "I think Sadie told more people than you would like, but I also think she was worried for her own safety and didn't want to be released back to the Juneau police."

The man sucked at his teeth and then frowned. "That's why I'm here, I suppose."

"Are you Grecko?" I asked.

"I am."

"Nice to meet you," I said.

"Welcome," Benny repeated. "Let me know what I can get for you."

"Thank you." He sighed and then seemed to fall into thought.

"Where did you come from? Is that okay to ask?"

"Tucson," he said.

"Long trip," I said.

He nodded. "Yes, ma'am. Do you know where else Sadie might have gone?"

"I have a few guesses, but it's probably not worth searching. Around here, we choose to stick to one place and wait. I'm pretty sure she'll get back to the Benedict House. Viola will for sure, and she'll know what to do next."

He grabbed his cell phone. "This is practically useless out here."

Benny nodded toward the room he'd peeked into. "There are pockets of service, but I have a landline if you need to make a call."

"Thank you, I might take you up on that. How does anything get done?"

"It's different," Benny conceded. She pointed at his water. "Something stronger?"

Grecko laughed, giving his whole demeanor a makeover from closed off to cute, with dimples in his cheeks and chin. The transformation was a little unsettling. I glanced at Benny, who also seemed to be surprised by it. "No thanks," he said.

"All righty then. Again, make yourself at home." Benny walked away to check on the Oosterhouses as well as attend to dishes and the other tasks she did behind the bar.

I should have left him to his water, but I couldn't resist. "Will you just take Sadie out of here?"

He'd gone back to serious, his face statue-like, but he didn't ignore me.

"As soon as possible."

"Oh. Tonight?"

"No. Probably not tonight."

He didn't explain further, but I figured her staying here had to do with the investigation of the dead man on the island as well as why he kidnapped her.

"You ran into some trouble, too?"

"I did."

He squinted in my direction. "You ever in WITSEC?"

I laughed, too. "No, not unless you could call mine self-imposed. I ran away, started using my real name more than my professional name. My methods wouldn't be quite as impressive as the professionals, but I got away from where I didn't feel safe. I'm glad for it."

"What's your professional name? If you're sharing it now, that is."

"Elizabeth Fairchild," I said, thinking he must have missed the splash in the national media my story had made when Walker was captured. It really had been over with quickly.

But he hadn't missed it. "Oh! That's you?" He looked at me again. "That was quite a story. Your captor is locked up, isn't he?"

"Trial in October."

"That's quick. Good news."

"His attorney is Clara Lytle."

Grecko whistled, shrill and sharp, causing Gus to perk up again. "She's something, but I don't think you need to worry. No one is that good."

"Right. Tell that to the family of the actor whose confessed killer got off scot-free."

Grecko nodded solemnly. "Get your ass down there. Get some PR going, get your story out there, and don't let any jury pool have not heard from you."

"Yeah?"

"Yes, ma'am."

PR? I hadn't ever considered something that proactive. I'd planned on going down for the trial but not any earlier. I'd certainly never considered manipulating the media.

But isn't that what Lytle would be doing?

Probably.

"Hmm. Thanks. I'll think about it."

"You should." He glanced at his watch. "I think I'll head back over to the Benedict House, see if they're there."

"Okay," I said. "I'll probably see you there later. I live there, too."

I could have gone with him, but that seemed weird. Besides, I was still hoping to sneak in later. Walking in with a US marshal might not be as covert.

Grecko stood and turned to leave, but his attention was caught by the stack of papers I'd put on the end of the bar.

"What's this?" He frowned and reached for the top paper on the stack.

Benny sent me a look and then answered, "It's our local paper."

I chewed the inside of my cheek.

Grecko's demeanor transformed again, into pure anger. "Where did this information come from?"

"It's our local paper," Benny said again.

"You . . . I . . ."

I jumped in. "I'm the publisher. Our police chief gave me the permission to print and distribute the information. It's legit." Whatever that meant.

"Your police chief doesn't have jurisdiction over this case," Grecko said as he pointed at the blurry mug shot.

I couldn't immediately understand what case he was talking about—Albert escaping prison or allegedly committing murder.

And, I didn't think he was necessarily correct. Gril had jurisdiction out here in Benedict and probably on Lilybook Island. But I didn't know for sure. I just shrugged and tried not to appear like I was arguing.

Grecko looked at me. "Where did you distribute these?"

"All over."

"Shit," he said with a heavy sigh. He tucked the stack under his arm and, without another word to anyone, made his way out the door.

"I should call Gril," I said to Benny.

"I think so. Go ahead." She nodded toward the back room.

I hurried to make the call.

Fifteen

I yawned, my jaw cracking loudly. Gus was the only one to hear it.

Gril hadn't answered my call the night before. Still using Benny's phone, I'd tried to reach Tex to no avail, so Gus and I had made our way into the Benedict House just as the sun was setting. I didn't see a soul as we hurried to my room. Possession was nine tenths of the law, after all. Viola wouldn't kick me out if she found me there sleeping. Would she? She hadn't yet.

I'd set my alarm for four A.M., unhappy that I'd made the commitment to Eddy but not wanting to flake on him—*like he had on me for approximately twenty-three years,* I noted ironically to myself—so when I awoke, I took care of Gus and then situated him outside Viola's room. I sensed she was there, but I had no idea where everyone else was. The door to Sadie's room was shut, but I didn't put my ear to it to see if I could hear anything. I had no idea if Grecko was maybe in another room.

"Be good," I whispered to Gus.

He was still tired enough to be okay with me leaving as he

curled up on his hallway bed. I watched as his beautiful blue eyes closed.

The sun was rising, and it was foggy-breath cold as I made my way to my truck. *Goodness, I hoped it warms up a little,* I thought as I peered at the sun. It was discombobulating, seeing both last night's sunset and this morning's sunrise while my body sensed the small number of hours between the two events.

Downtown was quiet, not a soul in sight. No lights on in any windows, but I knew the café would start serving breakfast soon. I hoped Eddy kept his word and had donuts. I didn't spot any police cars, and I wondered if Grecko had been driving one of the trucks I didn't immediately recognize.

As I made my way, my mind sifted through the events of the past two days. I felt more exhaustion just thinking about how much had happened.

I parked in the dock's empty parking lot and took the time to enjoy the sunrise from this location. The light diffused through the clouds, and for a moment, it was like butter and milk had spilled across the sky.

"Goodness."

I wished I'd brought Gus, but I had no idea what he thought of boats. I wasn't nervous for myself. I was sort of wishing I was still in bed, not about ready to head out on a boat, no matter who I was going with.

I laughed at myself. Maybe a boat ride would do me some good, shape me up.

Headlights appeared from up on the road. A vehicle turned onto the lot's sloped entryway. I figured it must be Eddy, which I confirmed once the car turned and the headlights were no longer blinding my vision.

Eddy brought the car to an easy stop and exited; the three Duponts followed directly after him. Eddy waved in the direction of my truck, and I flashed my lights to let him know I saw them. I gathered my backpack and decided to leave the truck keys under the mat. The parking lot would be much fuller by the time we returned, but I didn't think anyone would be bold enough to steal from it.

At first glance, no one might want such an old thing, but it was my favorite vehicle ever. It got me where I needed to go, it was paid for, and a new scratch here and there would never be noticed.

I closed the driver's side door gently, patting it appreciatively afterward. The window had been rattling some and I didn't want it to fall off track.

"Beth, hello!" Eddy called.

"Hey," I said as I approached them.

Betty Dupont stepped forward. "Ms. Rivers, thank you. You have made my daughter's day. Now, Greg and I have told her to chill a little, not go, too . . . what is the word? Fangirl? Just send me the signal if she gets on your nerves."

"Mom," Gracie said.

I laughed. "It's a pleasure to hang out with all of you."

"Well," Betty continued. "Time will tell, I suppose, but seriously, we don't want you to be uncomfortable."

"I've never been on a small boat, Betty. I might appreciate a little fangirl distraction before the day is over."

They all laughed.

Surprising me, Gracie threaded her arm through mine and led us to the dock. I tried not to act surprised by her familiarity, but even with Betty's implied warnings, I kind of was.

"Ignore my parents," she said. "I do. Greatest *thrill chiller* ever, you."

"Oh. Well, it's going to be a great day," I responded awkwardly, finding her words odd.

Eddy intervened quickly. "Okay, I need Beth to come aboard by herself first. You all have heard the safety rules, but Beth hasn't. I'd like to get her acclimated first. That okay?"

Noises of agreement were made by the other three.

Reluctantly, Gracie released my arm, and I hurried to join Eddy on the dock.

"Sorry about that," he muttered quietly. "Even on the ride over, her parents did tell her to keep it low-key, but I'm not sure she cares to listen to them."

"As long as she doesn't kidnap me and throw me in her van, I'm fine." I blanched at my own words. Hurriedly, I added, "Sorry. Dark, inappropriate humor, I guess."

"It's okay." He put his hands on his hips as we stopped next to his boat. "All right, so you've really never been on a fishing boat?"

"My first boat ride was two days ago, and we didn't make it to the glaciers. And that was a big tourist boat."

He studied me, both of us now lit by one of the dock lights as well as shadowed by the sun. "Are you concerned?"

"I thought I'd talked myself out of being concerned, but it's the unknown."

"Are you sure you want to do this? I would never force you."

I thought for a beat. I didn't want to disappoint Gracie, of course, but my main reason for wanting to go had nothing to do with either Eddy or any of the Duponts.

I decided to be honest. "You will stop at the island, let me look around?"

"Sure, if that's what you want."

"Eddy, I do think I should probably get past my fear of all of this, but my main reason for going is so I can explore that island. You okay with that?"

He wasn't offended in the least. In fact, I saw a smile spread wide on his face. "Whatever it takes, darlin'. I should have put it together by now. You worked with your grandfather. You probably had a healthy curiosity anyway, but if anyone could light that kind of fire, it was your gramps." Eddy shook his head. "He was one of the best men I've ever known."

My eyes suddenly burned. I swallowed away the emotion. No matter how much time passed, I would miss my grandfather forever. "I agree."

"Yeah. Yeah." Eddy put his hand lightly on my arm. "Come on, I'll show you the ropes—and all the other parts." He laughed.

Eddy stepped into the boat and then gave me a hand aboard. It wasn't as easy as he made it look, and my first step almost resulted in me face-planting on the cabin floor.

"Easy there." Eddy held on tight enough to keep me from hitting the ground.

I managed to straighten up and balance well, though a boat this small would probably never be completely still in the water.

"This is a thirty-footer," Eddy said. "Older model but in great shape. This back part is where everyone sits to enjoy the ride."

The cabin was equipped with two counter-like tables, well secured to the floor and surrounded by bolted-in bench seats. A canopy covered the top.

"We fish from out there, up by the cockpit or at the back of the cabin. I set up the fishing rods for everyone. All you have to do is watch them and reel in the fish. I help with the big ones or the fighters."

He moved to one of the benches and lifted the top, exposing life vests. "Everyone wears one of these, and we don't move along at too quick a clip. This boat has never gone under."

"Well, that's good," I said, but remembered my thought in Fred's plane—was I tempting too many fates? "Unless that means it's due."

Eddy laughed. "No, Beth, it's a safe boat. It even has a small living space under the cockpit, in case I want to move aboard. That's only a summer thing around here, though."

Eddy led the way toward the cockpit and opened a narrow door, exposing three steps that led down to the cutest tiny bedroom I'd ever seen.

"That's pretty convenient."

"Well, I'm not sure I'm ready to move in, but I do like having that option. Okay, the rules: No one gets too rowdy. I don't allow any alcohol aboard, but I do have waters, sodas, and snacks in the coolers. I'm the captain on this ship, and it's my way or the highway. I see something I don't like, I give some sort of command, you all have to obey what I say. That's just the way it is and the way I make sure to keep everyone safe."

"Got it." I felt like saluting, but I kept it to myself.

"Okay then." He sighed heavily again. "Here's the deal. If you want to explore that island, we'll go, but you'll be with me. I talked to Gril last night to let him know we'd be stopping there. He wanted to make sure I stayed with you. He doesn't like that the Duponts will be there, too, but he can't stop anyone from visiting any island. People kayak to it all the time, and it's no longer a crime scene. I've told the Duponts there are bears there and that they are welcome to stay on the boat or explore, but they should be aware. Beth, if any of them get freaked out about anything, I'll need to come back here as quick as possible. Okay?"

I appreciated his thoroughness as well as his frankness, though a part of me wished Gril hadn't been informed about my desire to explore the island. I hadn't even told Tex what I was going to be up to today. Eddy was staying with Gril, though, and if anyone was going to great lengths to be "legal" these days, it was my father.

"Got it." I nodded.

"All right. I'm going to call the others aboard, and we'll be on our way shortly."

I nodded again. "Just let me know what I can do to help."

By the time the Duponts boarded, there were a few other trucks and cars in the lot. Those working the big glacier tour boat were showing up for work, and other fishing boats were loading up, too. Glaciers, fishing, or whale watching, the summer boat industries here did very well.

The sun was over the horizon by the time we disembarked. The cool air was refreshing even as my eyes still felt a little tired. As Eddy steered the boat out into the bay, I sat in the cabin with the Duponts, watching the water and learning about their lives in Des Moines. So far, they'd loved their visit to Alaska.

Greg Dupont was a defense attorney, which he claimed, with a wry sense of humor, was not always a popular job. I took a quick liking to his self-deprecating way and quiet mannerisms. I filed away his profession. Maybe I'd talk to him about Clara Lytle, but I needed to get to know them all a little better first. Briefly, I also wondered if he might know the other defense attorney I'd recently learned about—Gina Rocco—but I didn't ask. I was sure that not all defense attorneys automatically knew one another, but there sure seemed to be a lot around the last couple of days. Thinking of Ms. Rocco made me wonder if Albert Jackson had been spotted yet as well as what happened after the marshal stormed out of the bar with the stack of *Petitions* containing the fugitive's photo. I was out of the loop of information, even more so out here on the water. I decided to let go of all of those concerns and try to enjoy these moments instead.

Betty was lovely, though chatty. She had something to say about everything, it seemed. Still, I couldn't help but like her, too.

It was Gracie who turned out to be the most difficult one to warm up to. She rolled her eyes at me as her parents made silly jokes or observations. I got that being a teenager automatically made you embarrassed by your parents, but she did seem a little bit over the top.

"Oh, Ms. Fairchild—I mean, Rivers—your character development is so superb; you write jaw-dropping twists, and readers are glued to the page," she said.

"Thank you," I said.

"You must have torture and murder on your mind."

"Oh." Not knowing how else to respond to that, I said, "I try."

Everyone laughed.

Her words were somewhat forced, but I appreciated her complimentary blurbs. After those initial introductory moments, though, we all relaxed into companionable water and island watching.

I noticed quickly that Eddy was pretty good at steering the boat over rocky waters with as minimal impact to the hull as possible. He seemed to know what he was doing, and he cut a confident figure as he stood at the helm.

"Tell me how you do it," Gracie asked after a few minutes. "How do you come up with the creepy stuff? I mean, you were writing scary things even before you were kidnapped, you know? You write so realistically."

I tried not to show the jolt of discomfort her fawning gave me. As much as I love that people read my books, I'm not one for public accolades. Nevertheless, her question was a version of *Where do you get your stories?* I'd been asked it plenty of times.

The answer was both "I'm not exactly sure" and "everywhere."

"It's kind of a mystery, Gracie. I don't live in those scary places in my head, even after Travis Walker, but when I sit down to tell a story, I can only work with the things that come to me. I've always been fascinated by darkness, by the sensation of being scared. If I manage to relay that on the page, I'm flattered."

"Oh, you do," Gracie said.

"Yes." Betty laughed. "You are terrifying. Not my cup of tea, though you seem so . . . normal."

"I guess I don't know what that is anymore, particularly after . . . what I went through." I shrugged. It was more honest than I was with most people. "But there's always scary stuff, and . . ."—I shrugged again—"for some strange reason that I can't quite understand myself, I'm compelled to write about it."

"I think that's a fine answer." Betty nodded at me and then looked at her daughter, who now seemed more perplexed than happy with my answer. "Don't you, Gracie?"

"I dunno." Gracie frowned but then peered up at Eddy. "When can we drown some worms?"

Just then Eddy slowed the boat, the engine noise whirring down from smooth to clunking, a noise I didn't think it was supposed to be making. I looked up at him and then around at the others. No one else seemed bothered by the sound. My brain was still trying to catch up to all these new experiences.

Eddy smiled at us. "Here we go!"

It turned out there wasn't a worm on that boat. We were fishing for halibut, which meant we needed something a little heartier to entice the ocean-bottom-dwelling fish to bite.

Herring did the trick. Before long, each of us had a line in the water. With the open bucket of herring bait in the middle of everything, the sun intermittently finding its way through the clouds, the spray of the cold ocean water on my face, I found myself having the time of my life.

Just being there, being in charge of one of the giant fishing poles, smelling the smells, seeing the sights; it was all so . . . *fun!* Why in the world hadn't I done something like this before now? Could this landlubber Midwesterner be a water person?

Ruke had warned me off of the ocean, the bay, but as I took it all in now, I couldn't believe I didn't live on this water.

We were all having a great time.

I felt a tug on my line. Eddy had explained that halibut were big, some of them really big, so if one bit, I would have to work hard to reel it in.

He wasn't kidding. With the first tug, I felt like I might have to reinsert my shoulders into their sockets.

"I got one!" I yelled, gleefully.

I grasped the pole, the end of it digging into my gut. I wrapped my left arm around it, trying to use the crook of my elbow to keep it from flying into the sea.

"Here, I'll help." Greg was by my side in only a moment. He put his hands on the pole, too. "You got a big one!"

"It feels like a whale." I laughed. "Wait, I couldn't catch a whale, could I?"

Greg laughed, too. "No, it's a halibut, I'm pretty sure."

"Gracious," Betty said as she came up to my other side. "That must be some fish."

"You got this, Beth! Reel it in!" Gracie exclaimed from somewhere behind me.

"Hang on tight there, Bethie," Eddy said.

It was a battle, no question. I reeled some, but then the fish tugged back, hard. I couldn't have held on to the pole by myself. I got winded, and my arms started to ache quickly.

But I wasn't going to give up.

That was, until Eddy made his way around Betty on my one side. I must have been the only one who'd seen the gun tucked in his waistband, because surely the others would have either tried to hide or tried to tackle him if they'd seen it, too.

"Gun!" I yelled.

I let go of the pole, leaving it to Greg, and turned to my father. Who was he trying to kill?

He looked at me with wide eyes and a confused expression. He held his hands up—and, yes, there was most definitely a gun in his waistband.

"Put the gun down, Eddy," I said.

Eddy looked at me, at the gun, and back at me again. I didn't understand why everyone else wasn't freaking out. Well, Greg was still struggling to hold on to the pole by himself.

"Right." Eddy took a couple of steps backward and set the gun down on the floor of the boat. "Beth, it's okay."

"Why do you have a gun?" I asked.

The line from my pole popped and the tension decreased immediately. Greg was propelled back a couple steps but remained on his feet.

The fish got away.

"Beth." Gracie came up to my side. "It's okay." She looked at Eddy. "You didn't tell her?"

"I forgot." Eddy's hands were still in the air.

Gracie continued to me, "The halibut are so big, you have to shoot them in the head. It's only a .22-caliber. It's not much of a gun, but it does help prevent them from suffering. Gets it over quickly and everything."

"What?" I looked around at my fellow shipmates.

"It's true, Bethie," Eddy said, his arms still raised. "It's okay."

"It's all right," Betty said. "Give her a moment; it'll be okay."

There was no one else around. The sea was so big that even with all the fishing and whale-watching tours that had disembarked from the dock today, I couldn't spot another boat anywhere.

But these people weren't trying to kill me. It took a moment, but I did realize that I was, in fact, safe. We all were.

My nervous system hadn't quite caught up to that reality, though. Before I could even utter one small laugh at myself, I threw up. At least I managed to aim over the railing and into the water.

Sixteen

'd taken a seat in the cabin.

"Hey there." Eddy joined me.

"I'm so sorry," I said to him. I'd said it to everyone, several times. "Please, I don't want to ruin everyone's day. Just let me finish my Sprite and I'll be good as new."

"You're not ruining our day. People can't help it if they get sick," Betty said from her spot on the bow. The boat wasn't big enough for any conversation anywhere to be private.

"I'm not sick. I just freaked out a little. I saw the gun, and . . . well, I am fine now. I'm so sorry."

"Sure?" she called, her focus on her pole and the sea, though.

"One hundred percent." I paused. "Although, I'm not sure I'm ready to shoot a fish in the head."

Gracie laughed. I would be forever grateful for her ability to see the humor I was so badly attempting. We'd moved well past her earlier seemingly scripted words. She seemed natural and relaxed now.

Eddy studied me.

"Eddy, I'm fine. In fact, that might have been good for me. I might have gotten something out of my system. Please. I don't need to fish, but I won't get in anyone's way, and I'm . . . I was having a great time, and I will get back to it. I just need a minute. More than anything, I'm embarrassed. A gun did that to me? Though I might never have seen you with one, I've seen plenty of them since moving here. I need to get a grip."

"I'm sorry I didn't tell you about it," Eddy said to me as the others worked to set up the poles again. We hadn't gone far and were still in a good pocket.

I laughed. "Me too."

"Hey, Beth," Gracie called as she sat on the bow. "Do you want us all to forget about it, act like it didn't happen?"

"Yes, in fact, that would be great."

"I can do that." Gracie looked at her parents.

"Me too," they said at the same time.

So that's what they did. Even Eddy did me the kindness.

After that, I did not fish. I helped fish. I was less bothered by touching the herring bait than I was by the idea of shooting an animal in its head, so I turned into the fishing assistant. And, again, I had a great time. Everyone did.

All three of the others caught big fish. Betty caught a seventy pounder, Greg a ninety-four, and Gracie a one-hundred-and-four pounder. I couldn't watch when Eddy used the gun and I was glad the fileting was left to him to do at the dock after we returned.

I'd been told more than once that if I was to find my way out here in this wild world of Alaska, I should consider accepting things that I hadn't thought I would be able to. This was one of those things. I wasn't going to accept it, but I certainly wasn't going to make a big deal out of it and ruin my father's paying clients' day. No matter what he'd done to me, I couldn't quite do that. I would also continue to hypocritically eat halibut. The café served a honey sauce for it that was divine.

As the fishing day ended, we all moved back to the cabin for snacks. Then, I sidled up next to Eddy as he steered the boat again—still very skillfully.

I looked up at the clouds. I'd seen skies more threatening, but it did appear that a doozy of a storm was on its way. "Can we still stop by the island?"

"Yes. You still want to?"

"I do, but I don't want to put anyone in danger." I nodded back toward the cabin.

Eddy shook his head. "It should be fine. I checked the weather—rain won't be here for about three more hours. Gril knows where we're going, too."

"He was really okay with it?"

"I wouldn't say that *okay* is the word, but he understood your nosiness."

I laughed. "I bet."

"I'm coming with you, and I'll have bear spray. And a gun."

"A little .22. What good will that do?" I was faking my gun expertise.

"Well, I have a more powerful one for the island. Gril approved it."

I sighed. Eddy had been staying with Gril, and their friendship seemed genuine. I knew both of them but probably knew Gril better than I did Eddy. Did they sit around at night and drink beer? Roast marshmallows? Did Gril have a satellite that allowed him access to sports or movies that they could watch together?

I hadn't inquired, and I didn't think I was ready to know anyway.

"Why the sigh?" Eddy asked.

"I can't believe Gril would get you, a felon, guns."

"I was never convicted. All statutes of limitations have long run out. My record is clean as a whistle." He paused. "Thanks to your grandfather."

"Right."

I knew my grandfather had intervened in my father's disappearance. I had a letter that told me some things regarding his assistance, but I was sure there was more. I wasn't ready to have such a heart-to-heart with Eddy, but maybe that time was coming closer.

"I'm grateful to be a free man, Beth, but I'm more grateful to be near you."

I looked at him and almost laughed, but his expression was genuine.

"When you are ready, I will be here. Well, I'll either be still living at Gril's or maybe I'll find a place on my own by then. Shoot, maybe it will have a spare bedroom. You could have another place to stay."

I held up my hand in a halt motion. "Not ready."

"Got it." He nodded ahead. "There's the island."

The last time I'd been on a boat approaching Lilybook, it had been from another angle, one farther east than where we were now. I couldn't see the beach where Sadie had been found, but I could see a forest all the way to the water's edge.

"Look at all the birds," I said as I pointed toward the trees. "I didn't see them from the other side."

Puffins, quite possibly the cutest bird ever created, filled the branches, their black-and-red markings standing out amid all the green.

"Huh. I haven't noticed them on Lilybook before, either," Eddy observed. "I've seen them on a few of the other islands. We're going around to the beach side, so you might not see the birds there."

"It's not that big an island, is it?" I asked.

"It's five square miles."

"Really? It doesn't seem like that." I wondered how in the world I was going to cover five square miles in an afternoon. I'd have to limit my search, but I'd decide just exactly how when we got there.

Eddy steered around a small peninsula. The beach was on the other side, two kayaks were leaning ashore.

"We won't be alone," Eddy said.

"Nope. That will be okay, though."

The police had cut off access to the island when they'd been looking for the body and then for only a few more hours so they could look for any other evidence. Tex had discovered the body, and nothing else had taken very long. The scene was considered processed.

I didn't expect to find anything at all, but I was thrilled about the idea of exploring.

The Duponts had all fallen asleep, Gracie with her head on her arms on the table, Greg and Betty leaning against each other. They'd had a big half day.

It crossed my mind to take a picture of them, but I didn't have a smartphone, and I didn't want to wake Gracie. The shot would have made a great post for someone who enjoyed social media, and I suspected Gracie was on at least one or two of the sites.

Eddy had me man the helm, though I didn't do anything with it. He jumped out, grabbed a rope, and wrapped it around a sturdy tree, securing it in some sort of fancy knot, before he signaled for me to join him.

"Leave a note for the Duponts," he called quietly up toward the cockpit.

I nodded and made my way back into the cabin, grabbed a brochure and a pen from a basket behind the counter, and jotted a quick note.

Eddy and I are ashore. Stick close by the
boat until we come back. Beth.

Gracie might be disappointed not to go with us, but maybe there would still be time if she woke up. Her parents hadn't expressed interest in exploring an island where it was certain that bears lived, but they'd seemed to be okay with Gracie looking around—a little.

I grabbed some waders and slipped them on before jumping off and into the shallow water near the shore. I was glad for Eddy's reach as he held on and helped me all the way onto the sand.

I took off the waders and hung them over the rope that was keeping the boat from sailing away.

"They should be fine," Eddy said. "If someone takes them, they might need them more than we do."

"Okay." I slung my pack over one arm. "Let's go."

Eddy sent one more look toward the boat.

"Are you worried about the Duponts?" I asked.

"No, not at all. Well, just in the way that I would be concerned for any customer. I do hope they aren't too confused when they wake up."

"I left the note."

"That works. Okay." Eddy turned and squinted into the woods. "Shall we get after it then?"

"We shall."

Before I could step in front of him, he started off ahead of me, walking surely into thick trees, though their trunks were smaller than those in the mainland woods. The undergrowth seemed mossier out here too and muddy. I'd taken the waders off but was glad I'd worn boots.

"Are we just looking around, or do you want to go someplace specific?" Eddy asked over his shoulder.

I could see he was hyperalert, his gaze darting almost everywhere at once, his shoulders tense. I didn't know what I could say to make him relax.

"I'd like to head over to the other side and look at where the body was found. I don't think that's five miles away, though."

"No. It's less than a mile. The island isn't round. It's long and fairly skinny. Okay, let's get across."

We trudged through the trees and brush. It wasn't cold out, but it was still cool enough to need a jacket. However, just a short time into the hike, I was too warm.

"Hey!" a voice called, while we were stopped for me to pull off my outer layer.

Eddy and I looked over to see two young people coming our way from the left, where I thought the caves were located. We waved and then Eddy, probably thinking he was being subtle, took a step so his body covered at least half of mine.

"Hey," a teenage girl with long bright yellow hair, pale skin, and a perfect complexion said again.

"Hi," I said.

The boy didn't join her as she approached us. Instead, he stayed back and pulled his pack off his shoulder and rummaged around in it.

"Hello," Eddy said. "You the ones with the kayaks?"

"Yep. Just wanted to see if we could find the killer bear," the girl said.

"What would you do if you found him?" Eddy asked.

The girl laughed. "Run like hell."

It didn't surprise me that local news and gossip had spread like wildfire. However, I knew these two weren't locals.

I also knew that looking for a "killer bear," whether that was an appropriate moniker or not, was downright stupid. I'd been a teenager once, too, though.

"I'm glad you're okay," I said.

"Oh, yes, we're fine," the girl said. "What are you guys doing here?"

"Just hiking, looking around."

The girl smiled knowingly. "You're looking for the bear, too, aren't you? Dang it, if you find him, I'm going to be jealous. What's your IG? I'll watch for your post."

"IG?" I asked.

"Instagram," Eddy said.

"Oh. I don't have one," I said.

The girl looked perplexed and disgusted. Eddy chuckled once.

"You?" the girl asked Eddy.

"Afraid not, but at least I knew what you meant."

"How will anyone know you found a bear?" she asked, perplexed.

I reached into my pack. "You two need any water?"

"No, we're good. Thanks, though." She seemed bored. "Okay then, have fun."

A second later, she turned to rejoin the boy, and they headed back toward the kayaks.

For an instant, I forgot my anger at Eddy, my irritation. That had happened a few times today, and I wasn't sure how I felt about that, except that I kept noticing it.

We did have a shared history—of course, it was only for the first seven years of my life, but it was real, and it had been good.

My dad's laughter at the dinner table had been one of the things I'd held on to when he'd disappeared. His happy chuckle at something my mother or I told him, his encouragement when it was needed.

I cleared my throat. "Let's go."

Eddy nodded and turned, leading the way again.

He was in as good shape as I was. The Mexican beach lifestyle had been kind to him.

And just like that, once again, irritation at the idea of him living well, having a good time, while Mill and I and my grandfather had been so worried about him, sizzled through me.

Let it go, Beth, let it go.

The hike wasn't too taxing, but it took a little longer than I'd hoped. I wasn't worried about the Duponts, but I did think that maybe Eddy's indulgence of my desire to explore might make them less than happy customers, and I didn't want to be responsible for that.

Once we were clear of the trees on the other side, though, it would have been impossible not to take a moment to soak in yet another stunning view.

This side's beach was narrower and rockier than the other side; the rocks were bigger than just pebbles and were colorful—gray, black, silver, burgundy, and even some that were yellowish.

"What is this?" I asked Eddy. "Why are the rocks like this?"

They reminded me a little of a toy I'd been given as a child—a rock polisher.

"I have no idea. Pretty, though."

"Definitely."

The shallow water gave way quickly to a murkier deepness that began only about five feet out.

Tex had told me that the body had been found in a small inlet. It was easy to spot the area. Next to big black boulders that stretched out into the sea, was a small, almost perfectly circular inlet. I spotted some detritus and a plastic water bottle there now, making me think that the area was some sort of natural draw.

We made our way over to it.

We gathered the water bottle so we could throw it away later. I put it in a plastic bag and then into my backpack.

"Gril told me that Tex found something else out here, but I couldn't reach him last night. Have you heard what he found?" I asked.

"I haven't." Eddy nodded at my pack. "Maybe the water bottle will be helpful."

I nodded. I doubted it, but I'd still give it to Gril.

We looked around. The view was spectacular, but there wasn't anything else to discover. I'd studied the ground and the trees as we'd hiked, but I hadn't seen any blood anywhere.

Eddy peered out toward the horizon. He closed one eye and lifted his right arm, seeming to gauge or measure something.

"What do you see?"

"I don't think I see anything, but look how the island curves around. I think that anything that might have come off that curve there would have been pulled to right here. So unless the body was left right here, it could have feasibly come off from up there."

"How far away is that?"

"Maybe half a mile."

"I hate to keep the Duponts waiting, but do you think we could head over that way?"

"Sure. We haven't been gone all that long. When I told them what the plans were, I mentioned a couple of hours."

"Thanks, Eddy."

"You're welcome. Let's go."

We were able to take a semi-forged path just inside the tree line, and we covered the half mile quickly.

"Look." I pointed, keeping my voice low.

To our left and only about twenty feet deeper into the trees, the entrance to a rocky cave gaped widely open.

"That's a big doorway," Eddy noted.

"There could be bears in there."

"Well, technically, there could be bears anywhere out here, but yes, that could be where they rest or take their kill to eat it."

I laughed lightly at his tone, but then I realized that he had a good point. My eyes went to the ground between where we stood and the cave's opening. There was most definitely a worn area there, a path of some sorts. "This isn't clear water, is it?" I nodded toward the ocean.

"I don't think there's any way it could be."

I took an even closer look at the greenery around, stepped closer to the water, and crouched.

"I think I get it now," I said as I pointed at the moving water.

Eddy crouched next to me. "Ah, a veritable bed and breakfast."

We watched fish swim around in the shallow tide not far from the shore. I didn't think any of them were salmon, but I didn't know my fish at all. Except maybe now halibut.

"They can just walk out of that cave, grab a bite to eat, and be on their way."

"Nice setup, if you can get it," Eddy said, though he glanced over his shoulder.

I looked in that direction, too. No bears watching us inspecting their next meal.

From the same position, I looked at everything else. "I guess a bear could have brought the body here and it floated over there." I nodded toward the inlet.

"But, remember, there were no claw marks or bites."

"And I'm not seeing any blood anywhere."

Eddy frowned. "None of anything that has occurred these last few days makes much sense to me, Beth. I'm sure we don't know enough of the facts to take a real guess as to what might have happened out here."

"Yeah, I don't know." I stood and did one circle of the area, still not seeing anything suspicious or any bears, for that matter.

"Want to explore the cave?" Eddy asked.

"I do, but there's no way I think we should."

"I agree. Good answer."

"Maybe some other time, then?"

"Sounds like a plan."

"Ready to head back?"

I nodded. I had enjoyed just exploring and would now wish for the chance to do it again. Shoot, I might even talk to Ruke about kayaking out here.

Okay, maybe not. But I knew I could convince Tex to bring me out for a look. He'd be thrilled and would see it as a proper teaching moment as well as a fun date. I smiled at the idea.

The journey back to the boat took a little longer than our outward trek, but while we were still hidden amid the trees, we were suddenly close enough to hear voices—and they weren't happy.

"Gracie! Where are you?" Betty called.

"Gracie! Come back right now!" Greg called.

"Eddy? Beth?" Betty called, her voice choked with emotion when she saw us emerge from the trees.

Eddy and I shared a worried expression and then set off in a run to join them.

Seventeen

Gracie was gone.

I'd often thought that Travis kidnapping me was the worst thing a person could go through. I'd been wrong. I'd never felt the fear and helplessness that now overwhelmed me.

Gracie was nowhere to be found.

Greg and Betty had awoken from their nap. Gracie wasn't on the boat. Because of the note, they realized quickly that we'd made it to the island, but they'd slept through the part where we'd disembarked, Gracie's departure included.

At first, they'd deduced that Gracie had gone with us, even though the note I'd written had said "Eddy and I" and I'd signed it.

They disembarked with the notion to look around the beach a little. They were concerned, but not overly so—at least until they saw Gracie's shoes on the beach, right next to the tree line.

Why wouldn't Gracie have her shoes on?

The question blossomed from worry into soul-consuming fear at lightning speed. They weren't sure what to do except to stay right where they were and keep calling for all of us.

"Where's Gracie?" Betty asked when she first saw Eddy and me. "Oh God, where's Gracie?"

We had to tell them that we didn't know, that she hadn't gone with us, that she'd been asleep just like they'd been when we'd left. The words were like rocks in my throat.

"She has to be here," Eddy said as he looked toward the trees.

"Her shoes!" Betty pointed.

It was a bothersome sight, those shoes on the sand as if they'd been kicked off purposefully, as if she was going to go for a swim or something.

But that couldn't be it. The water was too cold to swim, and the ocean was too dangerous to swim in, wasn't it?

"Maybe they got wet, so she just took them off." I hurried to the red Keds-like shoes and then looked up toward where I'd hung the waders. They were still there.

"Yes, they're wet. She just took them off because they were wet," I said as I held one of the shoes.

"She had no other shoes that I'm aware of," Greg added, his voice a forced steadiness. "She would wear wet shoes, not walk barefoot through the woods."

"I have boots on the boat," Eddy said. "Maybe she just grabbed a pair of those. She has to be around here. I'm going to take a look."

"Boots. You have boots?" Betty asked, the news giving her a bright enough glimmer of hope that she wiped at the tears running down her cheeks.

She wanted to fall apart, and she knew she needed to keep it together.

I knew that feeling all too well.

"Everybody, stay here. Give me a few minutes to look in the woods," Eddy said. "If I don't find her right away, we'll radio back to the dock and get some help."

Betty nodded. "How many pairs of boots do you have aboard? I'll go count."

"I'm not sure," Eddy said, "But I'll check after I search. I'll know if any are missing."

"I'm coming with you," Greg said.

There was no stopping him.

"Of course," Eddy said. "Let's go."

Betty and I remained on the rocky beach. She couldn't sit, didn't want to do anything but pace, look around, and call out for Gracie. I stuck by her side and called out, too.

"Where is she?" she asked a number of times.

"We'll find her," I said, though she wasn't really listening to me.

She turned back toward the trees. "Gracie!"

There was no answer, not even a birdcall. I wished for something, some sort of noise. I wished for Gracie to emerge from the woods, and look at us like we were being ridiculous. Say she was old enough to take care of herself, sheesh.

But that didn't happen.

Gracie didn't appear, and when Eddy and Greg came out without her, both of their faces ashen and full of fear, Betty collapsed into an emotional wreck.

Eddy hurried aboard the boat and made a call to the dock via the radio. We were told help would be on the way quickly. When Eddy returned, he confirmed that none of the pairs of boots were missing. It was horrible news to have to convey, worse to receive.

Never in my life, again including my time with Travis, had thirty minutes felt like three hours. But help did arrive, and I couldn't have been happier to see Gril, Donner, and Tex.

Tex and I shared a pained look, but we didn't speak immediately. There might not have been much to say, and the focus needed to be on finding the teenager.

It wasn't dark when the searchers set out, only about seven

o'clock. We still had a good two hours of light to help us. As much as I wanted to go with one of them, I chose to stay with Betty because she had grabbed my hand and didn't seem to want to let go.

Betty and I didn't re-board Eddy's boat but continued to sit on the beach, even as the air cooled substantially and the wind picked up. Gril had left thick coats, and I could see Betty start to shiver. Shock was a real danger here.

"Hey, we need to get this coat on you," I said as I patted the pile next to me.

She nodded, though her eyes looked out toward the boats.

"Here." I grabbed one with my free hand and slung it over her shoulders. "Slip your arms through."

She let go of me then as she threaded her arms through the sleeves. Hurriedly, I put one on, too, and then put my hand back where she could grab it if she wanted to. She didn't seem to notice.

She was crying again, though silently now, the noise in her head surely loud and awful. I didn't know how to comfort her in any way other than to just be there for her.

I pulled my knees up and wrapped my arms around them.

Gracie, where are you? I sent the thought out into the vast universe in front of us. From this vantage point, the world beyond was made of sky, dark clouds that hadn't brought the storm yet—thank goodness—and endless water, every single element a mystery on its own.

My own panic, on the other hand, made me laser focused.

"The kayaks!" I said as I stood and wiped sand off my backside.

They were gone. I hadn't noticed, hadn't thought about them, until then.

"What kayaks?" Betty asked, standing to join me.

"There were two kayaks right over there"—I pointed—"when Eddy and I first took off. We ran into a couple of teenagers in the woods. They said they'd kayaked ashore."

"So Gracie could have gone with them?" Betty asked, hope straining her voice.

"I don't know, Betty. Can kayaks hold more than one person? Would she have wanted to give one a try?"

"Sure. She's always about attempting an adventure." Betty ran toward the ocean and peered out into it. There were no kayaks visible, but there was so much ocean ahead of us that, feasibly, we might not be able to spot them if even they were there. She cupped her hands around her mouth. "Gracie!"

The only sounds we heard were water noises.

Betty turned to me. "Would they be back in Benedict by now?"

"I don't know," I said. I would have guessed they would be, if they didn't run into trouble along the way, but I couldn't be sure how fast they might have traveled.

Kayaks were each made for one person, not two. I knew this. Would the three of them—all teenagers—have wanted to try to put two people into one?

Of course they would. If anyone would, it would be adventurous, immortal-in-their-minds teenagers.

"We need to get back. We need to see." Betty put her hands on my arms.

I nodded. "Let's make sure the island gets thoroughly searched first, though. Gril will get us back there quickly when it's time." I knew there was a chance Betty might jump into the ocean and swim back to Benedict. I'd keep her with me, though. "We'll find out soon."

Again, time slowed as we waited. It was only ten minutes later, though it felt like an hour, that Tex joined Betty and me. He'd found nothing. I explained to him about the kayaks and the kids Eddy and I had seen. The others would surely be back in a few more minutes.

Tex made his way to the boat he, Gril, and Donner had come over on and grabbed the radio microphone. Why hadn't I thought of doing that?

"Benedict home, do you copy?" he asked.

No response.

"Benedict home, do you copy?"

"Benedict home here. Who is this?"

"Tex."

"Copy that, Tex. What's the word? Has the girl been found yet?"

"Not yet, but two kayaks were spotted on the island"—he paused and asked me how long ago and what colors they were—about three hours ago. Both were an orange-red, we think. Have they come ashore on your end?"

"Give me a second. I'll run and check the shed."

I knew the shed where the rentable kayaks and paddleboards were kept. It was down a hill from the radio office but not far away.

"Tex?" the voice came back a few minutes later.

"Copy," Tex said.

"I don't know how many kayaks are supposed to be accounted for, but most of them in the shed are that color. I will track down Henry, the guy who usually works the shed, and ask him—or ask someone—about inventory."

"Thanks. Also, hang on."

Tex asked me for a description of the teenagers, which I passed along to him. Betty made a strange squeaking noise and reaching for her phone when I described the girl.

Tex turned back to the radio and passed along the descriptions.

"Will you check the lodge? See if they are staying there? Let us know as soon as you can."

"Copy that. Jeff out for now, but I'll get back to you when I have more information."

Jeff was like the rest of us around Benedict. We helped out where we could. I didn't think he was the person who always manned the shore radio, but he'd be the one who had to do the following up tonight. I'd scrambled eggs with him one morning at the café when the cook was late getting in. My thoughts meandered back to Daniel Grecko again and his proclamation. *How did anything get done around here?*

"Thank you," Tex said.

He stepped out of the boat and made his way to us.

"What's up, Betty?" I asked her as she frantically worked the screen of her phone.

"I can't get to it."

"There's no internet connection out here," I said.

"Dammit to hell." She stomped her foot.

"What is it?" Tex asked.

"The girl." Betty looked at me. "The girl you described sounds like Gracie's best friend. I was trying to get to Facebook to show you a picture."

"What? From Iowa?" I asked.

"Yes!" She nodded adamantly.

I looked at Tex who shook his head. "We'll have to wait until we get a connection."

"Okay. Betty, we'll get it figured out," I said, wishing for the internet more than I ever had.

"Please."

"We will."

Though it felt like it took forever again, Gril, Donner, Greg, and Eddy reappeared. No one had seen anything, which was both good and bad news. There were no bodies anywhere. In fact, they searched the caves and they couldn't even find any bears. But there was also no Gracie, no sign of her.

I told everyone about the kayakers, and Tex shared about his call to shore.

"That's great," Gril said, enthusiastically. He looked back and forth between the Duponts. "Look, so far so good. No blood, no body, and we have a real lead. I think we should get back to Benedict and check it out."

It was good to have a plan. It gave us all, especially the Duponts, something to hope for.

Tex and I boarded Eddy's boat, while Donner and Gril took the Duponts with them. Gril's wasn't a speedboat, but it was speedier than Eddy's.

Though Eddy put his boat at full throttle, I felt like we were puttering along as I spotted the lights from the other boat ahead.

"You okay?" Tex asked me as we sat in the cabin and Eddy navigated. We had to raise voices above the engine noise.

"I'm worried sick," I said. "But I'm grateful I remembered the kayaks, and I really do hope she's with those kids. I need to look at a picture to see if the girl we saw was Gracie's friend—though, what in the world would that mean?"

Tex rubbed his chin as he thought. "You don't suppose Gracie wanted to get away, run away, and this is an elaborate plot to do it?"

"I don't know what I think. She sure didn't behave as if she wanted to run away."

I looked at my father then, who looked back at me sheepishly. He cleared his throat and spoke above the engine noise. "Sometimes you are given no choice but to run away. If that's what Gracie is doing, I would bet she wasn't given any choice in the matter. We should remember that."

He looked away, knowing how his words would land with me.

Tex smiled toward Eddy and then at me. He put his hand on my knee and then, knowing he probably didn't need to contribute to this conversation, turned his attention toward the front.

We couldn't get to Benedict fast enough.

Eighteen

Henry had been found and relayed to Jeff the number of kayaks that should be in the shed at the end of the day. There were exactly that many, but neither Henry nor Jeff had been around when the last few came in. They weren't required to be there until much later than about five because some people chose to stay out and camp overnight on an island rather than make their way back in. So much of the takeout and return was an honor system.

Counts were taken daily, but no one got too concerned unless a couple days passed with kayaks still out there, and then the missing people would be of more concern than the missing kayaks.

It wasn't a perfect system, but with no internet connection it seemed to be the best, and no one had been lost in the bay for almost six years now. We were all hoping that record would continue to hold up.

Eddy and Tex said they'd handle taking care of the boat as I hurried up to the lodge entrance. I pushed through the doors, hoping to find Gracie there inside, getting hugged and yelled at by her parents for what she'd done.

I wasn't that lucky, but I did get a few clarifications.

The lodge had recently ramped up their Wi-Fi connection but only during the summer season. Betty was able to pull up Facebook, and I was able to determine that the young woman Eddy and I had seen was indeed Gracie's best friend from Iowa, Laney Hooper. There was no doubt in my mind.

We spent a few minutes searching through pictures on both girls' pages to see if I could recognize the boy, but it was to no avail.

"He stayed back," I said. "I didn't think anything of it at the time, but he didn't seem as eager as Laney to be seen. Does Laney or Gracie have a boyfriend or a boy that, I don't know, they weren't supposed to be seeing?"

"Not to my knowledge." Betty shook her head. "The girls haven't dated that much. They prefer group activities, and I've shown you pictures of all those boys."

"How was she, Beth?" Gril asked.

"Do you mean was she scared or behaving strangely? No, in fact, she seemed very normal."

Betty continued, "They're sixteen, though, so I keep thinking the dating thing is bound to change. Maybe that's what's . . . I just don't know."

Betty and I were sitting on a couch in the lobby. Gril was on Betty's other side.

"The lodge folks don't have any Hoopers here. Do you have Laney's home phone number? I'd like to try to get ahold of her parents," Gril said.

"Sure. I wish I'd thought of that."

Instead of scrolling through and just giving Gril the number, she made the call herself, turning on the speakerphone feature.

The phone rang and rang with no voice mail picking up. Betty hung up. "This is their landline. I don't know their cell phones, but their names are Stephen and Holly Hooper."

Gril nodded as he made note of the number. "I'll track them down." He looked back up at Betty. "Tell me the circumstances of you coming to Alaska. You're here at the same time Laney is, but you didn't know she'd be here, too? Any inkling?"

Betty shook her head. "I don't know why we wouldn't know. We adore Laney and get along with her very well. There's no reason for her being here to be a secret. In fact, we would have brought her with us if that was something Gracie had wanted to do." She paused. "Maybe not a boyfriend, too, though. Anyway, it was Gracie's idea that we come here, I think." She looked at me. "Part of the reason was because Beth was here. She really wanted to find Beth and tell her how much she loves her books. She talked about that a lot."

"Okay. How long ago did you plan the trip?" Gril asked.

"Oh, just a month ago." She smiled, though it was a sad expression. "Greg is an attorney, and he finished up a big case. After a year, he could finally take a vacation. I don't remember the specifics, but now that I really think about it, I'm pretty sure Alaska *was* Gracie's idea." She frowned. "There was nothing forced about it, though. She brought it up like, 'Hey, how about this?'" She shook her head. "I can't remember thinking it was anything odd, but something must have been. There must have been something else behind it."

"Had you guys ever talked about Alaska before?" Gril asked.

"No, not really, but that's part of what made it fun."

Gril nodded. "Okay. Mrs. Dupont, we didn't find any evidence of trouble, and Gracie's best friend on that island at the same time can't be a coincidence. There's a plan here. Do you know what it could possibly mean?"

"I have no idea, Chief. None of it makes any sense at all."

Greg approached and sat in a chair across a large coffee table from us. He was a tall man, and though he hadn't appeared heavy until that moment, it seemed the weight of the world slowed his limbs, and even crossing his ankle over his knee was a laborious task.

"Mr. Dupont?" Gril turned to him.

Greg shook his head. "I've been racking my brain. I defend accused criminals, Gril. It's what I do. Of course, the media crucifies me. People hate me. That goes with the job. But we're careful. No one could easily find where we live in Iowa—"

"Anyone can be found," Gril interjected.

Greg nodded slowly. "Sure, but nevertheless, we do try to be careful. I can't think of a reason any of this has happened because of who I might have saved or not saved from going to prison. I guess anything is possible, but I have nothing."

"Have any of you had any threats or have any strange things happened lately? It's okay if you think you might have been overreacting. Has your intuition told you anything was off?"

Betty and Greg looked at each other as they both shook their heads and said, "No."

"I've put in a call to one of my associates back home," Greg added. "Just to see if anything has happened that I hadn't heard about, though I expect someone would have called me beforehand. I'll let you know what they say."

"Who knew you were coming to Alaska?" Gril asked.

"Everyone," Betty said weakly. "We told anyone and everyone. We were excited."

"Makes sense. Hey, you all did nothing wrong. Some sort of plan was put in place here, and that's good news when it comes to Gracie. She's . . . I don't know, *doing* something. We'll figure it out. I'm going to have to do some digging, though." He looked at them as if he was sending a potential warning.

"Of course! Dig all you want," Betty said.

"We are open books," Greg said. "I'm not aware that we have any skeletons in our closets, but if you find them and exposing them will help our daughter, do it. No holds barred. Anything."

Gril nodded and then asked the Duponts if he could escort them up to their room. Still stunned and glassy-eyed, they were afraid to leave the lobby, even if they couldn't logically understand why. Shortly, they agreed to allow Gril to lead them up.

I wasn't invited. After I watched them climb the natural-wood stairs, I left the lodge to look for Tex and Eddy at the dock or in the parking lot. They were making their way up the steps, probably planning to join the rest of us in the lodge. I let them know what had happened and that Gril was with the Duponts, so they reversed, and we climbed back down to the parking lot.

There were still a few vehicles along with each of ours. It was late; the sun was beginning to set. A familiar wave of exhaustion nudged away the adrenaline that had been giving me the energy to keep putting one foot in front of the other.

Eddy nodded at me—no hugs, but a handshake would have been too formal. He did shake Tex's hand before he hopped into his car and steered it out into the parking lot. He'd been traumatized, too. He felt responsible for what had happened even after I told him Gril's suspicion that Gracie had been planning all of this.

"I overheard Gril telling him it wasn't his fault," Tex said to me as we watched Eddy's taillights.

I opened my tailgate and hopped up to sit on it. "He takes his job pretty seriously."

"He does, but from what I saw and what you said Gril said, Gril doesn't blame him at all. I just hope for everyone's sake that it all turns out okay."

"Me too. Were you in town or did you come from Brayn?" I asked.

"Straight from Brayn. Left the girls with my mom." Tex hopped onto the tailgate, too.

"You have to head back tonight, I bet."

"Yes, ma'am, I do, but I thought we could take a minute and

look out at the sunset together—you know, count our blessings and see if we can summon Gracie Dupont to show herself."

I pushed away the thoughts of putting my head on my pillow. "Let's give it a try."

For a few long minutes, we did exactly that. Somewhere in those wishes and hopes and probably prayers, too, I sent out some gratitude. In a million years, I could never have imagined this moment, and despite the horrible circumstances we were all now faced with, I couldn't help but be grateful for it, too.

Nineteen

y the time I was attempting to make my way quietly into the Benedict House, the sun had set, Tex was well on his way back to his girls, and I was running on fumes. All lights were off downtown, all businesses closed for the night. It was unusually dark.

I was quiet as I entered the Benedict House, but not quiet enough for Gus.

Tonight, he was in the hallway, near the bed I'd left him in, sitting up, looking toward the front door as light splayed out of Viola's room.

"Hey, boy," I said in a whisper as he trotted to greet me.

A moment later, Viola—in her nightgown but still with her gun holstered around her waist—joined us.

"Hey, Vi," I said as she approached.

She signaled me into the dining room. I was probably about to be admonished for not finding another place to stay. I was so tired, I wondered if I just fell asleep with my head on a dining table, she might just leave me be.

But that's not what happened.

"What is going on?" she asked after we were seated, both of us with warm hot chocolates she'd made after directing me to a chair. "I have been charged with keeping my eye on Sadie, and Gril hasn't checked in with me. What can you tell me about everything? And don't leave out any details."

"Oh." I took a sip of my drink, rewinding everything in my mind, so I could determine the best place to start.

I began with a day earlier, when I'd first left her and Sadie in the restaurant and told her about the airfield and Buster. Then I told her about the goings-on on the island. Her concern deepened as I told her about Gracie, but she thought Gril was onto something— Gracie was part of a plan, hopefully one with a positive outcome soon. Her assignment had been Sadie, so the conversation moved back in that direction.

I remembered what I'd overheard, Sadie's Goose Creek call. I'd forgotten that part when I'd gone through things the first time. I grabbed a copy of the *Petition* from my pack. "Did the marshal, Grecko, find you?"

She seemed surprised. "Who?"

"Sadie's handler. He was looking for you last evening."

Viola shook her head. "No."

"You didn't even know he was in town? Would Sadie know?"

"I don't know how. I've been with her or in the room next to her at all times."

"The whole time?"

"Other than quick stops at the restaurant."

"That's weird. But Viola, there's something else I need to tell you. Before I do, I'm sorry I didn't before. I didn't want to mention it in front of Sadie, and then things got . . ."

"What is it?"

I shared the moments I'd eavesdropped on Sadie when she was

on the phone, her mention of Goose Creek, and then, as I slid the paper toward her, Orin's discovery.

"She hasn't said a word about Goose Creek to me." Viola looked at the *Petition*. "But this prisoner escaped from there, and he's the one accused of murdering the woman who was his biological mother? From Connecticut?"

"Yep. It's a murder that Sadie witnessed."

She studied the paper for a long moment. "Do you think Gril wants me to make sure Sadie sees this?"

I shrugged. "I don't know. I'm not used to you being out of the loop."

"Me neither, but the young girl's disappearance needs to be his priority." She sat back in her chair. "I'll call him in a few hours and ask him about Grecko. Surely, he's checked in with Gril."

My intuition conjured trouble, but my mind told me I was jumping too quickly to an unwarranted conclusion. Still . . . "Honestly, it's pretty weird Grecko hasn't made contact with you yet."

"I don't disagree."

"Maybe Gril has intervened with him." I paused, my tired mind trying to understand something I didn't have all the information to compute. I shook it off for now. "How is Sadie? Has she told you anything else about her past?"

Viola shook her head. "She's been sleeping, mostly. I keep trying to feed her, but she doesn't have much of an appetite."

A voracious appetite had kicked in when I arrived in Alaska. "She's going to be okay. I really do think so."

She paused, smiling a little at me, as if she was glad to have someone to talk to. It was something I'd come to enjoy: our chats. I'd been out of her hair for a couple days, but I realized that Viola liked my company, almost as much as I liked hers. "Here's a secret: I'm a really good cook. I don't enjoy it like I used to, so I make the clients do it. Oh, it's good for them to have a duty, of course, but I will fix Sadie up something she won't be able to resist."

"I'm not surprised. You're good at everything you do, Viola." I cleared my throat. "That sounded like sucking up, which is not the way we do things around here, I know. But you are pretty darn good at whatever you put your mind to."

Viola was tired, too, but she managed another smile. "How did you end up on that boat with your father and his clients?"

"The girl who is missing is a fan of mine. They asked Eddy if he could get me to join them. I didn't feel obliged, but I didn't hate the idea."

Viola nodded sagely, too sagely.

I nodded acquiescence. "Yes, I do want to find a way to get along with my father. I would very much like to want to spend time with him, to feel less angry about it."

"Talk to your therapist. She can help."

"She has, but I'm not all the way there yet."

She took another drink. "How old is the missing girl again?"

"Sixteen."

"And she's reading your books? I mean, everyone should read whatever they want, but I carry a gun and your books scare the breath out of me."

"You read one of my books?"

"Two. But that might be all. I didn't sleep well after either of them. Anyway, that sixteen-year-old must not dream much, or"— Viola scoffed—"she must have torture and murder on her mind."

There was something about what Viola said that rang a bell for me—unfortunately, it was a distant bell, something that I couldn't hold on to for very long.

"What is it, Beth?"

"Repeat what you just said."

"About the girl?"

"Yes."

"Okay." She repeated her words.

The bell rang again, but just as I was almost about to understand it, it fell silent and unknowable. "Something about what you're saying . . ."

"I'm sorry if I'm offending you."

"You aren't, but I feel like there's something important there."

I took out a notebook and pen from my backpack and wrote down what she'd said. There was that bell again. I was driving myself crazy. I tucked the notebook and pen back into my pack. "I'll look at it later."

"Okay."

"Did you hear from Orin today?" I asked.

"No, ma'am. I haven't talked to anyone but Sadie."

"Not even Benny?"

"No one's been here, Beth. I haven't talked to anyone, Benny included. That's why I waited up to see if you'd show up. I felt cut off from the world."

"That doesn't . . . Viola, did you call anyone?"

"No, I didn't. Gril told me to watch over Sadie, so that's what I've done, but I have certainly been a little miffed that no one has updated me on anything until now."

"Yeah. You are usually right in the middle of all of it." I stood. "What's up?"

"Have you checked your phone?"

"No."

One day in January, Viola's office phone didn't ring. Nothing special was going on in Benedict, but even on slow days, her phone rang once or twice at least, even if it was someone asking her to run over to the nearby café to see what soup was being served that day.

"It hasn't rung?"

"No." Viola's eyes darkened with understanding. She was remembering that day in January, too.

She made her way around me and Gus and led us all into her office. She lifted the handset.

"Nothing." She held it out so I could hear the silence, too.

"Your phone's not working," I said, stating the obvious.

"No, it isn't."

In January, after we discovered the quiet handpiece, we'd bundled up and trudged outside in our coats and boots to look at the outside phone line where it came out of the wall and snaked up to the power box, intermittent construction staples keeping the wire against the building.

The wind had been so strong one afternoon that two of the staples had worked free, and a gust must have pulled the cord out of the box.

Benedict didn't have phone repair people, but we had Orin, who liked to tinker and could fix just about anything, at least when he wasn't running a top-secret mission for the government.

It wasn't winter, but it was still cold enough at night to need coats and boots. Viola threw hers over her nightgown and slippers, and with Gus and a flashlight, we made our way outside and around to the back of the building.

Viola aimed the light.

A wind hadn't done anything back here this time, but something, or someone, else had. The cord had been cut—cleanly.

"What the hell?" Viola said.

"Someone didn't want you to have phone access today."

"Who in the hell would think this was a smart idea?"

"Good question."

"If I find who did this, I'll shoot 'em. Goddammit. I need to check on Sadie." She turned and stepped around me again, trudging back inside the Benedict House.

I looked at Gus. "I think she's serious."

Gus nodded in agreement.

We rejoined Viola as she was coming out of Sadie's room. She shut the door quietly. "Still fast asleep. She's fine."

Viola made her way back to her office and started riffling through one of the drawers.

"Can I help?"

She looked up at me. "I can't leave Sadie, and now I'm even more concerned." She opened a false bottom in the drawer and pulled out another gun.

My eyes went wide. "You have two?"

"Oh, I have more than two."

I wanted to offer another idea. I wanted to tell her we could just lock the doors, call the police, call Gril. Call Orin to fix the phone. But those weren't easy options out here.

"It was dark earlier, but do you want me to break into the bar and use the landline? Want me to drive out to Gril's place?"

"No, I don't want to break in," Viola said after a moment's thought. "And no, I don't want you driving anywhere alone."

"Where are the Juneau officers staying?" I asked.

"Last I heard, they went back to Juneau."

"Why?" As I asked the question, I realized that none of them had joined Gril and the others in searching for Gracie. If they'd still been in town, surely Gril would have asked at least some of them to help.

"I don't know. Wanted to sleep in their own beds, I guess."

Before the cut phone line, I might not have thought their leaving was the wrong decision, but I was seeing things differently now.

"We should all go somewhere else," I suggested.

"No, this is my place. I can handle anything here. Everything else is too unknown."

"I'm not leaving. Want me to hold a gun?"

"No, not until you've been properly trained through Viola's

gun-handling course. If you haven't been, then you're more dangerous and unsafe with a gun than without one."

A chill ran up my spine, and it was all I could do not to check the hallway for someone who might have sneaked inside. Gus immediately sensed my nerves and leaned in to me. I petted him to let him know I was okay. I didn't think he bought it.

"You'll stay with me. Let me check on Sadie again and set us up. We will be in the dining room together until sunrise. Then I'll have you head out and get Orin and try to talk to Gril."

"I think Gus would have noticed if anyone else came inside," I said.

"I agree." Viola nodded. "And that's exactly why I'm not forcing you to leave. I think we're okay, too, but I'm going to be ready for anything. Get what you need from your room and get to the dining room, Beth."

Gus was looking at me with probably the same sort of perplexed look that I was giving him. Neither of us would disobey this particular order.

"Come on, boy," I said.

Twenty

Viola was still awake by the time I fell asleep, my head on a table, Gus's head on my lap. I woke only when Sadie joined us, looking well rested and wondering what was for breakfast. As I came to, I realized that I must have slept hard—my neck was cricked, and Viola was cooking. I suspected she hadn't slept a wink.

The food smelled delicious, and hunger wrung my stomach.

"Hey, Sadie. Did you rest well?" Viola asked from behind the stove.

"I did." Sadie looked back and forth from Viola to me as I worked to get my eyes all the way opened. "You guys?"

"Oh, we did fine. Have a seat. Breakfast will be ready shortly."

"How are you feeling?" I asked.

"I feel a lot better, much less like I'm going to jump out of my skin." She sat.

"That's great. How's your appetite?"

"Enormous, I think."

I nodded. "That's probably a good thing."

"I agree."

I looked down at my backpack. Viola and I had talked about showing Sadie the copy of the *Petition,* but we weren't sure enough about anything to make that decision. In fact, Viola had asked me not to bring up Daniel Grecko. Viola might, but she felt the need to "get the temperature of everything first."

If Grecko hadn't gathered all the copies Orin and I had distributed, Sadie would be sure to see one if she set foot very far outside the Benedict House, though. Again, Viola asked me to let her deal with it.

We also decided not to tell her about the phone line being cut. I was to head over to the bar and use Benny's phone to try to call . . . everyone, but mostly Orin so he could fix it, and let them know what had happened as well as ask for further guidance.

Basically, we decided that Sadie didn't need anything else to worry her right now, so we weren't going to tell her much of anything.

I was sure that's what people did for me at first, kept me in the dark about Travis Walker's escape, for a few days at least, until it must have seemed cruel not to share. And to be fair, that news was the impetus for planning my escape to Alaska.

The bacon and eggs were delicious, and Viola had whipped up homemade blueberry muffins. They were to die for.

"Have you ever won a baking contest?" I asked her, working to keep everything as light as possible.

"No kidding," Sadie said as she grabbed her second muffin.

"Nope. Never entered one, though, so who knows where I could have gone with my talent?"

"Very far," Sadie said with a genuine laugh, though she sobered quickly. She looked at me. "I do not feel like I have the right to be happy right now."

"Here's the thing: when you realize you one hundred percent have the right to your happiness, you know you are back on the correct path. Be gentle with yourself. Life is for the living."

"Okay."

"That much I know." I shrugged. "But not much more."

I stood and grabbed one more muffin, knowing what my tasks were even if Viola had insisted that I eat first. "I need to run some errands. I'll be back, okay, Viola?"

"Absolutely."

"I'll see you soon, Sadie," I said.

"You will. I might just sit here and eat muffins all day."

"Nothing wrong with that." *Particularly because you'll be under the protection of a woman who is armed with at least two guns.* But I didn't add that part.

I told Gus to stay in the dining room and ran to my room, brushed my teeth, and splashed water on my face. After changing into clean clothes, I slipped a baseball cap over my increasingly crazy hair—it was almost to my shoulders now—and left the Benedict House.

The light of day always makes things seem better. The cut phone cord was deeply worrisome, but because it was now daytime and communication was easier, I wasn't as worried—even if maybe I should have been.

Viola would need a break today, though. I'd try to figure out how to get her one.

I was glad to find the bar's door unlocked and even happier to see Benny up front, sweeping the floor.

"Hey, Beth," she said. "It's awfully early."

"Could I use your phone?"

"Of course, but what's wrong with Vi's phone?"

"I'll tell you in a minute."

The first thing I asked Gril when he, thankfully, answered, was about Gracie. Had they found her? He said they hadn't and didn't have any new leads.

And then, I told him about the phone line.

"Are you sure it was cut—not an accident?" he asked.

"One hundred percent."

"God . . . I'll be right over—"

"Wait. I'm going to call Orin, too. He can fix it."

"Fine."

"Viola's been up all night, Gril. She won't admit it to you, but she needs a break."

"Got it. Thanks for telling me."

I called Orin next, and he answered, too. The secret to reaching people might be to try them very early in the morning.

He said he'd also be right over to fix the line. Worry filled his voice just as much as it had Gril's.

It had only taken me about ten minutes and two phone calls to talk to the people I needed to talk to. I wondered if that was some sort of Benedict record.

I stood to make my way back out to Benny but was stopped by the book she'd set on the corner of a tall dresser in the corner.

It was one of mine, one of the scarier ones. Benny had once told me that she'd read a few of my books, but we'd never had a real conversation about them.

I picked it up and turned to the author picture in the back, as I'd done more than a few times, since my looks had changed so drastically after my time with Travis.

For a while, I'd been sad about that now-missing long brown hair and happy smile, eyes that twinkled with either some good Photoshop or the ignorance of what one person in the world could do to ruin your life.

Then for a while, I hadn't recognized her. She'd seemed like another person.

Now she felt like a distant memory, even though it hadn't been all that long ago that I'd had the picture taken. Maybe only three years earlier. I didn't sense any other emotion—I wasn't happy nor was I sad to see her. She just was a part of something that wasn't reality any longer, and that was okay.

I closed the book, my eyes traveling over the back reviews. The bites of complimentary words, the snippets. The blurb my eyes landed on ended with "Fairchild must have torture and murder in mind."

"Torture and murder in mind?" I said aloud. Hadn't Viola said something about that just last night when we were talking about Gracie being a fan?

That was odd. Or just a coincidence.

But as I returned the book to the dresser, I realized something else. Gracie had been speaking to me in *review* blurbs. Specifically, two reviews. Her forced words on the boat. Viola had used some of the same words, pinging them again. I could understand why those words—torture and murder—might stick with anyone who'd even glanced at the reviews or blurbs of them.

I knew that though some people read all the reviews, lots of people didn't. I was pretty sure that most sixteen-year-olds didn't trust anyone else to make any sort of decision for them, including what they should read and what books they should like.

Did Gracie just want to have some talking points about my books, or maybe, just maybe, was she not a real fan? Was memorizing reviews her way of playing the part?

For an instant, something seemed to make sense. Gracie had wanted to come here so she could meet her best friend, and then . . . what? Well, we didn't know yet. Had she somehow used me being here—I'd been in the news—as a reason to get her parents to bring her here? Had she memorized the blurbs just so she might sound like she really had read my books if she and her parents happened upon me? It was a strange interpretation, but I couldn't help but be impressed by her plan, if that's what had happened. I didn't know if any of that was real or not; it was all speculation at this point.

It seemed completely weird and way too sophisticated but also, considering how little else we had to go on, somehow plausible.

I filed it away for later contemplation before I joined Benny out front.

"What's going on, Beth?" she asked with a tone that told me I wasn't going to be allowed to leave until I told her.

"You have one of my books?" I asked.

"Yeah. I haven't read it yet, but I plan to." Her eyebrows came together. "Does that bother you?"

"No. Thanks, Benny."

"Sure. What's going on?"

I told her about the phone line and then quickly decided maybe I shouldn't have. She reached around to the back of her apron as if to untie it.

"I'll come over. You should have called me at home, Beth."

"I don't have a key to the bar to use your phone."

"Shoot! I will make sure that gets taken care of."

"Viola didn't want to wake anyone up last night. Everything is okay, Benny, and Gril and Orin are on their way over. Let's just see how it goes—come over later."

Benny sighed, but then retied the apron. "I bet she's exhausted."

"We'll get her through it." I headed toward the door.

"Hey," Benny said. "Did you hear anything more from Grecko?"

"No." I paused. "He never found Viola and Sadie, though they were home all day yesterday."

"He never found them?" Benny shook her head. "That doesn't make sense."

"I don't think it does, either."

"That *really* doesn't make sense, Beth."

"Well, you know how plans get changed out here. Maybe he just needed some rest, so he decided to find them today. Maybe he found Gril? I'll ask."

"Okay. Maybe." Benny nodded, her frown deep, her eyes bright with worry.

"Benny, you know Viola can take care of herself and everybody else probably. I think we should let Gril tell us what to do. Don't come over now, but I'll keep you better updated."

Benny sighed. "I do. All right, Beth, find me, call me for anything."

"I will."

"I'll be over later."

I stepped outside just as Gril was opening the Benedict House front door. I called to him, but he moved too quickly to hear me.

I looked around as I hurried across the square. I didn't see Orin's truck yet, but he was probably close behind.

Inside, it appeared that Viola had sent Sadie back to her room, and she and Gril were already sitting across from each other in the dining room by the time I joined them.

"Beth, you okay?" Gril asked.

"Fine," I said, hesitating at the doorway.

"You need to get to work or go somewhere," Gril said.

I nodded. "Okay, but I need to tell you about Daniel Grecko first."

I shared with him about the interactions with the man at the bar.

When I finished, Gril shared a look with Viola before he looked back at me. "That's the name of her handler, but he hasn't made it to Benedict yet. I talked to him this morning. His flight from Seattle to Juneau was canceled. He might not be here until tomorrow."

"That's not good," I said.

"No, it isn't. I'm going to need you to describe . . . wait, a sketch artist is calling Sadie here later this afternoon. Will you talk to her, too?"

"Of course."

"Tell me what he looked like, what we all need to look out for."

"Tall, long legs. Average, until he smiled. He had some dimples that actually make him kind of cute." I shrugged. "It was weird. I'll try to remember more details for the artist."

"Look out for?" Viola asked. "You think he's . . . ?"

"Yeah, I'd bet money that he's someone from Sadie's past before she was Sadie, but unfortunately, I don't have any details from the Marshals. Even Orin hasn't been able to get anything. Not yet, at least. Maybe soon." Gril rubbed his chin. "For now, Beth, head out to your shed. I need one fewer person to worry about for a while. Okay?"

I nodded. "I need to grab a shower first. That okay?"

"Yes."

"When can I come back? When is the artist calling?"

"Be back by about three."

"Will do. I'll leave Gus here. He's a good watchdog."

"I'll be fine," Viola said.

"No, that's a good idea," Gril said. "Leave him here. I might take everyone someplace else, but I'm not sure of the best place yet. If we aren't here right when you get back, don't panic. I'll get it all worked out."

Gus was an adequate watchdog, but he *would* protect Viola no matter the cost. "Okay."

A sense of urgency hurried me back to my room. I took a real shower and then packed up for the day. I hesitated at the front door, listening as it seemed at least Viola and Gril were in Viola's office now, wondering if I should go back and tell them goodbye, but I chose not to.

I discovered Orin's truck parked next to mine. Hoping I'd find him out back, I redirected again.

"Beth, you were right. This was cut clean through," Orin said as he noticed me approaching. "A knife, probably. Maybe scissors."

"That's not good. Somebody wanted to cut off communication." I crossed my arms in front of myself.

I hadn't been too afraid last night, but maybe I'd just been too tired to be.

"Maybe," Orin said. He looked at me.

"Someone had something in mind, wanted to do something to someone inside," I said.

"Could be. But nothing happened." Orin looked at me. "Nothing happened, Beth, and you are safe. Everyone is safe."

I nodded. "Can you fix it?"

"Of course. I talked to Gril before I came out here. He told me about the man you met. Alleged Grecko?"

I nodded.

"I have a call in about an hour with someone from the Marshals office. As of today, I'm getting permission to open an official case. We'll figure out who that man was. Maybe get more help out here for Gril."

"I'll be talking to a sketch artist this afternoon."

"Good."

"Can I listen in on your call?"

Orin laughed. "No, but you can come over to the library when I'm done, and I'll tell you whatever I think I can tell you."

"Thanks. I'll be over around ten?"

"That'll work. See you then." He sat back on his heels. "I'm going to make this as good as new."

"Until someone does it again."

"I'm ready for that, too." He reached over to his right and gathered a big plastic boxlike thing. "I'm going to put a closure over it, with a lock."

"Can it be broken?"

Orin sighed. "Yeah, but it will take some work. I figure it's better than nothing."

"I agree."

I told Orin I'd see him later and then walked back to my truck. On the way to the shed, maybe as a way of pushing away the flashback heebie-jeebies over the cut phone line, thoughts of Gracie returned. I hoped she was okay. I could only imagine the pressure

Gril and Donner must be feeling, the multiple directions they were being pulled. Mistrust of Juneau authorities meant they wouldn't ask for the help they needed. It was going to be overwhelming at some point, though, if it wasn't already.

I was pleasantly surprised to see Tex sitting in his truck outside the shed, until I realized he probably wouldn't be there unless he wanted to tell me something in person that he wasn't keen on sharing over the phone.

We both got out of our vehicles at the same time.

"What's wrong?" I asked immediately.

"Nothing is wrong," Tex said. "Come on, let's go inside."

Tex started the coffee machine as I cranked up the heat. Once we were seated, I waited to hear what he'd come to tell me before I worried him about the phone line or Grecko.

"I'm heading out into the woods behind the lodge."

"To look for Gracie?"

"Exactly."

"What's happened?"

"Nothing. Except that all the kayaks were in their shed, so as far as anyone can tell, the kids you ran into did return them—if that's where they got them from, and that's the best guess anyone has."

"And that it's possible that Gracie is with her best friend in the woods?"

Tex nodded. "Yes, Betty still maintains that the young woman you pointed out is, indeed, Gracie's friend. The woods behind the lodge are a possibility, and right now it's the best we've got."

"I . . . I noticed something about Gracie," I said. "It's weird and might sound a little too self-involved, but I think Gracie quoted a bunch of reviews that were printed on my books."

"Really? Well, maybe she didn't know how to talk to you?"

"I considered that, like maybe she was just trying to connect. But why? Either she didn't know how to talk to me or she really isn't a fan but told her parents she was to get them to come out here. I don't know how long she claimed to have been reading my books. My story has been on the news quite a bit lately, including where I'm living now."

"So, maybe she used you to get here so she could run off with her friend."

"Or the boy." I shrugged. "I hope that's what it is, some teenage, misguided romance."

"Me too." Tex paused. "All right, I'll be gone at least twenty-four hours."

"I will worry about you."

"I'll be fine." Tex cocked his head. "But it's not bad to be worried. I'll probably spend a little time worrying about you, too. Stay out of trouble, Beth."

Nope, I wasn't telling him about the phone line. "I know it's sometimes hard for people to believe, but I never try to get into trouble. I'll be careful."

We finished our coffees, and I snuck a few extra candy bars from my desk into Tex's coat pocket.

He patted it and said, "Thanks."

As I watched him drive away, I wondered again about our relationship. What was it, and where was it going? And why was I dissecting something that felt just about perfect as it was? At least to me. Could Tex continue to coast on this path of hit and miss adventures and dinners and evenings together? I hoped so.

It wasn't until his truck was out of sight that I realized I'd forgotten to ask him what he'd found near the body. Everything had been so overwhelming. I'd missed two opportunities just a few moments ago and when we'd watched the sunset from the truck bed.

"Shoot," I said aloud.

It should just be something that could be handled with a quick cell phone call, but that wasn't how things worked out here. I told myself to remember it next time, or ask Gril if he would tell me the details.

My phone must have been connected to the library's signal because I felt it buzz in my back pocket.

I reached in to grab it, recognizing the name and number immediately.

Detective Majors was calling. I ran inside the shed and answered.

Twenty-one

"Detective? I'm here." I'd pushed my chair to the corner, near the window, where the reception was usually the best.

"Beth, hello. How are you?"

"Well, I'm fine so far. What's up?"

"I just wanted to give you a quick update. It's not terrible news, but it's not the best, either."

"I'm listening."

"Walker's attorney, Clara Lytle, succeeded in a motion to suppress the blanket as evidence."

"What? How did she win that?"

Detective Majors sighed heavily. "Chain of evidence mistakes. Minor things that Lytle managed to convince the judge weren't so minor."

"Judge? Did a trial judge get chosen? Did Lytle get her change of venue?" I asked. Hadn't it only been four days since I'd last talked to the detective?

"Yes, the judge has been appointed. No change of venue, which isn't good or bad news as far as we can figure. The attorney from the district attorney's office who's trying the case is keeping in close touch with me."

"Who are the judge and the attorney?" Milton might have been small, but because of my grandfather's position and my job in his office, at one point I'd been somewhat familiar with state judges and prosecutors.

"Judge Justine Bartles, and the lead attorney on the case is Harry Frederick."

"I don't know the attorney, but I remember Bartles. She's good, fair, but a real stickler."

"Yeah, that's what Harry told me."

"Was he upset?"

"He wasn't happy. He's sure there's still enough to convict. I just wanted to let you know."

It was a small pink blanket that the police had ultimately found both my DNA and Walker's on, as well as other women's. It had been a big win for us. Now, not so much.

I sighed, too. "Well, we'll just have to make it work."

"And it will. There's no doubt."

"Trial dates set?"

"Not yet. October still, but after 2020, everything is backed up." She paused. "I know you'll be here for the trial. Have you thought more about moving back?"

I laughed. "Every day, I think. I can't seem to get excited about the prospect of doing it right this minute, but I can't rule it out all the way yet, either. I just don't know."

Detective Majors waited a beat. "It's a different world up there, isn't it?"

"Completely." I laughed again. "I wouldn't have even known how to imagine it, and I have a pretty good imagination."

"A terrifying one at that."

"That is true." Gracie's blurb comments came to mind again. "Detective Majors, could I ask you a favor?"

"Anything."

"This is pretty far out of your normal duties."

"I could use something other than my normal duties to think about for a minute or two."

"A sixteen-year-old girl has gone missing up here. She might have left on her own with her friend, but the police resources are being used for another mystery. . . . Anyway, I wonder . . . well, if you could . . ."

"How can I help you from here?"

"The girl's name is Gracie Dupont. Her parents are Greg and Betty Dupont. Greg is a criminal defense attorney in Des Moines. Can you look them up, see if there's anything interesting to know about them? I'll do an internet search, but maybe you have something deeper?"

"Sure. Be happy to. If he's a defense attorney, I'll be particularly diligent. They aren't my favorite group of people right now. Well, they never really are, but sure, I'll try to get back to you tomorrow."

Her chair squeaked as if she was sitting up straighter, and I thought I heard her keyboard come to life.

"Thanks. And thanks for letting me know about the blanket. Any word on my mother?"

"Nothing new, but I kind of feel her presence in the air, if that makes any sense."

"Oh, it does. If anyone's presence can mess with the time and space continuum, it's Mill Rivers's."

"Good point. All right, let me get to work on the Duponts. You'll hear from me soon."

"Thanks again."

We disconnected the call. Leftover disappointment from the news she'd shared weighed me down a little, but I told myself to shake it off, that there was no way, blanket or not, that Travis Walker wouldn't be locked up forever.

I looked out the window. I hoped Tex would be all right, but there was no reason to think he wouldn't be. He'd been fine all the other times he'd assisted with search and rescue operations. He'd found people, some of them dead from having succumbed to the elements or the wildlife, and he was good at it. If I ever needed rescuing, or if I needed my body found, I'd want him on the case.

I stretched backward and peered over at the library. Orin's truck wasn't there yet.

I threaded a piece of paper through my old Royal, but instead of working, I typed up what had happened the last four days.

When I was done, I was further struck by the timing.

"This couldn't all be part of the same thing, could it?" I muttered aloud, first glancing at my feet to ask Gus, then disappointed he wasn't there.

But there was something that could possibly tie it all together—Lilybook Island.

Had it all been a coincidence? Had Laney and the boy just exited the woods, and found there her best friend from Iowa?

I believed in coincidences, in the universe sometimes nudging things along, but this was beginning to look and feel way too choreographed to be coincidental.

I was pretty sure Eddy had told me that he'd asked the Duponts about stopping at the island because it was something I'd wanted to do, but when had that been? Had there been enough time for Gracie to somehow make arrangements with Laney to meet there?

And how could any of this have anything to do with Sadie Milbourn? Or was that the coincidence, the fact that Sadie was found on the same island that Gracie had disappeared from?

I looked at my notes. I didn't sense the answer was there in front of me, but I sure thought I was onto something—that should lead to an answer or two.

I was so focused on the notes that I didn't hear a car approaching, which was unlike me. Usually, even in the deepest ends of my manuscripts, my ears were attuned to any unusual noises. I missed this one, though.

However, I did not miss the shed door bursting open, followed by the angry woman holding a copy of the BOLO *Petition*.

She held it high. "What. In. The. Hell. Is. This?"

Twenty-two

Gina Rocco could have been shot dead if I had a gun. As it was, her intrusion caused me to open a desk drawer and reach for the hunting knife I stored in there. Those few seconds erased the urge to pull the trigger I would have had if I'd had a gun on the corner of my desk. I left the knife in the drawer.

I couldn't contemplate that knee-jerk reaction now, but I decided that maybe that urge should be further examined at a later date.

My mind jumbled to a lot of conclusions fairly quickly, one of them being that this woman might be angry, but she wasn't here to hurt me—well, other than my feelings maybe. She was pissed.

I'd never seen her before, but the introductions happened quickly.

"Who the hell are you?" I asked in my best I'm-not-afraid voice, even though I was.

She gathered herself, and after a couple of heavy breaths out of her nose, she said, "My name is Gina Rocco, and this is my client." She held the paper up again.

I nodded. "Okay. I'm Beth."

"Who gave you the authority to publish my client's picture?"

"Can I get you a cup of coffee, Gina?" I stood and made my way to the coffee machine. Even if she didn't want a cup, I certainly did.

Gina sighed again but didn't answer. She was a pretty woman, probably in her fifties, with short gray hair and big blue eyes. Today, she wore clothes and had a scent about her that made me think she'd been fishing recently.

"Catch anything?" I asked.

As I poured two cups of coffee, I was struck by all the work I'd done to not allow people to see how they intimidated me. My heart was racing in my chest, but I was working to behave coolly. If I'd been truly afraid, I probably couldn't pull it off, but so far, I was proud of my even keel.

"What?" she asked.

I carried the two cups back to my desk. "You've been fishing. Catch anything?"

She frowned at me. "Who gave you the authority to publish this?"

"Have a seat, Gina." I nodded at the chair she was standing next to.

I held my jaw tight. I wasn't going to say another word until she sat down in *my office*. I did, however, slide one of the full mugs toward her.

She frowned but sat. "Who?"

"The local authorities gave me the authority to publish it. Gril."

"What authority does he have?"

"He is the police chief."

Finally, she deflated just a little. "Tell me what's going on."

I took a sip of my coffee. "I'm not sure if you noticed, but you are in my place of business. You have no authority here. You can't demand anything of me. However, if that man is your client, then you know he escaped from the Goose Creek prison."

Saying the words aloud made me remember Sadie muttering them in Viola's office, another note I needed to add to my list of coincidences. I wondered if I could sweet-talk Gina enough that she might share something with me. I didn't know what I wanted her to tell me, anything that might help me understand what was going on, but it didn't much matter anyway. It didn't appear that she and I were going to get along.

"Of course I know he escaped from Goose Creek. But why would there be a notice for him in Benedict?"

I worked hard not to say "duh" and instead said, "You're here, for one."

"My clients don't know I have a cabin in Benedict," she said. "My clients don't know any of my addresses."

"That makes sense. But we didn't put your address on there." I nodded at the paper. "Is that why you're upset? That he might find you?"

She took another breath and steeled herself. "Beth, has my client been spotted in the area?"

"Not to my knowledge."

"Goose Creek is in Wasilla. Why would anyone think he was here? What am I missing?" Her words were less clipped this time. She shook her head. "The reason I asked who authorized this was because I hadn't heard of any sort of statewide and official alert, so the fact that this, a local one-sheet paper, has Albert Jackson's picture on it? My only thought was that it was prompted by a sighting, and if he's here, I need to be speaking to the authorities. Not the local police chief, though. Bigger authorities. I've been in Benedict for a few days." She looked at her vest and then back at me. "Yes, fishing. I knew about his escape, but I wondered if I'd missed anything else of importance, something I need to attend to."

I thought for a moment. "I think you've missed a lot, but I'm not sure it has anything to do with your client. It might, but I'm not the person who should tell you anything else about it."

"You're the person who published the paper," she said, that accusatory tone raising the volume of her voice again. This time, though, she cleared her throat as if resetting.

"So?"

"I would appreciate it if you told me what you know."

I stared at her.

"Okay, has he been spotted nearby?"

"I did mention that he hasn't been seen, at least as far as I know."

She squinted at me. "Something is going on, and I feel like I have a right to know." She held up her hand. "I'm willing to admit I could be wrong about that, but . . . well, what if he is in the vicinity? If he's violent, this won't help calm him down."

"But it might make people wary of him, therefore keeping them safer."

She knew that part but probably wanted to see if I'd argue with her.

She nodded. "What if he's innocent?"

I laughed, but a tiny bit of rage ignited inside me. I would bet that's what Travis's attorney would say. "Isn't that what all defense attorneys say?"

She shook her head. "I just asked the question. I didn't say he was innocent. But what if he is?"

"Then he'll turn himself in."

"Or someone out here will shoot first and ask questions later." She held my gaze.

I tried not to blink. She had a point. I knew there were gun-happy people out here. I also knew that most gun owners were responsible and smart and safe.

Still, though, hadn't I just a few minutes earlier been glad there wasn't such a weapon sitting on my desk?

"I hope that doesn't happen," I finally said.

"I bet you do."

Again, I tried not to blink. "Gosh, Gina, nice to meet you and all, but I really do need to get to work."

She frowned a long moment before she stood and huffed her way out of the shed. This time I heard an engine start up and then head away, seemingly in a speedy fashion.

I relaxed, letting out a breath. I laughed nervously for a second and shook my head. It was too bad that Gina and I wouldn't ever be friends. I would love to bend a defense attorney's ear in preparation for Travis's trial.

I didn't have long to think about what she'd said or my missed opportunity for friendship before my phone buzzed with an alert. Orin texted me to come over. I texted back that I'd be right there.

Twenty-three

Orin was reaching for his landline handset as I entered and shut the door to his office. The weed smell was light again today. Maybe I was just looking to alleviate some stress, but I wouldn't have minded something stronger.

"How did it go?" I asked.

"It hasn't happened yet. Call me crazy, but I thought I'd let you listen in."

I smiled. I couldn't help myself. "Thank you!"

He nodded. "Have a seat. This phone will ring in ten seconds."

"Okay." I counted down in my mind from ten.

Surprising neither of us, the phone rang on cue.

"Six-seven-four," he answered.

I felt like I'd just stumbled onto the set of a Bond movie. My eyes got wide, but he put his finger up to his lips to make sure I understood I should be silent.

I air-locked my lips with my fingers and listened to this side of the conversation like it would tell me the secrets of the universe.

"Thanks," Orin said. "I really appreciate the connection. Yes, that's correct. Please repeat. Thank you."

He took no notes. He didn't have to; he had an eidetic memory. He could even remember long strings of numbers. I'd tested him once.

For probably a good three minutes, he was completely silent as he listened. I willed myself to frozen stillness, sending out a small prayer that my nose wouldn't whistle and my stomach wouldn't grumble.

"Got it. Right. I'm doing well, still in the same place. You? Your family? Oh gosh, I'm sorry about your mom. Condolences. Sure, sure." Long pause. "Well, thank you so much. Goodbye."

He placed the old handset back on the ancient rotary phone body. I'd just witnessed a covert meeting done with equipment my grandmother had thought was revolutionary.

Orin sat back in his chair and fell into thought. I didn't want to bother him. I knew he was mentally sifting through and organizing all the information he'd just received, and he'd share with me when he was ready—or he wouldn't have invited me over.

His eyes finally looked up to mine. I took it as an all clear.

"That was cool," I said. "Thanks for letting me sit in."

"Well, so you don't get too big a head, the conversation was set up so that I wasn't to say any names or specific details. I was only allowed to listen. As you heard, my responses made it all pretty generic."

"Honestly, that makes it even cooler. Top secret stuff. What can you share?"

"I probably need to talk to Gril first, but I can tell you that Sadie is, indeed, in witness protection, and she should not have told anyone—you, Gril, the Juneau police—her circumstance. WITSEC is not happy with her, and they want to move her quickly. Her handler is still on his way, though, and the Marshals don't trust anyone to move her but him."

"Grecko?"

"Yes, that's his name."

"Who was the guy pretending to be him?"

"I wish I knew, Beth. You haven't seen him again?"

"No."

"That's the most worrisome of all."

"Not the cut phone line?"

"I wouldn't be surprised if they're tied together somehow."

"Yikes."

Orin waved it away. "Just be careful out there. Carry your knife."

I nodded. "Well, speaking of that . . ."

I told him about my visitor and her admonitions.

"Oh boy, I hope she rethinks her attitude before she approaches Gril," he said when I finished.

"Or not. I wouldn't mind if Gril had to have a serious 'discussion' with her."

"I do not disagree." However, he said the words with little conviction. He was still thinking about the call.

"Anything else you can tell me?" I said.

"Sadie requested a transfer about a month ago."

"So she's been concerned about something for a month or so."

"Sadie is scared of something—*maybe* Juneau law enforcement."

"That's not news."

"No, but she was never clear as to her reasons why she wanted to leave. That's why they accepted me reaching out, opening a new case probably. They wondered if I had gotten to the bottom of any of it. She told them that she didn't need an urgent move, so they were planning on a meeting in another month. I think they wish they would have acted sooner, but I don't know that for sure."

"What could it be?"

"I don't have a clue what's going on, Beth. I sense all the issues are tied together, but I don't know how."

"I was thinking the same thing."

Orin shrugged. "I can't make the pieces fit."

"Did they tell you her real name, what happened to her?"

"They did." He bit his bottom lip. "But I can't tell you that, not right now. Suffice to say, the mysteries are still mysteries even with the new information. I want Gril to know the details first."

"What about the Duponts?" I asked.

"I wonder . . ."

"When I was thinking about it earlier, I realized that the constant is Lilybook."

Orin bit his lip again. "You have a good point. I'll think about it some." He paused and then looked back up at me. "Has the dead man been identified yet?"

"Not to my knowledge, but Gril might not tell me."

"I'll find out." Orin shrugged. "You might be onto something. Lilybook might be the thing to link it all together, though I don't know why."

"Did anyone find gold there, bury a treasure, something?" I asked.

Orin took my idea seriously. "Not to my knowledge. I'll keep thinking."

"Would you let me know if you come up with something?"

"Beth, do you know exactly how many people I've allowed to be in the room with me while I'm working, while I'm on a call?"

"I do not."

"Including you, one. Not even Gril has done such a thing."

"You trust me!"

"Yes, completely."

"Thank you."

"Yeah well, don't screw that up. I'm stingy with my trust, and if it's breached at all, things will get ugly."

He'd been so warm and friendly a moment before. He wasn't joking now. His voice turned icy with the warning, and I heard it loud and clear.

"I hear you. And, Orin?"

He looked up at me. "Yes?"

"Thank you," I said.

"You're welcome. And now you have to leave. I have work to do."

I stood and made my way to the door. I turned again. "Orin, do you read book reviews?"

"Never. Why? Did you get a bad review? Don't listen to reviews, Beth."

"Oh, no, I've had plenty of bad ones, but I'm just curious about who reads them. Gracie quoted things to me from my book reviews, I think. It was weird."

Orin gave me his attention again. "I don't disagree; it sounds weird. Or it could just be a way for her to communicate. I never, ever read them, though. Just not my thing."

"Me neither, but Gracie sure read them. Though I also wonder what her motives were."

"What were you reading at sixteen?" Orin asked.

"Everything, age appropriate and completely age inappropriate, whatever that means. No one ever monitored my reading, but there were books all around." Something came to me. "Huh. Did you know that I read *In Cold Blood* when I was twelve? I just remembered that."

Orin laughed. "That could explain a lot about the subject matter you write about."

"It could. That's what I'm going to tell everyone who asks me where I get my ideas now: Truman Capote."

"Seems apropos."

"It does, kind of. Okay, I'm out of here. I'll talk to you later."

"Later, Beth." His attention was already back on his computer screen.

Twenty-four

parked outside the shed but couldn't bring myself to turn off the engine. I had no desire to try to work. The deadline that had seemed so on track wasn't anymore. I wanted answers, and they weren't going to be found at my typewriter. Being your own boss sometimes spotlights just how bad an employee you can be.

I wasn't sure where to go. I could hang out with Benny at the bar. I could see if anything was going on at the community center. I could finally take up fishing.

It was that last thought that made me think about Eddy and what I'd thought was his sense of responsibility for Gracie missing. I'd noticed it, but I hadn't said much of anything to ease his concern. He had been doing me a favor by exploring the island, after all. Maybe I should feel guilty, too.

I swallowed hard as I steered the truck toward the dock.

I didn't know Eddy's schedule. I gambled on the fact that he'd be on his boat. I did know that when he didn't have customers, he spent a lot of his time working on the boat, *puttering* he'd said.

There was always something that needed to be fine-tuned or fixed or improved.

I spotted him quickly. In fact, his was the only boat still in the dock, which made me feel even worse. It was the busy season, and he was missing out. I noticed him in the cabin area.

I parked the truck and wove my way through the crowded parking lot and onto the dock. It swayed slightly with my footsteps, and I thought about the time fishing with the Duponts. It had begun as something I'd joined in grudgingly. I'd made a fool of myself over the gun. But then, it had all been fun. Really fun.

"Hey, Eddy," I said from the dock.

He turned and smiled. "Bethie. Hey. What's up?"

"Can I come aboard?"

"Of course." He stepped out of the cabin and held a hand out for me to grab.

Once aboard, we moved back to the cabin.

"Water? Soda?" he asked as he looked at a shelf. "Uh. Granola bar? I need to replenish the treats, I think."

"Water would be perfect. Thanks."

The boat rocked pleasantly. I'd seen the result of bigger waves, storms that tipped smaller boats on their sides. I'd heard about sinking ships and boats, but that sort of tragedy hadn't occurred since I'd moved here.

Out on the horizon, heading back from the tour of the glaciers, I spotted one of the cruise ships. All those people had a chance to see the glaciers. I still hadn't, but that's not why I'd come to talk to Eddy.

"How are you?" I asked him after we were both sitting, our arms and water bottles on the table in front of us.

"I'm fine, darlin'. How are you?" he said cautiously.

Of course he was suspicious. I didn't often express much interest in how he was doing. I suppose I hadn't been very nice, but on the other hand, he'd . . . well, he'd done what he'd done.

My therapist Leia, who I visited with on Zoom, had asked me a question a couple weeks ago when I brought up my sassy attitude toward my father.

Does tit for tat make you feel better?

I'd answered in the affirmative. Leia had only nodded and then said, "Okay."

I hadn't lied. Being angry at Eddy did feel better than trying to forgive him. But it certainly didn't feel good.

"I'm okay. Worried about Gracie," I said. "And her friend Laney."

"Me too. I went back out to that island this morning."

"You did?" Shoot, I'd missed an opportunity by that much.

He nodded. "I didn't find anything, but I took it slow and really looked. Nothing, Beth. Not even a bear."

I nodded. "Because Laney was there, I'm thinking it was planned. Do you?"

"I don't know what to think. I just know Gracie's missing. I don't know if Laney is considered missing yet. Did Gril talk to her parents?"

"I don't know."

"I keep hoping the answers are out there, and they just haven't filtered their way to me yet."

"Me too." I paused. "I feel guilty about asking you to take me to Lilybook, but I do keep telling myself that somehow it was just convenient for them to meet there. It was nobody's fault, Eddy."

He nodded slowly. "I know, and I appreciate your support, Beth, but I sure would like to find that girl and get her back to her folks."

I nodded.

"Anyway, did you come out here just to talk to me?"

"Kind of. I've been kicked out of the Benedict House, at least temporarily. I was in the way, I guess."

"Still like living there?"

"I do. Viola is family now, too, and it . . . well, it just works."

"I get that. I'm still looking for my own place." He hesitated. "You okay with that?"

I nodded. "Sure, but there's a chance I might go back down to Missouri. Don't stay here for me."

"Well, I won't say that I won't go back to Missouri, too, if you go, but I've come to love it out here. We'll see how I do over the winter, but Gril has been good to me. Better than I probably deserve."

"He wouldn't have helped you if he didn't . . . believe in you."

Eddy laughed and looked up toward the lodge. "Hey, I have an idea. Want to go check on the Duponts with me? I've been thinking about trying to talk to them all day, but I didn't want to disturb them. If you're with me it might be easier."

"Sure, I'd love to."

We disembarked, leaving the still-lone boat in the dock. I hoped the day of inactivity wasn't too painful on his bank account. I knew Eddy had some money from his life in Mexico, but I didn't know how much. He'd mentioned that he could pay Gril rent now and that was looking for a place to live, so he was probably fine.

We walked across the parking lot and took the stairway up the hill to the lodge. The building was well hidden by trees, so it was always such a surprise to see how busy it was when you came right upon it. The parking lot was full, and there were a lot of people hanging out in the lobby and visiting the tourist information center located up on a second-floor balcony.

We wove our way around the crowd and to the front desk. We asked the receptionist to ring the Duponts' room. After she dialed, she gave me the handset.

"Betty, it's Beth. Eddy and I are here. Just seeing how things are going. You want some company or would you rather we just leave you be?" I asked.

"Beth, yes, come up. We're in room 14, second floor." She disconnected the call.

I handed the phone back to the receptionist and turned to Eddy. "Her tone was clipped, but she told us to come up."

Eddy nodded and followed me up the stairs to the second floor. The door to room 14 was ajar. I knocked as we stepped inside.

"Betty? Greg?"

"Greg's somewhere with your police chief, I think." Betty came around the half wall that separated the suite's bed area from its small living area. "Come. Sit."

Her face was drawn, her eyes red and heavy with dark circles.

We sat in the small space, Betty and I on the couch and Eddy on the desk chair.

"Any news?" I asked.

"Not one thing." She looked at her phone sitting on the side table. "The cell coverage out here is ridiculous. I don't understand how a place can be so primitive."

Before her daughter had gone missing, Betty seemed to like the seclusion, but I understood why it frustrated her now.

"Do you have everyone's landline number?"

"Who is everyone?"

"Gril, Viola; she's the woman who owns the place where I live. She helps Gril sometimes. I can also give you the library's and the bar's numbers, too. If you want to talk to someone, sometimes you just call all the landlines until someone can find who you're looking for. Have a piece of paper and a pen?"

Betty nodded, but it was Eddy who reached around to the desk and grabbed the complimentary notepad and pen and handed them to me.

I jotted the numbers quickly and handed Betty the list. It had been a long time since I'd memorized a phone number, but these had become part of my everyday life.

"I'm glad the hotel has a connection. They told me they shut it off in the winter, even if they have guests. I can't imagine being so out of touch," Betty said.

Again, I knew she was feeling the disappearance of her daughter more than anything else.

"What can we do for you?" I asked. "Can we get some food? Something?"

Betty put her hand on her stomach. "I have no appetite at all."

"You need to eat," I said. I looked at Eddy. We'd figure out a way to bring them some food.

"I will. At some point."

Surprising us all, my phone buzzed loudly from my pocket. I didn't remember ever signing on to the lodge's Wi-Fi, but my phone recognized it somehow.

I grabbed the phone. "Gril?"

"Beth, do you know where your father is?"

"Um. Yes. Eddy and I are visiting with Betty, in her room at the lodge."

"Stay there."

"We wi—" But the call had been ended.

I turned to Betty, not Eddy even though that's who Gril had asked for. "Gril's on his way."

He must have been close by because he was in the room only moments later, and Donner was with him.

"Eddy, you need to come with me," Gril said.

"Why?" Eddy asked.

"Come on, Eddy. Come with me."

"Uh. Sure." Eddy stood, confusion squinting his eyes.

"Gril, what's going on?" I asked.

"Chief!" Betty exclaimed as she stood, her eyes darting between Eddy and Gril. "What's going on? Any news?"

Gril stopped herding Eddy and turned to Betty. "Nothing new. I'm sorry if this visit gave you false hope, but, no, nothing yet. I'll let you know."

"Where's Greg?"

Gril shook his head but gave Betty even more focused attention. "I haven't seen him. When's the last time you saw him?"

"A couple hours ago. I thought he was going to talk to you."

"Not that I'm aware of. Give him a little longer. Call me when he returns. He'll be back."

Betty nodded and then sat back down. I didn't realize that I'd stood, too, but I remained standing as Gril nodded at Betty and then at me before he, Donner, and Eddy left the room.

For the longest moment, I just stood there looking at the door and wondering what in the hell was going on. I heard Betty start crying. I turned to her.

"I'm so sorry," I said as I sat again, too. "What can I do?"

The look in her eyes as she brought her gaze back up to mine was nothing short of murderous. I tried not to jump, but I probably blinked in surprise. "I knew we couldn't trust him. Your father. I just knew it."

I shook my head. I was even more confused than my father had looked. Nevertheless, now wasn't the time to defend him—though, I didn't feel the need to. I was simply confuzzled. I patted Betty's arm for a moment before I told her I needed to go, that I needed to understand what was happening.

"Beth!" she said as I got to the door.

I looked at her.

"Call me with any news. Any. Please."

I nodded. "I will. I promise."

I hurried out of the lodge and down to the parking lot. Eddy's boat was still the only one in the dock, and I suddenly wondered if he'd ever see it again.

I also wondered if he deserved to.

Twenty-five

made my way to the shed. I would have redirected to the library if I'd seen Orin's truck there, but it appeared that he'd left—probably to find Gril, who'd come for Eddy. What was going on?

From the shed, I tried to call Viola, Benny, the police station, just in case someone might answer. But no one did.

I should have asked Betty more questions. Did she know something about Eddy that I didn't? Why had she suspected him? Did she really, or was she just distraught and looking for answers anywhere they might present themselves? I wasn't going to go back and bother her, but I needed to know what was happening.

"Dammit!" I exclaimed as I ended the last unanswered call.

Okay, I was going to have to get answers on my own. Sure, I could storm the police station, but that would not be met with good cheer. I wasn't ready to rule it out completely, but I did have another idea.

Eddy's boat. He'd been living with Gril, so he probably wouldn't keep anything incriminating at the house, but the boat might be a place he would hide something.

But what?

I had no idea, but I was ready to find out.

I hopped back in the truck. As I made my way to the dock again, I told myself to calm down. I didn't know why Gril wanted to talk to Eddy. He hadn't thrown the cuffs on him, but that might have been for my benefit. My concern could just be stemming from Betty's words—they'd been ominous and so certain.

I hadn't been suspicious of Eddy.

Or had I?

When perspective is shaken up, it's sometimes hard to remember how you felt about something before the way you feel about it now. I shook my head at myself.

Since nothing was too far away from anything in Benedict, it took only a few minutes to get back to the dock's parking lot. There were two other boats there now, but the rest were still on the water.

If Gril or Donner had searched Eddy's boat, they'd probably done it before they picked Eddy up. They'd been up to the room so quickly; it was feasible that they'd been that close by.

I parked and hurried to the boat. I leapt from the dock, catching myself on the rail as everything rocked with the impact, but I managed to balance a moment later.

I went to the cockpit first, opening the small panel doors with twist knobs behind the helm.

I found extra keys strung on chains with floaters. I found the boat's registration and a copy of its bill of sale. I was curious enough to examine the receipt. Eddy had paid sixteen thousand for the boat, in cash, it appeared.

I stuffed everything back into the cubbyholes and then made my way to the cabin.

I lifted the bench seats, only to find the same things I'd seen before—life vests and extra gear, some I couldn't identify.

Small cabinets ran along the perimeter of the top of the cabin, three on each side. A quick glance in the first three uncovered granola bars and water and a few cans of soda. But when I opened one of the doors on the other side, I finally found something to slow me down.

A ledger. In fact, it reminded me of one my grandfather had kept at the police station.

Oversized with a thick green hard cover, the inside was full of lines to be filled out for transactions. Gramps had used the one in the police station to keep track of everything in and out of there, from new pens to petty cash to computer purchases. He liked the sense of organization the ledger gave him.

Eddy's was similar in that it listed transactions, but of course, his was about his fishing business—more specifically, his customer list. I didn't spot receipts for supplies or parts.

Three pages had been written upon. I started on page one, and with my finger trailing down the page, read every name.

At the end of page two, my intuition pinged on something, but I couldn't hold on to the idea long enough to figure out which name might be doing it, so I kept going to the end where I found the Duponts and the dates of their tour listed.

I went backward. What was ringing that intuition bell? I still couldn't place it.

I started at the beginning and read each name aloud, letting it fill the air a minute, see if it wanted to tell me anything else.

I came to the name Jack Albert and stopped. Could that be Albert Jackson, the escaped prisoner?

In Eddy's scratchy handwriting, I saw that Jack didn't give a home address, but he did have a phone number, and I knew the area code. I'd just been given a 515 area code, and it was from Iowa. More pinging.

"Okay," I said, knowing what I'd found could mean absolutely nothing. "What else?"

In tiny writing in the block of the last column, Eddy had written, *Client asked specifically for a visit to Lilybook Island, wherever the hell that is.*

He certainly knew now.

"Jack Albert?" I pondered aloud again.

I looked at the date on the ledger. Five days ago. If I remembered correctly, that was the day after Albert Jackson had escaped from Goose Creek. Next to most of the rest of the names was a check mark. There wasn't one next to Jack Albert.

"Shit. What is going on?" This was a stretch, and I wouldn't have given it much weight if not for that Iowa area code. Even that might be coincidental.

I didn't have a camera on my burner flip, so I ripped the page from the ledger. I took it with me as I hurried back to my truck, then sped up to the main road.

There was only one person I wanted to talk to now, and I was going to find him.

I parked outside the station—glad to see both Gril's and Donner's trucks in the lot, disappointed not to see Orin's—and hurried into the building. I hadn't "stormed" inside on purpose, but forces I didn't quite understand had taken over my actions.

"Beth?" Donner asked as I stood inside the doorway, the door that I'd let slam. "Can I help you?"

"Where's Gril?" I looked toward his closed office door. "Eddy?"

"Beth, we are working."

I reached into my backpack. "Has the dead man been identified?" I pulled out the water bottle I'd taken from the island.

This was the idea that had come to me on the way over. It was probably even weaker than the Iowa area code, but it was the only thing I had that I thought I might be able to use for leverage, a reason to be there.

"No, but why do you need to know that?"

I held the water bottle out for Donner. "There's a chance this was his water. Maybe you can get his DNA from it."

Donner squinted and crossed his arms in front of himself. "Beth, did you just grab that from the refrigerator?"

"No, Donner. I picked it up on the island the other day. It was in the area where the body was found. I forgot about it until now."

Donner sat up. "Really?"

I nodded. "I'm not making that up. It was after the body had been taken away, but, yes."

"That water bottle could have floated in from anywhere. Chances of it belonging to the dead man are . . ."

"Not nil. I mean, chances are low, but even if there is a tiny chance this could identify him, shouldn't you and Gril explore it?" I looked at Gril's door again. I was simply using the water bottle to get to Gril and my father, though that idea was beginning to feel as ridiculous as it probably was. "Could I talk to Gril?"

Donner studied me for a minute. Finally, he stood. "Have a seat."

I nodded but I didn't sit. I watched as Donner made his way into Gril's office. I leaned a little to the right and saw Eddy sitting in the chair across from the police chief. He still wasn't handcuffed, didn't seem bothered, which was such a relief that I took a noisy deep breath after Donner disappeared inside.

A long moment later, he opened the door again. "Come on in, Beth."

I hurried before the invitation expired.

Once inside, Donner closed the door behind me and signaled to another chair. It was crowded with four people inside, but no one brought up moving to the bigger outer office.

"What's going on?" Gril asked, though there was a tinge of sympathy to his irritation. "What's this about a water bottle?"

I looked at Eddy, who sent me a strained smile, before I turned back to Gril. I told him what I'd told Donner.

"That's true, Gril. We did find it at that spot," Eddy added.

Gril frowned but then said, "Okay, give it to Donner. It could be something, but that's highly doubtful." He paused. "But you're here because you're worried about your father, right?"

I handed the bottle to Donner. "Not . . ." I was going to say that I wasn't worried, but I was. Dammit. I didn't want to worry about Eddy Rivers. "Maybe, but there is something else." I reached into my pocket this time. "I got this out of Eddy's ledger." I unfolded the page and spread it on Gril's desk.

"You took a page from the ledger on my boat?"

"I did."

"Okay."

"Why, Beth?" Gril asked.

I pointed. "Jack Albert. He asked for a tour to Lilybook, and he had an Iowa area code."

"Who's Jack Albert?" Eddy asked.

Gril looked at me.

"Maybe it's Albert Jackson," I said.

"The kid who escaped the prison?" Donner asked.

"Maybe?" I said. "Look, he wanted to go to Lilybook and . . ." I looked at my father. "Remember the boy who was with Laney?"

"He was off in the distance a bit, but sure," Eddy said.

"What if that was Albert Jackson?"

"I remember the kid being blond."

"I remember that he had a hat and sunglasses on."

"I don't remember that part."

I shrugged. "He might have had a wig on, too, or maybe he bleached his hair. I didn't pay attention, but when I think back about it, it kind of . . . fits."

I reached over to the corner of Gril's desk, where he still had a few copies of the *Petition*. I showed it to Eddy. "See?"

"I don't know."

"What about Jack Albert?" I pointed to the ledger sheet.

"That customer never showed. Look." He took the sheet. "Jack wanted a ride from Lilybook four days ago. He said he was going to call me, use his satellite . . ." Eddy looked at Gril. "I was supposed to pick him up after I dropped off the Duponts that day, but I never heard from him." He paused. "Gril, what if the dead guy is Jack Albert? What if he wanted to use my boat?"

"Albert Jackson is young, remember. The body was that of middle-aged man," Gril said.

"The Iowa area code?" I said.

"Yeah." Gril paused. "Yeah. I need to look at it."

He picked up his phone and dialed the number. A voice mail picked up. "This is Albert. I'll get back to you." *Beep*. It was impossible to distinguish what age of man the voice belonged to.

"Sadie told me she would recognize her captor's voice if she heard it again," I said.

"Donner, get over there and have her listen, then get someone to track this number."

"Got it." Donner put his hand on the door.

"Wait! Why are you talking to Eddy?" I asked.

"Police business, Beth," Gril said, but he looked at Eddy, who after a few seconds' thought, nodded, then Gril returned the nod as if to tell Eddy it was up to him to continue. Donner took his hand off the doorknob.

"Travis Walker's attorney has contacted Gril, looking for me," Eddy said.

Of all the things going on now, this was the last on my list of things Eddy might have been brought into the police station for.

"What? Why?"

"They want to depose me about Walker."

"From twenty-three years ago?" I asked.

Eddy nodded. "As much as it pains me to say it because of what he did to you, at one time, I thought Walker and I were friends. We weren't, of course. We were just business associates who somehow found each other in Milton, Missouri, and got up to some bad things."

"All of which have expired statutes of limitations," Gril added.

I paused. "So why is this so important right now?"

Gril sent me a sheepish look. He didn't do sheepish, so I was caught off guard.

"Eddy's being served, and I didn't want him to be afraid. Also, I didn't want him to be served in front of you or his paying guests. That's never a good look," Gril said.

So in the middle of all of these crazy mysteries, Gril had considered my feelings. Eddy's, too. My grandfather would have been that thoughtful, but no one else would.

"Oh, Gril. Thank you," I said.

He nodded.

I turned to Eddy. "What are you going to do?"

"If I'm subpoenaed, I'll have no choice but to talk to them."

"In effect then, will you be a witness for the defense?" I was incredulous.

"Well, as I've been telling Gril, I don't remember much of anything from back then, so I doubt I'll have much to say."

"I also wanted to give him a chance to get out of town if he didn't want to be served," Gril said. "Beth, this is how we take care of our own around here. Your father's been a good member of our community."

I cleared my throat and turned to Eddy and asked again, "What are you going to do?"

"I'm never going to run away again, particularly from you, which might make me sound noble. I'm not. I was a shitty husband and father for what I did; there's no denying that. But I'm done running. I told that to Gril when I first got to Benedict. It's awfully kind of him to give me a chance to get gone again. But I'm not hiding. I'll be served, and I'll show up at the trial. I'll be as honest as I can be, but I sure don't remember much."

"That's good, Eddy. That's good," I said.

"Now," Gril said, "could we get back to police business?" He turned to Donner. "Get that bottle bagged so we can send it over to Juneau today and have Sadie listen to the voice mail message. Then go get the Duponts. I want to ask them if they know anything about Albert Jackson, or Jack Albert, but don't tell them that. Do tell them that we don't have any news on Gracie, though—good or bad. Lead with that."

"Yes, sir," Donner said before he left the office and then the station.

"Feel better?" Gril asked me.

"I do. Thanks."

"Well, I gotta admit, as long of a shot as that water bottle is, it's something. Thanks," he said.

Since I was there, I didn't think a couple more questions would matter. "Gril, can you tell me what Tex found with the body?"

"You haven't asked him?"

"I keep forgetting."

He lifted his eyebrows. "No, not right now, Beth. The moving pieces of all of these things seem to keep changing directions."

I nodded. "Okay. What about Gina Rocco?"

"What about her?"

"She stopped by the shed. She wasn't happy about the BOLO *Petition.*"

"Ah. No, I haven't heard from Ms. Rocco." He paused. "I hope I do. In fact, I should try to reach her."

They had plenty to do and they'd taken the time to talk to Eddy. "Thanks, Gril."

"Of course. Now, go. We have a lot to do."

I looked at my father. "Want a ride back to your boat?"

Eddy looked at Gril who gave him the good-to-go and said, "Thanks. I would love one."

There was no drive in Benedict long enough to get too deep into any conversation, but on the ride back to the dock, Eddy and

I rehashed what had happened, and discussed what might happen next. We didn't have any solutions.

As I dropped him off and watched him board his boat, I did have one thought that kept going through my mind amid all the other scattered ones.

What a strange life this is turning out to be.

Twenty-six

I hurried back to the shed. I had a decent enough internet connection there to look up the Duponts, and I was even more curious than before about them and their lives in Iowa.

However, I got slightly diverted. Orin's truck still wasn't at the library. I wished I'd asked Gril if he knew where Orin had gone. Ruke's truck was there, though, and I knew he'd been helping out at the library for the last few months.

I made my way to Orin's office. The door was open, and Ruke was behind the desk reading a book.

"Beth. Hi," he said as he reluctantly looked up from the book.

"I promise I won't be long. I just have a couple questions."

Ruke closed the book and put it on the desk. "Sure. What's up?"

"At one time you revised your warning to me about going on the bay water."

"Right. I said it didn't feel right for you to venture out on a kayak or something small. I remember."

"How do you feel about that now?"

"Oh." Ruke's eyebrows came together. "I'm not prescient, you know that, don't you? It's not something I call up, but something that just comes to me. I can't summon it but only listen when it speaks."

"Intuition?"

"Yes." He fell into thought. "I haven't experienced any other moments that might tell me differently. I'm sorry." He studied me. "Maybe, though, since you've been here a while, all is fine. Maybe what I sensed was something as simple as you were new to this place, and I could tell it was unlike anywhere you'd ever lived in before."

I laughed. "It was that obvious, huh?"

"It was obvious, but you don't appear that way to me anymore. And, it's rare to meet a new person to Benedict who doesn't need some time of adjustment. When I see you or think of you, I don't even think of you as the girl with the scar anymore. Just as Beth who lives downtown."

"I like being known as Beth who lives downtown."

"Makes sense to me." Ruke leaned back in the chair a little. "Just be careful, no matter what you do. You'll be fine."

I didn't understand why Ruke's words and warnings had had such an impact on me. Though he was not a medicine man, because that title wasn't used anymore, there was something spiritual about him. Members of his tribe *did* go to him for healing remedies. Maybe it was just his kind smile. Maybe his aura was comforting. I didn't know, but I trusted and believed him.

"Thanks, Ruke."

"No problem." He reached for the book.

"What are you reading?" I asked as I made my way to the door.

Ruke held up the book. "Spy novel. It's so good." He flipped it around and read the back. "*Publishers Weekly* calls it 'groundbreaking in the age-old game of spies.'"

Maybe lots of people read the reviews.

"See you later, Ruke."

"Later, Beth." But the book was already open again.

I hurried back to the shed, where once again, I squeezed myself and my laptop close to the window to better access the Wi-Fi and started my search with "Greg, Betty, Gracie Dupont, Des Moines, Iowa."

I got a lot of hits.

Greg was, indeed, a well-known and successful defense attorney. His picture graced many articles and publications. He was active in Des Moines–area charities, too—there for groundbreakings and celebratory anniversaries.

Betty wasn't as public as Greg was, but she was in some photos next to him, appearing uncomfortable, as if she didn't like having her picture taken.

I didn't immediately find any family pictures with Gracie included, but a few pages in, I came across something.

It was an article dated back when Gracie had been a first grader. The title was "First Day of School Milk and Cookies, a New Tradition."

The article went on to talk about Greenwood Elementary's inaugural first-day cookies-and-milk event. The parents were invited to walk their children to their classrooms. Once there, they were offered the treats. The article said that even the sixth graders, who were much more comfortable with their parents out of the way, seemed to enjoy (well, at least not mind) having their parents there.

A black-and-white picture sat to the right of the first column of the article. A group of adults stood together, most of them holding cookies and containers of milk, all of them smiling or in conversation with one another. Kids milled around. The caption said, "Parents enjoying the morning. And yes, that's Greg Dupont, our local celebrity attorney."

Betty was there, too. Unaware of the camera, she smiled at another parent as she held the hand of a child.

I wouldn't have thought much about the almost-decade-old picture except that I spent a few moments looking at it, noticing how relaxed Betty seemed when she didn't know someone was taking her picture. She was a lovely lady.

As I looked more closely, I realized that Gracie was standing next to her father. I could see her profile as she looked toward—or so I deduced—the person who was holding her mother's hand.

Who would be holding Betty's hand other than Gracie? Hadn't they mentioned that Gracie was an only child?

Maybe Laney? Maybe Gracie and Laney had been friends all their lives. I hadn't had a friendship like that, but some people did.

I looked at the picture a little longer before I printed it, just to have it. It wasn't anything, really, but I couldn't help but wonder whose hand Betty was holding, and why Gracie was smiling so big in that direction.

My curiosity grew quickly and I wondered if I could get ahold of the publication, ask to see the original picture. It didn't seem possible that they would keep a picture that old on file, though.

I exited that article and then followed the links deeper into the search engine list but didn't come up with anything else interesting.

The Duponts were a nice family from Des Moines. Greg might not be beloved, but I didn't spot anything that made me think he was vilified. The Duponts of Des Moines were respected.

My next search was Gracie by herself. That took me to a number of Facebook pages, but for a reason I couldn't understand, none of them were hers.

Surely, Betty hadn't gotten her page taken down that quickly, had she? And why would she want it taken down anyway? I chalked it up to there just being too many Duponts to make Gracie's page any sort of search engine priority for whatever algorithms were associated with me.

Next I searched for Laney Hooper from Des Moines. I found her Facebook page immediately, as well as other notifications. Laney was very into FFA, the Future Farmers of America. Being from a small town in Missouri, I knew all about FFA.

Laney didn't fit any mold I'd ever known of any FFA member. From the photos on her page, she had a style that said "City Girl" much more than "Farmer."

Nonetheless, and having known people who had used FFA to formulate an interesting future, I was glad to see that stereotypes might be changing.

On Laney's page, I clicked on a video. She was talking about the scientific names of plants as someone flipped through pictures. The person with the pictures was also holding the phone to record, so it wasn't a smooth take.

But Laney was good. Quickly and without having to think much, she named the plants, their common names, and then their scientific names.

"White yarrow, Achillea Millefolium," she said without missing a beat as she looked at another picture.

I was fascinated by her sheer speed at recognition, so I kept watching. It might be a parlor trick of sorts, but if it was real recall, Laney had a wonderful mind.

She continued, "Small-flowered anemone, Anemone parviflora; Alpine aster, Aster alpinus; etcetera."

But it was when she said, "Beach strawberry, Fragaria chiloensis," that my attention was even more piqued. I had to rewatch the video and write everything down before I could confirm what I was thinking.

I'd heard of the beach strawberry. Surprising me, strawberries grew well out here, and Benedict and the surrounding areas celebrated the strawberries. The variety grown in and around Benedict were called *beach strawberries.*

I started the video over and wrote down all the plants—

phonetically spelling their scientific names. And then I searched for each plant, using their common names.

Every single plant Laney mentioned in the video was native to Alaska. Of course, they were also in other places, but the commonality for this list was that they *all* could be found in Alaska.

That had to mean something.

I glanced at the date the video was posted. It was a month earlier. Maybe she was just readying herself for the trip to Alaska. She was a plant nerd, who was incredibly cool, I thought, but it certainly wasn't the way most people would ready themselves for a trip up here.

I sat back in my chair and pondered what in the world had been her motive. And then something else occurred to me. I'm not sure why, but for some reason it seemed like a logical next step.

I searched for "Alaska poisonous plants." I found a few, two of which were also mentioned on Laney's video.

One caused cardiac arrest; the other was listed as toxic.

Was I forcing something? I didn't think so.

I went deeper. Where specifically in Alaska would I find the two poisonous plants Laney had mentioned: baneberry and poison hemlock? I found a map broken up by regions. Not only did baneberry and poison hemlock grow in this area of Alaska, according to what I read, they both probably thrived in marshy areas—like those that could be found on Lilybook.

Everything kept pointing back to that island: Sadie, Gracie, and now Laney. What was happening on that island?

I needed to talk to Gril again.

Twenty-seven

The police station door was locked tight, no vehicles in the parking spaces. Maybe Gril had gone out to talk to the Duponts instead of having Donner bring them in. There were still a couple hours before I was supposed to be back at the Benedict House for the sketch artist, but after debating what to do next, I decided to check on Viola and Sadie, see if I would be pushing my welcome back at the Benedict House. It was two-thirty, so I wouldn't be too early for the sketch artist.

No one guarded the door, and I didn't spot either Gril's or Donner's trucks. I announced myself as I went inside. "Hey, it's Beth!"

Gus peered out from the dining room and then trotted to greet me.

"Hey, boy, I have missed you today." Just his presence seemed to clear the racing thoughts in my head or at least slow them down a little.

"Beth, in the dining room," Viola called.

"Hey," I said tentatively at the doorway.

"I've been trying to call you," Viola said. "Come on in. I'm making some snacks."

Sadie looked at me. "Donner was here. I didn't recognize the voice on the message. It wasn't him."

"Oh, I'm sorry."

Sadie shrugged. "I still don't know quite what it all means."

"Everyone will keep working." I looked at Viola. "So it's okay I'm here?"

She nodded. "I don't know. Sadie's marshal should be here tomorrow, probably early but we're not sure yet."

I looked at Sadie again. "You'll be leaving?"

"I'm all packed."

I turned back to Viola again. "What about the sketch artist?"

"Canceled for now. That's why I was trying to call." Viola's tone was tight.

I didn't want to ask aloud, but I suspected that it had become important to get Sadie out of there.

Viola hadn't had a break, but she looked okay. In fact, I thought maybe I saw some relief in her actions, the set of her shoulders even as she prepared the food. She was about to be free of this particular babysitting job.

"Excuse me," I said to Sadie, planning to lend Viola a hand.

"I got this," Viola said.

"I know, but I can help carry in."

"Okay."

We ate turkey sandwiches, mostly in companionable silence, but Sadie seemed more circumspect than before. She'd been easy about sharing so much with me, but I sensed her keeping her words inside now, holding on to them.

I asked her what she did for a living.

"I cut hair." She looked pointedly at me.

I laughed. "Well, you're not the most subtle."

"I didn't mean to be." She paused. "Look, I'm nervous, anxious, waiting for my handler to get here." She took a deep breath. "I'd rather not think about some things. Want me to cut your hair? You really do need it."

I thought about my mom and what she'd said to me before she'd disappeared—she'd wanted me to get a haircut. "I guess I can't come up with one good reason why not. I don't have appropriate scissors, though."

"I can round something up," Viola said.

It would give us all some distraction. I shrugged. "Let's do it."

We moved to Viola's room, using the full-length mirror on the back of her door. Sadie started by trimming Viola's long, straight hair, keeping it long enough that she could still pull it back into a ponytail but cutting it short enough that it was easier to take care of. Viola had nodded and made an agreeable noise, which I explained to Sadie, was her way of expressing her satisfaction.

Then it was my turn in the chair.

Sadie asked, "Can I just do whatever I want?"

"Um. Sure. Wash and go, though."

"Will do."

In the reflection, I watched her brow furrow as she looked at my head from all angles and then cut quickly and with precision.

It wasn't too long later that I didn't recognize the person in the mirror. Sadie was good at cutting hair, really good.

Less than fifteen minutes later, my hair had not only been cut but also shaped. It was a short style: angled on one side, slightly asymmetrical, stopping at chin length on the non-scar side, shorter on the scar side. Before Travis Walker, I'd always worn my brown hair long. I'd never had a short, stylish haircut. Until now.

"I didn't try to hide the scar. Let's use it, give it a starring role. I'm a firm believer that scars tell important stories," Sadie said.

"Okay," I said. I would have argued if I'd felt differently.

My hair suddenly looked damn good even if I said so myself.

The way the incision had healed would make it next to impossible to cover the scar completely. But she'd added some shorter layers that didn't stick straight up, like my hair had done when it had first been growing out after the surgery. She said she understood the angles as they would fall. She'd told me to trust her. I had.

I looked older than before I'd run away to Alaska, but there was something in my eyes that was also wiser, and this cut somehow highlighted that glimmer a little more than before.

Sadie had delivered, making me look like I actually cared a little about my hair but not enough to need to spend too much time working on it.

I realized that I'd forgotten that I really did care a little—used to, at least. It was good to be reminded.

Viola whistled, and Sadie blushed at the accolades.

"It's what I do," she said.

"Well, it was needed," Viola added.

Mill would be speechless. Well, as speechless as she could possibly be. I hoped she'd reappear and see it soon, prove me either wrong or right.

"Thank you, Sadie," I said.

"You are welcome."

I saw Sadie's eyes darken as she looked away from my gaze.

"Hey, you okay?" I asked her.

"Thank you for letting me cut your hair," she said.

"What's wrong, Sadie?" Viola was sitting on the corner of her bed.

Sadie sighed again as she sat down on the other corner of the bed. "There were no bears. I killed that man."

For a long moment, Viola and I looked at Sadie with our mouths open.

"Um," I said eloquently.

"Well," Viola jumped in. "I . . . I think maybe you shouldn't tell us any more," Viola said, real surprise in her tone. It wasn't easy to surprise Viola.

"But I want to. I think I need to."

I turned the chair to better face the two of them.

"Sadie, you don't owe us any explanation. You should wait for Gril," Viola said.

She shook her head. "No. I'll tell him. I'll tell Grecko. Truly, I didn't remember until this morning. But I didn't tell Donner when he was here to play the voice mail message. I should have. I don't know why I didn't. Now I feel like I need to—quickly."

She spoke so casually, but if she had, in fact, killed the man who'd abducted her, she'd had every right. At least in my book. I didn't know if she'd just remembered, but it was possible. I didn't think it mattered.

"I'm kind of jealous. I wish I'd been able to do the same." It was the purest of truths. I would have killed Walker if I'd had the chance.

Sadie nodded but still frowned.

"Okay, Sadie. What happened on the island?" Viola asked.

Sadie nodded. "He was pushing me along. We were headed for a cave, I think. I saw a broken off branch on the ground. It had a sharp end, like part had peeled away leaving something weapon-like. I didn't even think; I reached down and grabbed it and stabbed him with it. I caught him by surprise. He dropped the gun he had at my back, and I just kept stabbing." Tears filled her eyes but, she steeled herself and blinked them away. "I couldn't stop myself."

"What did you do with the branch?" Viola asked.

"I don't remember that part, but I probably just dropped it."

"There was no sign of any of that on the island."

Sadie shrugged. "I don't know why. Maybe they just missed it or it somehow got hidden. I just don't know."

"He kidnapped you. You were just defending your life," I said.

"It was his blood all over you?" Viola asked.

She nodded.

"Gril told me the lab confirmed it was human blood," Viola added.

Sadie nodded. "It was his."

"Your hands were fine, though," I said.

"Well." Sadie frowned. "I remembered this part before, but I didn't understand it. I had gloves on. I took them off at some point."

"Gloves, why?" I asked.

Sadie shook her head again. "I think my hands were cold and he had the gloves. I don't know."

I'd been working on understanding what was going on, but I realized that the people whose real job it was to solve the mysteries were way ahead of me, as they should be. Still, though, some answers weren't clear yet, and as my grandfather used to say, *"Nothing's over until all the question marks turn into periods."*

Sadie laughed and wiped the tears away. "Gril told me I way overstepped my bounds. I should never have told anyone about WITSEC, but thank you for listening. And letting me cut your hair."

"What else do you remember?" Viola asked, pushing now, even though she'd first recommended Sadie not to tell us. "Any other details?"

Sadie closed her eyes and appeared to be working very hard to think about things. She opened them a long moment later. "Not one more thing. Yet. I'd like to rest."

We thanked her again for our hair and took her to her room.

The circumstances—the haircut followed by a confession—were discombobulating. Was there some motive to her timing?

In the hallway, I sent Viola some raised eyebrows.

She put her finger to her lips. "There's more to all of this, Beth," she said quietly.

I nodded and whispered, "Right, but what?"

She shook her head and then disappeared into her office, closing the door behind her.

I looked at Gus, who'd been waiting in the hallway. I felt very left out.

"Let's take a walk."

Gus seemed to think that was a great idea.

I grabbed my coat, and Gus and I made our way out to his patch of woods across the road from the Benedict House.

I didn't see anyone, which meant no one saw us. Not one person to notice my new hair. I thought about showing it to Benny just to have someone else see it but decided I was too tired. There would be time tomorrow.

It was cold outside. Though it was only July, consistent cold weather would be here sooner than I was used to. I'd been through one winter, but it would take at least another one to get used to the Benedict winter quirks—the cold and dark, the wind.

I looked at Gus enjoying his time in the woods. If I left Benedict, he would come with me. How would he feel about Missouri?

My property had woods, St. Louis had winters.

But not like Alaska. Would Gus be fine with the differences?

A wave of sadness washed over me at the thought of taking him away from his home, the only home he'd known.

He trotted to me, looking up as if to tell me he was done now and that he wondered what was bothering me. He didn't want me to be sad about anything.

"Okay, boy. I'm fine." I smiled. "Let's get some rest."

We still saw no one as Gus and I went inside. After a quick

glance down the hallway toward Viola and Sadie's rooms, Gus and I went the other direction. It was still kind of early, but I was pretty sure both of us fell asleep quickly, me even before my new haircut hit the pillow.

Twenty-eight

I woke up at four-thirty with no hope of falling back to sleep. My mind was racing. Again, Gus wasn't ready to face a new day. Viola wouldn't be up for an hour, and it appeared that Sadie was still asleep behind the door to her room.

I left Gus on the dog bed outside Viola's room again and took off for the shed. I had things to do and things to think about. I needed internet access, and if I didn't want to pack up and go to the airport, I would have to tuck myself and my laptop into the corner of the shed to get what I could from the library's connection.

But on the road, I redirected, and I turned toward the boat dock instead. Eddy might be there this early, and something drew me toward it, something that had been part of what had awakened me, even if none of it was making any sort of clear picture in my mind.

Mine wasn't the only vehicle in the parking lot this time. There was one other truck, though I didn't recognize it.

I drove close enough to the water that I could see onto Eddy's boat. It appeared that no one was aboard. I wondered who might have driven the other truck, so I took a quick scan of all the boats. I didn't spot anyone aboard any of them.

As I looked out toward the bay, though, I saw the lights of a boat, probably about the same size as Eddy's, making its way along the familiar route. It was out a ways, though, and I couldn't see anything distinctive about it.

There was nothing else for me to do. I shook my head and made my way to work.

I didn't need to tuck into a corner this morning. In fact, I had such a great connection just from the desk that I wondered if the library's Wi-Fi had somehow been upgraded. If anyone could do it on their own, Orin, superspy and master tinkerer, could. In fact, I wondered why I hadn't asked him if he'd consider an upgrade—I should. I'd offer to pay for it.

I searched for everything I'd searched for before, all the players of the craziness that had been happening in and around Benedict. I emailed Tex, hoping he had made it back by now or would soon enough.

I also hoped he hadn't found more bad news.

"Not just Lilybook but Iowa connects everything, too, except for Sadie," I said aloud.

Sadie had allegedly been in Connecticut before she'd been in Juneau, but I suddenly wondered if that wasn't true. Could that just be something she'd said? Though she'd shared her WITSEC status, she hadn't been completely truthful.

I shrugged and typed into the search bar: *Sadie Milbourn in Des Moines, Iowa.*

There were at least ten Sadie Milbourns living in Iowa, two in the Des Moines area. I dug a little deeper into each one of them, finding absolutely nothing that indicated that any of these Sadie Milbourns were the same one sleeping in a room in the Benedict House. I didn't really think I'd find her that way. No matter that she was Sadie now, I was pretty sure she had been someone else before moving to Juneau.

I sat back in my chair and made a noise that sounded exactly like *harrumph*.

I remembered that Detective Majors was going to research the Duponts for me. I hadn't heard from her, but there was a chance I'd missed her call. St. Louis was three hours ahead, so I grabbed my phone.

"Beth?" she answered on the first ring. "All's well?"

"Yes, it is. Any news—Walker or my mom?"

"Nothing new, I'm afraid."

"Well, I don't mean to bother you, but I wondered if you'd found anything on the Duponts?"

"Not bothering me at all. Yes, in fact I did find some things of interest—well, *I* think they're interesting. I was going to call you this morning, but I was going to let you sleep a little longer."

I laughed. "I couldn't sleep. I tried. Is now okay?" I readied a pen and paper.

"It is. Okay, well, you know Greg Dupont is a defense attorney?"

"Yes."

"I looked for something with a client that might cause him or his family some trouble, but I couldn't find one thing. I mean, normal clients—drunk drivers, car theft, drug dealing . . ."

"The usual suspects?"

"Yep."

"Until I found something unexpected. Greg wasn't an attorney in this case, though."

"Okay."

"About ten years ago, one of Dupont's associates, Smith is his last name, represented a man named Southright who killed a man named Harrison Weidler. Both the victim and the killer were involved in a Chicago mafia group who'd bled over into Des Moines from Chicago. Bad guys."

"Mafia in Des Moines, Iowa? Who would have guessed?"

"Well, drugs are everywhere, and that's a big part of this group's modus operandi. Anyway, and I'll get to the point quickly—Southright was found guilty and is locked up in Leavenworth."

"He's still there?"

"Yep. I confirmed it. Anyway, Southright was only convicted because there had been an eyewitness."

My Spidey-Sense tingled. "And that was?"

"Weidler's wife. Her name was Tasha."

"Was?"

"I can't find her anywhere, Beth. Considering mafia was involved and even though it was murder, it was probably considered infighting by the man who headed up the group back then. He would have killed whoever threw one of his men to the wolves. They would have wanted to handle everything in-house, if you know what I mean."

"I do. So is Greg Dupont a part of this story, because his associate represented Southright?"

"No. Well, that's what caused me to search for the other things. I couldn't find where Tasha went, but there was a kid. I think."

"You think?"

"I found an article about Weidler's murder that included a mention of a son, but then I couldn't find anything anywhere else. I'm guessing that the media were told to keep things on the down-low, and Tasha and the boy were put into witness protection, but those are things I don't get full access to. I did find one other thing, but I'm only guessing that it's tied together. When a child goes into foster care, there's a paper trail. I found Greg and Betty Dupont's names listed as temporary foster parents for a boy, name and age unknown."

"Temporary?"

"Yes, that probably means there were clearly plans for him to move someplace else, but I couldn't find anything to help me understand where or when a move might have happened. Maybe Tasha got situated and the boy joined her later. I have no idea."

"Was there a date on the form?"

"Yes."

When she told me the date, I did quick math and determined that the time frame might fit with the first-grade cookies-and-milk picture.

Detective Majors continued, "It was the date, right near the end of the trial, that made me wonder if the kid was the Weidlers'. I can't figure out any way to confirm or deny that, Beth. I can't understand why, other than that Dupont and Southpoint's attorney were business associates, that the Duponts would have taken the boy in. I've dug deep, but some records are sealed for safety's sake."

I agreed with her guess—but I thought I had a name for the boy: Albert Jackson. I hadn't given her all the details of what had been happening, but she'd done the research anyway. She probably hadn't told me anything that I couldn't have found if I'd thought to look. She was just better at knowing what to look for. She didn't ask for more of the story from me.

"Detective, I can't thank you enough for this information."

"You are welcome, Beth. I hope it helps. Your chief up there is a good guy. Should I call him?"

"Sure. I will try to get to him, too, but it wouldn't hurt for you to let him know what you found. You might have to leave a message."

"I can do that."

We disconnected the call, and I said to the air, "I think we're getting somewhere."

I found the cookies-and-milk article and spotted the name of the reporter. Josh Jensen had written about the first-grade event ten years ago. I was sure he didn't remember any of it, but thought maybe I could use some questions about it as a way to grease the wheel, see if he knew more about any of the players in these mysteries. I pulled up *The Des Moines Register* website and did a search for the reporter. There were no Joshes and no Jensens.

Finding the paper's number on the site, I dialed. Once I danced through an irritating phone tree system, a person finally answered.

"Newsroom. Brady here."

"Yes, hello," I said. "I'm looking for a reporter I know worked there about ten years ago, but I've lost track of him. His name was Josh Jensen."

Brady laughed. "Ten years? That's an eon in the newspaper business. Hang on, let me think. Yeah, if I remember him correctly, he hasn't been here for a while."

"Do you know where he went?"

"Between you and me, darlin', I think he was canned, kicked to the curb . . ."

"I'm sorry to hear that," I said. "I really need to talk to him."

"Why?"

"I work at a paper in Alaska." So far, not a lie. "I'm doing some follow-up on something he wrote about." Still not lying.

"Which something?"

"Zoo safety." A complete lie.

"Huh. I don't remember that one, but that's what he usually wrote about—boring stuff."

"Okay." I hesitated because I knew that Brady could give me an answer to something, if only I had the right questions. "Do you have archives?"

"We're a newspaper. We're all archives."

"This is going to seem weird."

"That's all I do around here. Weird."

"Okay, well, other than zoo safety, Josh wrote an article about a first-grade event ten years ago. There was a picture. I wonder if I could see the original picture."

"Huh. Why?"

"I think my niece is in it. I want to frame a copy for her." More lies.

"Huh. Well, I'll see what I can find. Email?"

I gave him the article's details and my email. He disconnected the call before I could finish saying "thank you" again.

I made notes and then sat back in my chair. The conclusions I could jump to were now obvious. Sadie was Tasha and it was, for whatever reason, no coincidence that she was here when the Duponts were also here because Albert Jackson was her son. Was he nearby, too? Why were they all here together?

"But Albert was arrested for killing his biological mother, and Sadie is alive," I spoke aloud again. Gus would have been entertained.

Either I'd been given clues, or I was forcing them.

I looked at the window and almost cheered when I saw Orin's truck at the library. Shoot, he might have all of this information, might have given it to Gril, but if anyone could help me sift through it, it was him.

I loaded up and headed to the library.

Twenty-nine

B eth! Your hair—it looks great."

"Oh." I couldn't help but smile. "Thank you."

And then I told him everything.

"Wow, Beth, that is something," Orin said after I finished going over the details.

"These aren't things you knew?"

Orin frowned a moment, but then said, "I knew her name was Tasha and that she witnessed a murder, but that was it."

Maybe Orin's contacts wouldn't have discovered the foster-care form, wouldn't have thought it was pertinent.

But, surely, they would have.

"Orin, that's weird that your people didn't know. Maybe this is the wrong track."

"Nope. I knew her name was Tasha. The murder details, too. We're on the right track, just not with all the right details."

"Gril knows what you know?"

"He does."

"But what about the woman Albert Jackson allegedly killed? It was reported that she was his biological mother. That couldn't be Sadie then. She's very alive. Should we just ask her? Our bigger goal is to find Gracie. I'm pretty sure everything is connected, but if we confront her with what we know, maybe she could help fill in the pieces. I . . ." I closed my mouth but continued a few moments later, "Orin, I don't think anyone has told her about Gracie. I mean, she was a victim, too. We've all been being careful around her, not wanting to worry her. She might not even know."

"Oh." Orin frowned. "Oh, well, that might need some attention, but we should do it through Gril. Hang on. Let me look something up."

He turned back to his laptop. "Okay, here's the story of the woman who was killed in the shoe store. Her name was Linda Robin. Let me do some searching, see what Linda was up to before she was killed." He typed a little longer. "Okay, well, a woman with the same name lived in Iowa before she was in Juneau. I need driver's licenses to confirm it was the same woman. That much I can find easily."

"That name is familiar."

"Linda's?"

"Yes. Linda Robin. How do I know it?"

"I don't know."

It needled at me, but I couldn't immediately remember why it was so familiar. I hoped it would come to me later. "I think we should talk to Gril."

"You're probably right. I'll get the licenses later." Orin shut his laptop and put it in his bag. "Let's go."

I led us out of his office. It seemed the library was full of readers today, not just internet users. Orin and I sent distracted greetings to everyone as we made our way out. One person, a woman I'd met at Pip's Packing, the local fish processing facility, was sitting in a corner chair reading a copy of one of my books.

Those kinds of moments were both thrilling and confusing.

Sometimes it was difficult to connect myself to the books, but it was always wonderful to see people reading them. The book she'd picked was about a serial killer who found a secret way into a big tourist cave—I based it on a real place, Meramec Caverns in Sullivan, Missouri. There in a mostly hidden "room," he was storing dead bodies. He would send the victims' families on "scavenger hunts" to find them, but they could never gain access to the hidden parts. Not only were the murders gruesome, but the families' frustration at not solving the hunts was rage inducing.

It had been one of my most difficult books to write because I was claustrophobic. *Scavenger Hunt* had sold well, still sold well.

I stopped in my tracks. Orin almost ran into me.

"Beth?"

"Oh." I hurried over to Veronica.

"Hi! I'm loving this," she said.

I resisted the urge to just grab it out of her hands. "May I look at that a second?"

"Of course. You should sign it for the library."

I turned to the back cover where some reviews had been quoted, and I mumbled some of them aloud. "Absolute perfection! Greatest thrill chiller! Fairchild has torture and murder on her mind!"

I gave the book back to Veronica and then turned to Orin.

A wave of clarity hit me so hard, it almost knocked me over. "Orin, they're in the caves."

"What? Who?"

"I'm not sure who, but I hope Gracie is there. No one has seen any bears on Lilybook, right?"

"I have."

"When?"

"A long time ago."

"Okay, recently?"

"I haven't looked recently."

I nodded. "They're in a cave on the island. It's what Gracie was trying to tell me. She quoted reviewers specifically for that book," I pointed, "and it's about caves. She was communicating with me."

"The caves were searched, weren't they?"

I shook my head. "Maybe not thoroughly. Everyone's been concerned about bears."

Orin processed my words. He looked at the book, now back in Veronica's hands. His eyebrows rose as he looked at me again. "That book scared the shit out of me."

"When Gracie was talking to me, she wasn't sucking up or trying to build a rapport, she was trying to tell me something. I don't know everything that's going on, but for some reason, she wanted me to figure out how to save her."

"Well, then I think we should get to saving her."

Orin and I sped to the police station.

Thirty

Donner wasn't there, but Gril was. He was on his way out the door, though.

"Your hair looks wonderful," Gril said.

I thanked him. Another day, I would be drinking in these compliments. Today, I just wanted him to know what we knew.

Without going inside, we shared with him the things we'd found or concluded or thought might be relevant. He'd already heard from Detective Majors, so some of it was repetition.

He listened intently and then said, "All right. Let's go."

Orin and I looked at each other.

"Where are we going?" I asked.

"To talk to Sadie. I'll search those caves, but if all of this is pertinent, she knows much more than she's saying."

"You think Gracie's involved?"

"I hope this is a lead to Gracie."

"I don't think Sadie knows about Gracie. Everyone's been trying to protect her."

"Time for her to know."

"Orin, you're with me," Gril said. "Beth, you can take your own truck."

I was disappointed not to be included in whatever conversation Gril and Orin would have on the way over to the Benedict House, but a glance from Orin reassured me he'd tell me later.

But before we could pull out of the parking lot, Tex pulled into it. We all waited for him to exit his truck. I was happy to see him, but now wasn't the time for PDA.

Tex looked at all of us. "What's going on? Beth? Looks great." He pointed at his own head.

"Did you find anything?" Gril asked.

"No, sir," Tex said.

"We're going over to the Benedict House. You can join us or ride with Beth if you'd like."

"I'll ride with Beth."

Inside my truck, I filled Tex in on as much as I could on the short ride over.

"You think they're—someone is—in the caves on Lilybook?" Tex asked when I was finished.

"I do."

"We looked inside them, some at least."

"In my book, there's a secret entrance that the killer found. There must be one here, too, maybe a secret room or space. No one has seen a bear on that island since this all happened."

"I didn't see anything that might indicate a secret room, but I suppose that's what would make it a secret."

"Is there another way onto the island, other than the two beaches I've seen?"

"The south end of the island doesn't offer an easy way to anchor a boat. There's a cliff blocking it."

"That's where the secret entrance is then, I'm sure."

Tex shook his head. "I think I should head out there right now."

"I don't know, Tex. Gril wants to talk to Sadie first, I think. It would be better if you didn't go out alone."

My mind went to my book. The bodies the killer had hidden in Meramec Caverns were mutilated, killed in gruesome ways. A wave of fear iced through me as I thought about more bodies on Lilybook. I hoped it hadn't gone that far, whatever it all was.

I swallowed hard.

Tex was watching me. "What?"

"My book, *Scavenger Hunt,* is pretty bloody."

"Right. Well, it's fiction. This is real life." Tex paused. "Gracie wanted you to know. You figured it out. There's time to save her."

"Kayaks," I said. "Could people on kayaks access the south side of the island?"

"Better than boats, but it still wouldn't be easy."

And then that other thing that had been in the back of my mind, nudging at me to pay attention, came to the front, with a clarity that now made me gasp and slam on the brakes.

"Beth?" Tex asked after we both righted ourselves.

"The boat."

"What boat?"

"There was no other way for Sadie and the man to get to Lilybook other than on a boat, and—"

I didn't have to finish my thought.

"We need to find that boat."

I just hoped it wasn't, by some twist of fate, my father's boat. "We do."

"Okay, so are we going to the boat dock or the Benedict House?" Tex asked. "I'm game for doing either."

The seconds ticked by, but I decided quickly. "Benedict House first. Sadie said she was drugged, but maybe she can now remember something about the boat." I looked at Tex quickly. "Sadie told Viola and me that she killed him with a branch, on purpose. She claims to only just remember it."

"I see."

"You're not surprised?"

"I'm just trying to remain calm and think through everything, but, honestly, I'm not too surprised."

"I wasn't, either. Not really."

Tex nodded.

As we hopped out of the truck, I remembered something else. I hoped Gril was okay with me asking. "Tex—you found something with the body?"

He registered my words. "Oh. The glove?"

"You found *a* glove?"

He nodded. "A gardening glove. I didn't think it was much of anything, but we brought it in with the body."

It wasn't winter gloves, it was a gardening glove. Sadie had been in her yard when the man had taken her. She'd had it on her. "It must have been Sadie's."

"Why her hands weren't too torn up?"

I nodded.

"Do you think that means premeditation on her part? Somehow?"

"I don't know. Let's get inside."

Gril had already set up the dining room, leaving two chairs empty for Tex and me. He nodded toward them as we came in.

"Okay, everyone's here," he said.

Flanked by Viola and Orin, Sadie sat on the far side of the table. Short of leaping over the table, she had no escape, which was probably what Gril had wanted. Her eyes held that trapped-animal glassy panic. I felt terrible for doing that to her, but I was sure her story had something to do with Gracie, and that was our most important mystery at the moment.

Tex and I sat, quickly and silently.

"Sadie," Gril began. "I'm going to need you to tell me some

truths. I don't care what happened in your past, but I've got no choice but to bring it up. I need to know some things."

Sadie looked around. "But . . ."

"Nope," Gril said. "I'm not in the mood to argue."

"I was just going to say that there are so many people here."

"Yes, there are. These are people who've been working hard to figure out who might have abducted you from your home, and they have also been worried sick and looking for a missing teenage girl. They have a right to be here."

"Missing teenage girl?"

Gril nodded. "Do you know the Dupont family?"

"No," Sadie lied. She was so bad at it that even she knew. Her cheeks flushed, and she looked at her hands on the table.

"Sadie?" Gril pressed.

The rest of us waited silently. The room felt like a pressure cooker.

"Look, I'm not supposed to talk about my past. It could put me in danger," she said.

"Nope, you don't get to use that. You're not in danger. You're safe, and we'll make sure you stay safe. We need to find Gracie Dupont, and we think you can help. Just tell us what might help us find her."

Sadie deflated. "Where is Grecko?"

"Still on his way from Seattle," Gril said.

"When he gets here, I'll ask him for guidance and tell you what I can."

Gril slammed his fist on the table, causing us all to jump and making Gus bark once. I put my hand on his neck.

"No. We need to find that girl, and I know you know something. Tell me now," Gril said.

"Or what?"

"Or we'll all do everything in our power to get you removed

from witness protection. You'll be on your own." Gril looked at Orin, who nodded, and then back at Sadie. "And we can do that."

Sadie laughed somewhat maniacally. "This is the strangest place. You are all so . . . unexpected. I should have done my research better."

"What does that mean?" Gril asked.

Sadie shook her head. "Doesn't matter."

"All that matters is whatever you know that can help us find Gracie," Gril said sternly.

A long moment later, Sadie nodded. "I don't know that I can help. That's the truth. But I can tell you some things."

"We're waiting," Gril said.

Sadie nodded again. "I didn't know the Duponts would be out here. Honestly, I don't quite understand how they got involved unless Albert somehow stayed in touch with them over the years."

"You sound like you were planning on being here?"

"Well, I won't explain that part, but I can tell you that Albert orchestrated all of this, including me being here."

"Your son?" I interjected.

She frowned at me. "He's not my son."

I looked at Gril. He gave me a nod of approval, so I continued. "If you're Tasha Weidler, he's your son."

She laughed once. "No, Beth, if I'm Tasha, he's not my son. However, Tasha's husband might have had a child with another woman."

I nodded. "Oh. Well, that makes more sense." I had to pause and let the pieces of the mystery puzzle move around in my mind a little. "Who?"

Sadie sighed. "Her name was Linda Robin."

Orin and I shared a look.

"The woman who was killed in the shoe store?" Orin asked.

Sadie seemed surprised. "Wow, that's impressive."

We all looked at her expectantly.

She didn't want to continue, but she did. "Yes, Linda was at one time my best friend. Until she slept with my husband, got pregnant, and had a child."

"She's the reason you moved to Juneau. You killed her. Albert didn't. You did, and you got away with it," I said after I thought about it for a moment.

Sadie was more prepared now. "I didn't hear a question there, but I'm not commenting on any of those things."

Gril held up his hand. "Okay, okay. Sadie, I don't care about any of this right now. I want to find Gracie. Where is she?"

"I don't—"

"She's in a cave on Lilybook. A secret cave, one that hasn't been discovered by most of the rest of the world," I said.

Sadie shook her head at me. "My goodness, you figured that out?"

Gril stood. "That's where she is?"

Sadie looked at him. "Gril, I really don't know, but based upon the information I was given, I would guess she is on that island, in a cave probably. I swear, though, I really don't know. I did not know that Gracie would be here. It just makes sense, though."

"Why does it make sense?" Gril asked.

"Because this whole thing is about Albert's vengeance. It's a miracle I'm still alive." She bit her bottom lip. "I shouldn't say more, not without Grecko."

"We're going out to that island. If she's not there, be prepared to plan for a whole different existence," Gril said.

"You can't—"

"Oh, yes, we can." Gril looked at the rest of us. "Viola, Orin, and Beth, stay here with Sadie. Tex and Donner, come with me."

I wanted to protest, beg to go with them, but it felt way too wrong.

"We'll need a boat, Gril," Tex said. "Eddy's will do. Beth should come."

Well, if I hadn't loved him before, I felt a big old surge of it now. I looked at Gril.

"Good point. Come on, let's go."

Gril led us out of the dining room, and we raced to the dock.

Thirty-one

We found Eddy on his boat. As we all climbed aboard, Gril asked him a slew of questions.

Eddy, as he followed Gril's command to get us all to Lilybook by first steering us out of the bay, listened intently and then answered one of the questions. "I never took anyone but Beth and the Duponts to Lilybook. That guy never returned my call or called me again."

"That's what you said before, Eddy. Are you sure?" Gril asked.

"One hundred percent. I'd tell you, Gril."

"Did you ever take anyone to the far side of the island, where there might be some secret cave entrances?" I asked.

Everyone listened for the answer.

"Never."

"Have you been served yet, for Beth's kidnapper's trial?" Donner asked him now.

"Not yet."

I remembered the man who'd pretended to be Daniel Grecko

and wondered if he was there for the purpose of serving Eddy, but that didn't fit. How would a process server from a Missouri trial even know Grecko's name? It would explain how he knew so much about me, but it was currently the least of my worries.

"All right, everybody, listen up," Gril said.

We all turned our attention to him.

"I'm going to need Tex to help me understand if there's . . . a secret entrance."

"I can do that," Tex offered.

"Then, Donner and I will lead the way. Tex, are you comfortable being right behind us?"

"Affirmative."

"Eddy and Beth." He looked pointedly at me. "I want you to stay on the boat."

"Of course," Eddy said.

I nodded agreeably. Even Tex couldn't help me with this one. It didn't make sense for me to follow along in some sort of raid. I didn't have a weapon. My thoughts went to Eddy's .22—I could have a weapon, if Eddy would let me. He wouldn't.

Eddy powered the boat down as we entered the wake zone at the back of the island. There were, indeed, rocky cliffs on this side. Puffins had made nests in ledges and trees that grew atop some of them, but there was no obvious sign of a cave entrance.

"Head around that outcropping," Tex pointed. "Be careful—the cliffs extend out."

Eddy piloted the boat in that direction, expertly I thought. Suddenly, true to Tex's guess, an outcropping came into view. Near the shore next to the cliff wall, there was a ledge that extended far into the water. It looked like something anyone with a sense of curiosity would want to explore.

"See that gap in there?" Tex pointed again.

A gap in the cliff walls made the seeming "walkway" even more intriguing.

"That might be a way into one or more of the caves, I'm not sure," Tex said.

"Through that gap?" Gril asked.

"Yes."

Gril looked at Tex. "Any other options?"

Tex shook his head. "I don't know if the land openings lead here or not. We could check it out first."

"We have no choice. We won't fit in that gap."

"Wait," I said. "I will."

"No, Beth—"

"Gril, we don't have any choice. Sure, go look from the land side, but at least let me explore. I'll be careful. We have no choice—Gracie and Laney might be in there!"

Gril looked at Donner. It was rare that Gril looked at anyone for an answer. Donner shrugged.

"All right, Beth," Gril finally said. "Just see what you can find. The good news is that a bear can't fit in that slot."

"That is very good news." It occurred to me that Gracie and Laney could fit, and if I'd gauged that young man's skinny body correctly, he could, too.

"Eddy, can you get the boat near enough to that outcropping?" Gril said.

"I think I can," Eddy said.

A few seconds later, I was able to jump from the boat directly onto the ledge. I stood up and told them I was fine.

Gril had given me a flashlight and a knife, but he wouldn't allow a gun, though he did think about it a second.

"Beth!" Eddy called. "Be careful. Do you hear me?"

I nodded. In my head only, I said, *Yes, Dad, I'll be careful.*

"Listen to your father," Tex said as he peered at me, his hands on his hips.

"Just look, Beth. Get back out here quickly," Gril said. "Don't do anything . . . well, more unreasonable than you're already doing."

Donner just sent me a stern expression.

I approached the gap, surprised by how dark it really was on the other side of the opening. I flipped on the light and shone it inside.

"It's definitely a gap. I can't see the end of it. I'm going in."

"Be careful," Eddy called again.

We weren't being quiet or covert. Nevertheless, I tried not to make too much noise as I squeezed myself into the slot.

It was tight. I wouldn't get stuck if it didn't narrow, but I wouldn't be able to move quickly.

In my story, *Scavenger Hunt*, it's a female police officer who makes her way into the secret opening inside the cavern to ultimately make a gruesome discovery. The claustrophobia I felt while writing it had nothing on this. I told myself to ignore the crushing sensation.

I took a couple of deep breaths.

One side step at a time, I moved deeper into the darkness. It was cold in there. I was sweating down my back and into my eyes. If I stopped moving for too long, I could get dangerously cold.

Again, I told myself not to think about it. Just keep going.

As I aimed the light, I thought maybe I was seeing a space ahead that opened up some. I wanted to hurry to get to it, but hurrying was impossible. I did the best I could.

As I approached the widening, I thought I heard something. Instinctually, I flipped off the light and worked to quiet my breathing. My heart pounded in my ears, but I didn't think I'd been noticed by anyone.

For a long, cold moment, I listened hard. Did I hear voices?

I needed to keep on, but I was going to have to do it without the light and without making a sound. Man, it was dark.

A few minutes earlier, I'd been out in the big world, only the clouds above acting as any sort of barrier. I told myself I would be back out there again soon. I just needed to keep going and figure out what I was hearing.

I almost fell as I emerged from the gap. I hadn't seen it coming, but I was glad not to be closed in anymore. I had no choice but to turn on the light again, though. I was completely blind without it. Hang on, maybe I wasn't. I held the flashlight at the ready, but off, as my eyes landed on something coming from a corner of the space. Was that light?

Even after another few moments of allowing my eyes to adjust, I couldn't tell exactly what I was seeing. I still heard what I thought were voices, but I couldn't understand the words being spoken.

This was probably the point where Gril had hoped I'd turn around. I'd heard voices, and that was enough for him to know that this whole cave needed further exploration. He wouldn't have wanted me to do said exploration. But none of the others would fit in that slot. I needed more information.

I flipped the light back on and aimed it toward the corner. There was another opening there, and light was definitely coming through. That opening wasn't tall and narrow, but short and squat, wider, too. I could crawl into it, presumably through it.

As I got on all fours, the voices I heard ramped up in volume. I peered into the tunnel. I could see a lot more light, but I couldn't see the end of the tunnel, where it might lead to.

"She's an idiot," a male said. "She knew what she was supposed to do and now she's holed up in that weird hotel."

"It's okay, Albert," a female said. I was pretty sure it was Gracie, and a wave of glee ran through me.

"It's not all right!" the male yelled.

Then the voices fell back to unintelligible.

I looked back at the slot I'd come through. I'd reached another waypost, another point Gril would have wanted me to turn around.

But I didn't. I turned off the light again and crawled into the tunnel.

I traveled about ten feet, when the tunnel jogged sharply to the left. Carefully I peered around the rocky corner. A large room opened up about five feet down that tunnel. From my vantage point, I could see a few battery-powered lanterns, some blankets, and a pair of boot-covered feet as they marched by. I pulled back into the tunnel, covering my mouth with my hand to stop a gasp.

Weirdly, I couldn't make out the words being spoken from here, even though I was closer to them. The tunnel must have served as some sort of amplifier to the other side. However, I could distinguish one male voice and probably two female voices.

Relief relaxed me, took away the claustrophobia. Gracie and Laney were alive—hopefully. Albert was alive, too. I didn't know the dynamics of what was going on, but if no dead bodies were in that cave-walled room, the outcome was on the way to becoming much more positive than the story I'd written.

I had to get out of there and tell Gril. He'd figure out a way to do whatever was needed.

I couldn't turn around, but I could back out, relatively easily. I made a move to go backward when the male voice rose to an angry level.

"Fine! I'll get you some food. Jesus, I fed you yesterday!"

I quickly concluded that the man attached to the voice was just about to join me in this tunnel. The panic turned the easy backward motion into a disaster. I hit my back on the top of the tunnel, scraped my pants-covered knees on the floor, painfully ran into the walls, bumped my head.

I decided to brace myself for the interaction instead. I didn't know what that meant other than to grab the knife, but I knew he was coming, and he didn't know I was there. The element of surprise would be on my side.

The knife in hand, I was ready.

But he never appeared. Thirty seconds passed, then a minute.

I listened hard, but didn't hear any voices.

I redirected again and moved forward, cautiously turned the corner and then hurry-crawled to the wider opening.

I peered out.

Gracie and Laney were there. Alive. I almost cried, but now wasn't the time.

"Hey," I whisper-shouted, my voice strained with emotion.

The two girls jumped and looked at me. It was then that I noticed a few more things I probably should have registered before letting my presence be known. Laney was sitting on a blanket, looking bored and maybe concerned, but she wasn't tied up in any way.

Gracie was tied up, her hands behind her, her ankles crossed.

"Beth!" Gracie said. She looked at Laney and back at me. "She's . . . in on it."

I didn't know what she was in on, I didn't understand anything except it was clear that Gracie was being restrained and Laney wasn't.

"Oh, look, it's that nosey woman I met the other day," Laney said.

I scrambled into the room and stood. "We're getting out of here. All of us."

Laney laughed. Gracie just looked at me wide-eyed.

"Come on." I looked around the room, spotting another slot, thinking that's how Albert must have exited. "Before he comes back."

Laney shook her head and stood, but she didn't have a weapon. "No, that's not happening. We're not done here."

"What does that mean?"

Gracie looked back and forth between me and Laney. "They're going to ask my parents for money, and then they're going to kill them. Laney knows about poisonous plants on this island—"

"Shut up," Laney said to Gracie.

"Why?" I asked them.

"Because they sent Albert away when he was a kid. He was happy in my family's house, but then he was sent away to a terrible situation. He's angry at them. He got Laney aboard," Gracie said.

"But you knew?"

"No. They tricked me into being here. I didn't know the plan. I thought we were just going to explore, spend time with Albert. He was like a brother to me. I missed him. He hasn't killed anyone—yet, but he wants to kill my parents. Things started to feel weird. I . . . I tried to give you clues just in case something like this happened—"

"Shut up!" Laney yelled at Gracie.

I didn't doubt what I now saw. Clearly, Gracie was the one being kept here against her will.

Her mouth made a straight line as her eyes pleaded with me. I needed to get her out of here, hopefully before Albert got back.

"Laney, Gracie is your best friend," I said.

I thought she might laugh, but she didn't. "No one is going to hurt Gracie, but Albert needs her here."

"No, you are wrong. Albert will hurt Gracie and probably you, too. I don't know what Albert told you, but this is wrong. You know this is wrong. Come on, Laney. Let's get out of here. The police are waiting right through that tunnel."

A distant noise sounded from the slat I presumed Albert had gone through.

"He's coming back," Gracie said.

"Come on, Laney," I said. I gripped the knife in my hand by my side. "Let's go. Now."

I stepped toward the girls. Laney was a kid. Both of them were kids. Laney didn't know what to make of my approach. With the knife, I sliced the ropes around Gracie's ankles and her arms. Laney didn't know how to stop me, maybe didn't want to. I helped Gracie up. "Go. Now."

She stumbled some, as if her legs might have fallen asleep, but she got there, got down on her knees, and crawled through. She was going to need a flashlight, but I wasn't going to be far behind.

I held the knife, but not threateningly. "You have seconds to decide. Go. I'm going without you if you don't come right now!"

Laney's face scrunched up. I turned and hurried to the tunnel. I looked at her one more time. Finally, she ran to me and fell to her knees.

"Go! Now!" I pushed her into the tunnel.

Once she was all the way in, I crawled in, too.

"Hey!" Albert said from behind me. "Stop!"

"Shit," I muttered, though the moment might have called for something stronger. I disappeared all the way into the tunnel. "Go, girls, go!"

I didn't look behind me, but I heard Albert enter the tunnel.

"Go!" I yelled.

I exited the tunnel into the bigger room, which was just as dark as it had been before. I fumbled but managed to get the flashlight turned on and pointed at the slat. "There. Quickly!"

Gracie and Laney went through. I was right behind them, but Albert joined us in the slat only about five seconds after I was all the way in. None of us could move quickly. We all fit, though. I held the knife in the hand toward Albert, but kept the light faced ahead so the girls could see.

We were all noisy, the girls upset, Albert yelling, me continuing to tell the girls to just keep going.

It seemed like forever, but finally light from the slat's opening to the world greeted us.

"Right out there, girls. The police are right out there."

I felt Albert grab my hand. Somehow, I yanked it free but lost hold of the knife. I just kept going.

With Laney in front of me, I couldn't see Gracie exit, but I heard her call to the people on the boat. Laney was next.

I found some speed in my feet, managing to scrape my face on the rock wall, and felt warm blood ooze down my cheek.

Albert made one more grab for me but missed as I emerged out into the open. The girls were being helped aboard the boat, but I fell onto my backside on the long ledge.

"He's—" I was going to say *He's coming*, but he was there too soon.

In only a second or two, Albert appraised the situation and made a decision. He ran at me, maybe to hit me, throw me in the water—or to stab me with my own knife, which he'd managed to gather.

"No!" I yelled as he came in my direction.

A gunshot rang out just as Albert lifted the knife.

Thirty-two

I t was Eddy who shot Albert, with the .22. He got the young man in the shoulder. It wasn't a lethal blow, but it threw Albert backward and onto his back. Somehow, Tex managed to get off the boat and to me. In a flash, he lifted me aboard and then grabbed the injured Albert.

"What do you want me to do with him?" Tex asked Gril.

"Bring him aboard. We need to get pressure on that wound."

The boat was crowded on the way back to the dock. Gracie wanted to explain what had happened, but Gril stopped her.

"No. We'll get you back to your parents and then we'll all talk. I don't want to hear a word from anyone while we're on this boat, unless I speak to you directly. Got it?"

Gril used Eddy's radio to ask someone to get the Duponts down to the dock as quickly as possible and find Dr. Powder, too. With a nod from Gril, Eddy sped up the boat.

I sat between Tex and Donner. Albert's wound was bandaged, but his eyes were closed as he lay along one of the cabin benches. The two girls were, oddly, finding quiet comfort in each other.

I couldn't wait to hear the rest of this story, but Gril was right, getting the girls back to land safely was the goal.

"Laney," Gril said. "I've been trying to call your parents. They haven't answered."

"They're in Europe," Laney said.

"Good to know. Thanks." Gril's gaze moved over all of us. Clearly, he was telling us to return to silence.

We did. None of us said a word, but Tex did attend to the cuts on my face. They weren't deep and he kissed me on the forehead when he was done, making it much better.

When we hit the no-wake zone for the dock, Eddy slowed the boat. We could see the Duponts standing on the shore. They were both hopeful and terrified. I wondered if Gril should have allowed them to know more, like the fact that Gracie was alive. It was too late now.

Gracie stood from the seat and made her way to the bow of the boat.

"Mommy, Daddy! I'm okay," she yelled.

Greg had to hold Betty back from going into the water. She fell to her knees instead as Greg held her arm, keeping her from going all the way in.

The boat couldn't dock quick enough, and Gril had to hold Gracie back from jumping out. "Let's not get hurt now. Hang on."

A few minutes later, the family was reunited, holding on to one another and crying on the beach. We all shed a tear or two.

"Laney, come." Betty signaled the girl over to join in the group hug.

Laney shook her head, and Gracie said something to her mother. A second later, Betty signaled to Laney again. "It doesn't matter. Come."

Laney went to them and joined in the hugs and the tears.

Gril talked to them before rejoining the rest of us, and the Duponts and Laney sat on the beach and talked and cried. Dr.

Powder appeared a few moments later and jumped on the boat to attend to the gunshot victim.

Gril, Donner, Tex, and I disembarked and sat on the beach as well, though a distance away from the others. We were all tired, and sitting seemed like the thing to do. Dr. Powder told me not to leave until he looked at my face.

We talked through what had happened. Gril would question Gracie and Laney within the hour, after he understood the severity of Albert's wound and any prognosis.

"Gril?" I asked. "What else is going on here?"

His eyes still on the nearby family reunion, he rubbed his chin. He looked at me. "The dead man on the island was Michael Smith, the attorney who worked with Greg Dupont and defended a man named Southright."

"I don't understand that at all," I said. "Why was he here? Did Sadie lure him out here?"

"I don't think so. I think Albert Jackson got Smith to pick up Sadie and bring her out here. She killed him before he could deliver Sadie to Albert. She did know him and went with him willingly, according to witnesses, but he probably kept her in the abandoned hangar against her will. I'll have to get her to tell me any more than that."

"Why would an attorney do that?" Donner asked.

"Money, pure and simple. Albert Jackson had money, had grown up with a family that was dysfunctional but rich in Westport."

"Did he kill his birth mother?"

"He was convicted of it."

"Sadie said she killed Smith; she admitted it," I said.

"We figured. We have the branch, had it the whole time."

I looked at Tex, who shrugged. "Gril and I thought it best to keep it quiet until a body was found. After that . . ."

"After that," Gril said, "I just needed to figure out all the moving parts, and I didn't want anyone to know until I knew more.

I nodded, though I wish I'd known.

"Tex also found a glove near the body. We're sure that was Sadie's, too. Just got confirmation that the blood on it came from Smith."

"Smith agreed to do that for Albert?" I asked.

"Smith needed the money." Gril shrugged.

"Jesus," Tex uttered.

"Where's Grecko?" I asked.

"He should be here soon. Harvingtons went to pick him up from Juneau," Gril said.

"Did anyone ever identify the man who was claiming to be him?" I asked.

"Nope," Gril said.

"Who could that have been?" I asked.

"Who would know about Grecko?" Tex asked.

"No one should." Gril rubbed at his chin. "We figured out where the van came from, though."

"Where?" Tex and I asked together.

"Taken from a cleaning company in Juneau. Robin's Nest Cleaning or something." Gril looked at Donner.

"Robin?" I asked.

"Yes," Gril said.

The pieces came together quickly now. There was only one more person to identify. "Gril, the woman killed in the Juneau shoe store was Linda Robin. Fred and I found a Robin's Nest Cleaning Company business card in Buster's things. We thought it was something left over from the old days, and didn't think Robin was a name. Why would Buster have it? I bet it came from that van. And I would not be surprised if the man who pretended to be Grecko was Linda Robin's husband. He might know who Sadie is and was. He might know about Grecko."

Gril stood. "Shit. Someone needs to check on her. Donner, stay here. Bring Albert back to the station if he's well enough. I'm heading back to the Benedict House." Gril stood and hurried up to the parking lot.

I looked at Tex and then Donner. "We're going back, too."

"Makes sense," Donner said. "Be careful."

Tex and I hurried to my truck, leaving Donner alone on the beach, but I suspected he was glad to be rid of us so he could simply do his job.

We weren't far behind Gril, but as we turned and the Benedict House came into view, we noticed that Gril's truck was parked out front, not in a designated parking space. His door was left open.

I parked my truck, but Tex and I hurried into the house. The adrenaline from the cave hadn't dissipated before a new wave took over. I was buzzing with it.

We burst through the front door, hearing noises from the dining room. We hurried in that direction, shocked but not surprised by the sight inside.

The man who'd claimed to be Grecko had Sadie in the small space, a knife held to her throat.

Orin and Viola were fine, sitting in the chairs I'd last seen them in. Viola's gun was on the floor, far away from the skirmish. Tex and I remained back as Gril talked to the man. Sadie struggled in his arms, her face distorted in terror. Gus was seated next to Viola, growling. Viola held his collar.

"Come on, let her go. She's in trouble. Let the justice system take care of her," Gril said with no preamble that we'd seen.

The man laughed. "Like it did before? I told the police she was the one who killed my wife. They didn't care. They were happy to have their man, an innocent man by the way."

The pieces of that part of what felt like this never-ending puzzle came together even more in my head. This was definitely Linda Robin's husband. Linda Robin, the woman killed in Juneau, most likely by Sadie. Fred Harvington and I *had* found the business card—Robin's Nest Cleaning. It hadn't given us pause other than

266 • PAIGE SHELTON

that it seemed an odd thing to find under Buster's bedding. Albert had known exactly who might help with his revenge. Of course, Mr. Robin wanted to help Albert somehow hurt Sadie, but that didn't feel completely right.

"You knew Sadie and Smith were at the airport," I said.

"Of course, but they left before I could take care of . . . her." He pulled the knife tighter.

It occurred to me that that business card that Fred and I had shrugged off had actually been a big clue. If someone had looked closer, realized Robin was a last name, and then found the company's owner, we might have learned things so much more quickly.

"Wait. You weren't just a part of this—you orchestrated all of it, didn't you?" I asked him. "You might have even helped Albert escape."

He sneered at me.

"Why didn't you just kill her?" I said.

"Too many people wanted the honor."

Sadie's eyes pinched; tears rolled down her cheeks. She croaked, "I'm sorry!"

Gril said, "The Juneau police thought she was guilty of something. There just wasn't enough evidence. I can convince them otherwise. Work with me here. You don't need to do this: ruin your own life. Let her go."

"I will kill her right here if you don't let me take her out of here." He pushed the knife a little deeper into the skin on her neck. Sadie made fearful noises.

"No, you won't. You're not a killer," Gril said. He nodded in my direction. "Or you would have just killed her already."

"She's a killer. She killed my wife."

"I know, and I will make sure she pays for that," Gril said. "I promise you."

"You will—"

We hadn't heard the front door open again, but the person

who'd come in had probably decided to enter more covertly than the rest of us.

Next to Tex and me, a man took a shot. The noise was terrifying and deafening—this was no wimpy .22.

The man holding Sadie was shot in the knee. He went down; Sadie moved to the corner of the room.

We all looked at the man and his smoking gun. He was probably in his late forties, with a pleasant face and a mostly bald head. He wore jeans and a green-and-white golf shirt.

Gril was drawing his own weapon when the man put his on the floor. "Daniel Grecko, US marshal. You must be Gril?" He paused. "I'm here for her, and from the looks of you, you all might be glad to get rid of her."

We were all frozen in our spots, afraid and processing what had just happened.

Finally, Gril looked at Tex and me. "Go get Dr. Powder. He has another gunshot wound to attend to."

Thirty-three

They are spectacular," I said, meaning it. "Look at all the blue and white. So beautiful."

"They are," Eddy agreed as he piloted the boat along the route.

I was finally seeing the glaciers. Eddy had offered, and Tex had come along, too.

"Of course, they used to be bigger," Tex said. "You know, when they first came about, the ice grew so quickly that villagers had to pick up and move with very little notice or they'd be covered by it. The ice was a real force, moved with a terrifying speed."

"That had to be rough."

"It was, but they survived. People think this land isn't made for growing things, but it was before the ice, and then other places had to be found. Survival, that's the name of the game."

"I hope the ice grows again."

"Me too."

As we watched, a chunk broke off and fell into the ocean. It was called calving, and not everyone got to see it.

I ooohed and ahhhed.

Tex and Eddy smiled.

I'd finished my book, and Benedict had calmed down. Sadie, the Duponts, Albert, Laney, and the rest of them were all gone. Viola slept for two days straight after they left.

Everything that had occurred had been sparked by Linda Robin's husband, Marcus. He'd wanted revenge for his wife's murder and had known Albert had been set up. He'd contacted the young man and did, indeed, assist in his escape from Goose Creek.

After that, they worked together. It was all about vengeance, of course, and money. Money is always involved somehow.

Albert had also wanted to kill Sadie for managing to convince the police that he'd killed his biological mother. He hadn't; Sadie had, but they'd believed her more than him—even as they harbored suspicions about her, keeping an eye on her over the years. Albert had used Smith, a man desperate for money, who had pretended to stop by to say hello to Sadie that day and ask her to lunch with him. He'd been paid handsomely to get her out to the island, but she'd turned the tide and killed her captor before he could hurt her. She'd remembered it all but had lived so many lies, including the ones she'd been living in witness protection, that after she killed Smith, she wasn't sure which ones to stick with. She'd thought that telling me about her witness protection would put me on her side. She'd been right, my sympathy and then our shared "kidnapping" had made me trust her more than I should have. She'd never even been to Connecticut, but it's what she'd told me to protect some of her story. But Albert had. It's where he'd gone after leaving the temporary care of the Duponts' and where Sadie somehow found him. She'd told him about Linda being in Juneau, encouraged him to come out to Alaska, and then framed him for Linda's murder. Viola had said that Sadie was "a clever one."

When Sadie had been introduced to me, she'd remembered

the recent news play of my story, but us meeting had been as much a surprise to her as it was to me. Same with Marcus Robin. He'd come into the bar that night behaving with authority and then played along when I asked if he was the marshal. I'd made it pretty easy for him, and he'd remembered my story, too, using it against me as if it was something his client, Sadie, had told him.

Albert had convinced Gracie to come to Alaska by just acting like he wanted to see her. His escape from prison the week before had shocked her. Her original motivation for wanting to come to Alaska was to convince her parents to travel to Goose Creek to visit him. She'd used my recent and weird story of fame to convince her parents she wanted to go to Alaska—she knew they'd never make the trip just to visit Albert.

On the down-low, though, Albert had also written to Laney— Laney and Gracie *were* close friends, and Albert had known her, too. He'd written to her only to get her to help him convince Gracie, but via their letters, a relationship had blossomed. Teenage Laney had become "in love" with twenty-year-old Albert and was willing to do whatever he wanted.

Gracie did become suspicious, though. When using me to convince her parents to come to Alaska, she had perused my books, mostly the stuff on the covers. After his escape, Albert had told Gracie to meet him on Lilybook, an island with caves that would make great hiding places.

As Gracie's suspicion grew, she thought to use me and the blurbs from *Scavenger Hunt* to lay out a trail of bread crumb clues, just in case something happened to her, something that she didn't want to believe would happen, but things certainly hadn't gone the way she thought they would. She was a smart girl, but she was still a kid, and kids were known to make a bad choice or two along the way. In fact, Laney and Albert were planning to try to get money from Greg and Betty and then kill them, though all of the Duponts are sure Laney would have never let the murder happen.

I wasn't so sure, but I hadn't spoken to any of them after the day they were reunited. I hoped they'd all pay attention to the video on Laney's Facebook page. She might need some more help.

A boat had been used by all of them, but it wasn't Eddy's. He hadn't called Albert back in time, so Albert had called someone else, another fishing boat captain who had no idea what his trips back and forth to the island had meant.

Smith had hired yet another boat, one in Juneau, to get him and Sadie to the island originally. He'd come aboard with a drugged Sadie, but that boat captain had also been paid handsomely, so he'd ignored the obviously strange circumstances. That captain would probably be in trouble. I was glad it hadn't been Eddy.

Laney was in trouble, Albert (his wound healing) would now go back in Goose Creek, though maybe not for long. He hadn't killed Linda Robin, but the court would have to go through appropriate motions to get that conviction set aside. He would still have to answer for his actions, but that would be via new indictments. Sadie would be arraigned for the murder of Linda Robin. Marcus was also in all kinds of trouble, and he would have a bum knee for the rest of his life. In a twist that I thought must be somewhat unfair, Gril didn't think anyone would be charged with Smith's murder, because there was a strong enough case that he got Sadie to go with him for wrongful purposes, most likely so Albert or Marcus Robin could kill her.

Very, very messy.

Albert's defense attorney, Gina, was angry about it all, but Gril wouldn't tell anyone details about his conversations with her. He did smile when he was asked about them, though.

My email had pinged just this morning with the picture from *The Des Moines Register*. The full picture did show Albert smiling at Gracie. More than anything, it had made me sad to see it. Such happiness had ultimately gone so wrong.

"You okay?" Tex asked as my eyes unfocused from the glaciers.

"Oh. Yes, fine. I think. I'm still reeling a little."

"It was . . . crazy. Everyone's fine, though, at least everyone who should be."

I nodded. "Hey, Eddy, thanks for bringing us out here."

"You're welcome. Anytime. If I can't take my daughter to see the glaciers, what good is having a boat?"

I laughed.

Suddenly, my phone buzzed and rang. "What in the world? We're out in the middle of nowhere." I reached into my pocket.

"It's the Nat Geo ship." Tex nodded toward the big National Geographic ship ahead of us. "They have their own tower. It happens a lot out here."

"Really?" I looked at the phone. It was Detective Majors. I answered. "Hello."

"Beth, you okay?" she asked.

"Sure, I'm fine." But I heard the tight pull of her tone. "Why?"

She sighed. "Look, I'm sorry to have to tell you this, but Travis Walker escaped last night. He's on the run again."

I collapsed to the bench seat. "That can't be. No. How?"

"I don't have all the details. I'm sorry, Beth. Maybe get out of there, or at least be on the lookout for him."

"My mom?"

"We haven't seen her. We don't know if she was involved, but he's in the wind."

Tex took a seat next to me, and Eddy's concerned attention was moving back and forth between the route ahead and me.

"You think he's coming after me?"

She paused for so long that I wondered if we'd lost the connection.

"Beth, he left a note. It says he's coming after you. I quote, 'It will be the last thing I do, but I will take her with me to the great beyond.' I'm sorry, Beth, but his escape is sure to hit the news any minute now, if it hasn't already. I wanted to be the one to tell you."

"Okay." I didn't have any other words.

"Where are you?"

"On the ocean, looking at the glaciers. I'm with people."

"Good. He hasn't been gone long enough to make it up there yet, but he'll be there, I'm sure of it."

My story had been all over the news, my location. Even Gracie had known. He would find me easily.

"Okay," I said again.

"I'll keep you up-to-date."

"Okay." I nodded.

The call disconnected and I looked at Eddy and Tex.

"What?" they both asked.

I didn't want to say the words aloud, but I did, and then we made a plan.

Acknowledgments

I'm so lucky to get to work with some of the most talented people in publishing. My agent, Jessica Faust, and my editor, Hannah O'Grady, are astounding. I'm so grateful for them both.

Thank you to everyone at Minotaur who works so hard to make sure readers know about the books. Kayla Janus, Allison Ziegler, and Sara Eslami are only a few. Editors, copy editors, artists, and marketing folks are magical.

Thanks to my plot group—Jenn McKinlay and Kate Carlisle—and their patience for my pantser ways.

My husband, Charlie, is always supportive and, thankfully, his glass is always at least half full. My son, Tyler, and daughter-in-law, Lauren, give me many hours of joy—even more now that my grandson, Wesley, is here. Goodness, there is nothing better.

Thank you to my readers. I guess it goes without saying that I couldn't do this without you, but, really, I couldn't. And to all of you who battle for ARCs or early copies and get reviews out into the world, I don't know how to thank you enough. Drinks or milk and cookies on me if we meet in person.